PENGUIN CLASSICS

ROMANCE IN MARSEILLE

CLAUDE MCKAY (1889–1948), born Festus Claudius McKay, is widely regarded as one of the most important literary and political writers of the interwar period and the Harlem Renaissance. Born in Jamaica, he moved to the United States in 1912 to study at the Tuskegee Institute. In 1928, he published his most famous novel, *Home to Harlem*, which won a Harmon Foundation award for literature. He also published two other novels, *Banjo* and *Banana Bottom*, as well as a collection of short stories, *Gingertown*, two autobiographical books, *A Long Way from Home* and *My Green Hills of Jamaica*, and a work of nonfiction, *Harlem: Negro Metropolis*. His *Complete Poems* were published posthumously, and in 1977 he was named the national poet of Jamaica.

GARY EDWARD HOLCOMB is professor of African American Literature and Studies in the Department of African American Studies at Ohio University. His books are *Teaching Hemingway and Race* (2018), *Hemingway and the Black Renaissance* (2012), and *Claude McKay, Code Name Sasha: Queer Black Marxism and the Harlem Renaissance* (2007), a study that includes a chapter devoted to *Romance in Marseille*.

WILLIAM J. MAXWELL is professor of English and African and African American Studies at Washington University in St. Louis. He is the author of *F.B. Eyes: How J. Edgar Hoover's Ghostreaders Framed African American Literature* (2015), which won the American Book Award in 2016, and *New Negro, Old Left: African-American Writing and Communism Between the Wars* (1999). He is the editor of *James Baldwin: The FBI File* (2017) and Claude McKay's *Complete Poems* (2004).

Claude McKay, 1926. Photographed by Berenice Abbott / National Portrait Gallery, Smithsonian Institution / Getty Images.

CLAUDE MCKAY

Romance in Marseille

Edited and with an Introduction by
GARY EDWARD HOLCOMB
and
WILLIAM J. MAXWELL

PENGUIN BOOKS

PENGUIN BOOKS
An imprint of Penguin Random House LLC
penguinrandomhouse.com

PHOTO AND FACSIMILE CREDITS:
Page ii: Berenice Abbott / Getty Images
Page lii: page 26 of typescript titled "Romance in Marseille by Claude McKay"
from the Claude McKay Collection owned by the Yale Collection of American Literature,
Beinecke Rare Book and Manuscript Library, Yale University, is used with the
permission of the Literary Estate for the Works of Claude McKay.
Page liii: page 124 of typescript titled "Romance in Marseille by Claude McKay"
owned by the Manuscripts, Archives and Rare Books Division, Schomburg Center for
Research in Black Culture, New York Public Library, is used with the permission
of the Literary Estate for the Works of Claude McKay.

LIBRARY OF CONGRESS CATALOGING-IN-PUBLICATION DATA
Names: McKay, Claude, 1890–1948, author. | Holcomb, Gary Edward, writer of
introduction. | Maxwell, William J. (College teacher), writer of introduction.
Title: Romance in Marseille / Claude McKay ; introduction by
Gary Edward Holcomb and William J. Maxwell.
Description: New York : Penguin Books, 2020. | Includes bibliographical references.
Identifiers: LCCN 2019025262 (print) | LCCN 2019025263 (ebook) |
ISBN 9780143134220 (paperback) | ISBN 9780525505983 (ebook)
Classification: LCC PS3525.A24785 R66 2020 (print) |
LCC PS3525.A24785 (ebook) | DDC 813/.52—dc23
LC record available at https://lccn.loc.gov/2019025262
LC ebook record available at https://lccn.loc.gov/2019025263

Printed in the United States of America
5   7   9   10   8   6

Set in Sabon LT Std

Contents

Introduction

New readers are advised that this introduction makes details of the plot explicit.

Visiting Barcelona in September 1929, Claude McKay (1889–1948), one of the earliest stars of the Harlem Renaissance, set to work on a novel he then called "The Jungle and the Bottoms." Seven years earlier, during the annus mirabilis he shared with *Ulysses*, *The Waste Land*, and *Jacob's Room*, the Jamaican-born, hard-traveling McKay had published the Harlem movement's first substantial book of poetry, *Harlem Shadows* (1922), in New York. Six years after that, his first novel, *Home to Harlem* (1928), had enjoyed multiple printings as the Harlem Renaissance's first certified American bestseller. Launching "The Jungle and the Bottoms" in Spain in the autumn of the stock market crash, however, an author recognized for originality planned to rework already covered material. As McKay initially sketched it, his new book would recycle both the Marseille dockside setting and the loose, picaresque storytelling of his second novel, *Banjo: A Story Without a Plot* (1929), a rambling tale of black life led as "a dream of vagabondage."[1] Yet within months he was rethinking "The Jungle and the Bottoms" wholesale, aiming to break with *Banjo* by drafting an uncluttered, linear plot combining his rowdy troupe of sailors, dockworkers, and *filles de joie*—collectively straight and queer, disabled and able-bodied, African, European, Caribbean, and American.

In the summer of 1930, following transatlantic debates with his New York publisher and Paris literary agent over the merits of the novel, McKay lost his enthusiasm for this story with a plot, and set the manuscript aside. Hoping he could salvage the work, he took it up again in 1932, the interracial history and fluid sexual landscape of his new home of Morocco spurring a return to the raw miscellany of his "Jungle." Adding scores of pages and an operatically violent ending, McKay restyled the novel as "Savage Loving," a title calculated to attract the carnal imagination and the sales figures he had not earned since *Home to Harlem*. But a now ill and impoverished author again faced editorial obstacles, not to mention harassment from British consular agents and French colonial administrators suspicious of his doings around Tangier's International Zone. By the time he abandoned the project for good in the Great Depression depths of 1933, he had given the completed novel its least sensational and most place-bound name, *Romance in Marseille*. (In another break from *Banjo*, McKay finally preferred the de-Anglicized French spelling of the city without a final *s*, fulfilling his self-description as a cosmopolitan "bad nationalist."²) Whatever the politics of its orthography, what you hold in your hands or read on your screen is the first version of *Romance in Marseille* published in any form, anywhere. After nearly ninety years in waiting, this descendant of "The Jungle and the Bottoms" and "Savage Loving" has escaped its tangled transnational composition history to make its public debut. McKay's legacy will never look the same, and neither will the Harlem Renaissance, Black Atlantic modernism, Caribbean postcolonialism, twentieth-century LGBTQ writing, the Lost Generation, and the radical novel between the world wars. Above all, perhaps, our understanding of the literature of disability will need to account for a strange and absorbing new view of colonial racism and the heritage of European slavery as triggers of physical impairment.

Although its population of roving and loving black workers ensures its family resemblance to *Home to Harlem* and *Banjo*, *Romance in Marseille* stands apart from all five of McKay's previously published novels, two of them, *Harlem Glory* (1990) and *Amiable with Big Teeth* (2017), also recovered after his early death. Most distinctively, it places an acutely disabled African at the heart of its lean but eventful three-part narrative. *Romance*'s male lead, Lafala, has next to nothing in common with the traditional literary character marked by a physical disability, the angelic icon or spectacular alien confined to a book's margins and obliged to draw pity and horror from its major players. Lafala instead serves as McKay's never freakish, rarely saintly protagonist, a sailor born in an unspecified part of English West Africa who seeks self-respect after his betrayal by Aslima, a black Moroccan prostitute he falls for in the Mediterranean port of Marseille sometime in the 1920s. Fighting "self-disgust"[3] with quick action, he ditches the city Alexandre Dumas dubbed "the meeting place of the entire world"[4] and stows away on a ship to New York, expecting that his dark complexion will allow him "to escape detection in the gloominess of the bunker."[5] But he is discovered and forced from his hiding place, and jailed in a freezing toilet. Badly frostbitten by the time the boat docks, the once-nimble dancer loses both of his lower legs, emerging from life-saving surgery as what he terms "an amputated man."[6]

Thanks to a successful lawsuit against the shipping line, however, the down-for-the-count Lafala scores big in the litigious United States. Anticipating Toni Morrison's one-legged, insurance-enriched character Eva Peace, the matriarch of the black "Bottom" neighborhood in the novel *Sula* (1973), he schemes to convert stolen mobility into social ascent. Feeling flush after his legal payout, and tempted "like all vain humanity who love to revisit the scenes of their sufferings and defeats after they have conquered their world,"[7] Lafala doubles back to Marseille and resumes his liaison with Aslima, who had fleeced and jilted him. Though now a wealthy local "personage"[8] equipped for a leisurely life in the Vieux Port's "caves and dens,"[9] he finds his troubles far from over, his affair with Aslima complicated by more than his double amputation and the lurking presence of her covetous pimp. Adding another coat of irony to the "Pyrrhic victory"[10] of limbs traded for gold, the shipping line conspires with French police to imprison Lafala for the unforgiven offense of stowing away for profit. To McKay's unnamed maritime company, a messenger of Europe's greed for obedient black bodies, the African's extremities are insufficient sacrifice. By the novel's end, an international crew of mostly black allies, led by a McKay-like Caribbean intellectual, has set

Lafala free once more, easing his return to his native land. But the good fortune he brings back to West Africa does not include Aslima's companionship. While Lafala keeps his African birthright, he sells his healing intraracial romance for a pile of dollars.

Flanking its pivotal affair between two representative Africans, McKay's jazz- and beguine-soaked narrative is stocked with memorable supporting actors. The matter-of-factly gay longshoreman Big Blonde joins Lafala in standing out against McKay's typical cast list. This strapping and unrepressed white American qualifies as a different kind of Lost Generation expatriate. Queerly reminiscent of "a hero straight out of Joseph Conrad,"[11] he is "an outstanding enigma" of the Marseille docks, rumored to "have once held a respectable position in the merchant service" and to employ the Casbah-like "Quayside" district as a hideout besides a pleasure den. Unlike Conrad's similarly strong and inscrutable Lord Jim, however, Big Blonde's legend is fed by his instinctive socialism, unorganizable though it may be. Among the outsized laborer's co-conspirators is the writer and Communist recruiter Etienne St. Dominique, a "mulatto from Martinique"[12] who leverages his "cultivated accent and his refined manners"[13] on Lafala's behalf when he lands in jail. Big Blonde's "Little Brother" and younger lover is Petit Frère, "fascinating with his pale prettiness"[14] and always eager for a good meal and a taste of intrigue. Still another queer figure, the single well-developed lesbian character in McKay's work, is the independent black courtesan La Fleur Noire ("the Black Flower"), who connives against Aslima, her only worthy rival in the Vieux Port sex trade. In one of *Romance*'s concluding episodes, La Fleur's antipathy toward Aslima is revealed as camouflage for admiration and desire. Throughout the novel, forms of queer love suggested or sidelined in McKay's previous fiction are drawn in bold strokes and allowed to intrude on Lafala and Aslima's central passion.

The genesis of *Romance in Marseille* is as distinctive as its dramatis personae. McKay derived the novel's outline from an acquaintance's experience of shattering amputation and extraordinary recovery. Even before he wrote the first page, McKay

identified the model for Lafala as Nelson Simeon Dede, a Nigerian seaman he had befriended in Marseille. A minor character
influenced by Dede also appears in *Banjo*, to some extent a
roman à clef of McKay's nomadic circle in the south of France.
In this earlier Marseille-set novel, Dede takes the form of a race-
proud Nigerian named Taloufa, a talented guitarist and "good
luck baby"[15] who stows away to America without a hitch. When
embarking on *Romance*, McKay gave his disabled protagonist
this same name.[16] As the drafts mounted, "Taloufa" morphed
into "Lafala," the latter a would-be Africanism, perhaps repur-
posed from Ruwaili Arabic, just a short distance from the former in sound and syllable. McKay had been introduced to
Lafala's template, the flesh-and-blood Dede, during his first visit
to Marseille in 1926. He reencountered him in January 1928,
after Dede had stowed away, been captured, suffered the loss of
both feet, unexpectedly won restitution, and returned to the
city's teeming, low-lying "Bottoms" with prostheses and a wad
of cash. In a February 1928 letter to his literary agent,[17] William
Aspenwall Bradley, McKay excitedly discussed his Nigerian
friend's wildly mixed "fortune and misfortune."[18] His next
novel would cast the paradoxical drama of the abruptly disabled yet suddenly prosperous stowaway as a key to the modern
African diaspora.

The 1920s, the high season of the Jazz Age, the New Negro,
the Harlem Renaissance, and the so-called Negro Vogue, was
also the era of the high seas black stowaway. The decade that
liberated millions from the mechanized slaughter of the Great
War became "a time of universal excitement,"[19] as *Romance
in Marseille* explains it, and "even among Negroes there were
signs of a stirring and from the New World a dark cry of 'Back
to Africa' came over the air." The blooming desire of New
World blacks for reconnection with Africa, and of Africans
for reconnection with their New and Old World kin, assumed
many institutional forms. Marcus Garvey's Universal Negro
Improvement Association (UNIA), complete with tens of thousands of uniformed members and its own Black Star steamship
line, was the most popular, the most spectacular, and finally the

most tragic of these. But practically every month of the 1920s brought news of individual black men slipping onto ships, risking limb and liberty to sail in various international directions and bend Garvey's seafaring vision to their own designs.

In April 1923, for example, the Baltimore *Afro-American* reported on the brave and angry stowaway of Battling Siki, a Senegalese boxing champion. Marooned in Ireland after a bout "because both American and British ships refused to haul him home," the light heavyweight crept onto a "small cargo boat" heading from Dublin to Le Havre. Strength derived from "righteous indignation,"[20] Siki affirmed, delivered him securely to France. Five years later, in August 1928, the *Afro-American* told the roguish tale of Sherlock and O. Granville Grinage, a pair of black brothers from Maryland who stole "aboard a merchant marine vessel" headed to "the Pacific Coast." On their way through the Panama Canal and across California, the latter by car, they met with "thrills which would give inspiration to an O. Henry,"[21] the famous American author of plot-twisting stories. Earlier that summer, the *New York Amsterdam News* relished "the adventuresome experience of Frank Murray Byrd,"[22] a Harlem student discovered on the *Berengaria*, a luxurious transatlantic Cunard liner, "sitting in the first-class library writing in his diary." Another *Amsterdam News* item painted Byrd as a colorful dandy despite his lack of a paid fare, a beau on a budget tossed into an English jail "in pearl spats, a soigné purple suit, a velour hat, yellow suede shoes, sauterne chamois gloves, a pink shirt, a claret cravat, and a lavender topcoat."[23]

Closer to the end of the decade, African American papers devoted columns to a stowaway saga mixed up with another adventurous Byrd. Robert White Lanier, a black teenager from Jersey City, had packed up a camera, "hired a rowboat, dodged the police patrol,"[24] and sneaked under cover of night into the forecastle of Commander Richard Byrd's flagship in New York Harbor. Lanier's well-prepared aim was to join Byrd's expedition to Antarctica and become the first black man to reach the South Pole. Disregarding the achievement of black explorer Matthew Henson, the first man of any color to leave footprints on the North Pole, Byrd dropped Lanier off in Panama, deciding that he "lacked the stamina necessary to withstand the rigors of an Antarctic voyage."²⁵ "I'm a lad that's always been righteous. They're jealous of my upcoming. They don't want to see me get ahead,"²⁶ Lanier protested to the *Chicago Defender*. Lanier never surmounted either pole, but he gained his portion of fame as the most determined black stowaway profiled in a long journalistic series. Stylishly and unapologetically hijacking the means of nautical transportation was one dependable route to press attention in the years when "the Negro mind,"²⁷ as W. E. B. Du Bois had it, reached out "to know, to sympathize, to inquire" beyond national borders.

In addition to the true story of Nelson Simeon Dede, other more-or-less nonfictional tales of ocean tramping filtered into *Romance in Marseille*. McKay, an eager if cynical reader of the African American press even while globetrotting in Western Europe and North Africa, supplied *Romance* with related yarns of black wanderers lighting out without tickets, passports, or portfolios, relying on their wits alone to ply the Atlantic and the deep-water port of Marseille. Close to the heart of McKay's *Romance*, in fact, is a set of searching, big-picture questions suggested by the whole body of New Negro stowaway tales. Can black internationalism flourish as a personal, even erotic attachment in the absence of studied Pan-Africanist convictions? Can black selves return to Africa, spiritually or otherwise, without the benefit of Garveyism, Communism, or other collective movements capable of raising armies, purchasing steamships, and resettling formerly colonized lands? Can reparations for past centuries of racial slavery and for the ongoing plunder of black working bodies somehow be earned on a case-by-case basis, and, if so, would these reparations implant incurable materialism in those granted them? Finally, can the modern reunion of the peoples of the black diaspora, dispersed and wounded by the violence of slavery and imperialism, be plotted as a changeable, passionate romance instead of a resolute political epic? Du Bois, McKay's fiercest critic among the African American intelligentsia, once characterized *Banjo* as "a sort of international philosophy of the Negro race."²⁸ Had he been able to read *Romance in Marseille*, he might have typed it as an international philosophy of a race reconsidered as a network of broad-minded, love-driven, but ultimately detached individuals.

Notwithstanding the single city pinpointed in its title, *Romance in Marseille* is thus a work of stowaway fiction, like *Banjo* a reflection on the art of improvised movement around a black world rediscovering its far-flung corners and relations. Unlike *Banjo*, however, *Romance* is stowaway fiction incited by the prospect that black fugitives would seek restitution for losing too much while making the world smaller. A consistent feature of McKay's dispatches from abroad is his appetite for news and gossip. Again and again, the Jamaican traveler implores his American correspondents to bundle and send him whatever engaging local journalism they can. Before he learned firsthand that Dede had lost his feet but won his lawsuit, McKay could not have missed press reports of another remarkable case of legal resistance to "brutality on the high seas."[29] In the spring of 1927, both the *New York Times* and the black-owned *Amsterdam News* prominently shared the "unusual story" of "Jonathan Gibson, a 21-year-old Negro of Kingston," Jamaica, who had pressed a "suit against the steamship *Princess May*, operated and owned by the Di Giorgio & Co., Inc.," of New York City. The *Princess May* reliably hauled fruit and passengers from West Indian ports to Manhattan Island, and Gibson, an underemployed tailor chasing opportunity in America, chose it as a safe craft on which to hitch a ride. Four days after the *Princess May* shoved off from Kingston—the Jamaican capital where McKay had briefly worked as a policeman—Gibson was spotted by an officer, however, "and dragged from his hiding place."

What followed, alleged Gibson, was an ordeal reprising some of the worst punishments of slavery. "Gibson said his hands were manacled behind his back"[30] and fixed by handcuffs "to an upright stanchion at a point level with the deck rail." "Every time the vessel rolled," Gibson testified, "the deck fell away and he was left suspended by the handcuffs, leaving him in agony until the ship righted itself." Waves "washed over the rail and soaked his shoes, causing the leather to contract and his feet to swell." Near the end of his agonizing voyage, he was removed from the deck and penned in a cabin, "crazy with pain." Like McKay's friend Dede, Gibson was detained at the immigrant hospital on Ellis Island after landing. There, similar to Dede, "gangrene necessitated the amputation of the fore portion of each foot. Gibson . . . charged that the gangrene caused him to suffer from toxic psychosis and that for part of the time at the hospital he was insane and placed in the psychopathic ward." In the eyes of the Jamaican stowaway, his initially voluntary ocean voyage descended into a reenactment of the physically tormenting and psychologically traumatic Middle Passage once forced on his African ancestors. The Statue of Liberty, its torch raised less than a mile from the Ellis Island hospital,[31] welcomed him to anything but.

Yet Gibson employed an emphatically modern and especially American weapon in seeking revenge on the living ghosts of slavery, a disabling as well as peculiar institution. According to the *Times*, he filed suit against the *Princess May* in the U.S. District Court in Brooklyn, hiring lawyers to argue his case—an official "action in admiralty"—before Federal Judge Grover M. Moscowitz. Gibson and his team sought no less than $100,000 in damages, about $1,500,000 in 2020 currency. Dr. William H. Egan, a New York physician, was introduced as a prosecution witness to testify that "the condition which necessitated amputation of part of Gibson's feet could have been caused only by some physical pressure which constricted the bloodvessels [sic]."[32] Another stowaway on the *Princess May*, Sidney Gunter of Jamaica, was called to the stand and "substantiated Gibson's story." Not surprisingly, the ship's captain conceded none of this, attesting "that Gibson had been treated humanely. He denied that the stowaway had been manacled to a stanchion, and produced the log of the vessel to show that the weather on May 24, 1926," the longest day of Gibson's nightmare, "was clear and only a small amount of spray came over the side." Regardless of the height of the waves, continued the defense, the poor state of Gibson's feet "before he boarded the vessel could have caused his later condition."[33] On the third day of the trial, the judge sided with the company, curtly dismissing the charges. Simply put, "Moscowitz said he did not believe Gibson's story,"[34] and the Jamaican failed to match Dede's coup and recover damages.

Consciously or not, on one of its lower frequencies, *Romance in Marseille* retries Jonathan Gibson's case. In the courtroom of the novel, McKay judges his countryman's suit in place of the Honorable Grover Moscowitz, and rules, with prejudice, in favor of the prosecution. Lafala, *Romance*'s Gibson, is a comparably English-speaking, non-American black protagonist. He too stows away, is detected in his hiding place, is locked up and to all intents tortured by his white captors, and brings suit after losing both feet in a New York hospital. (McKay's novel begins with the just-amputated Lafala stranded in a sick bay somewhere in the city, feeling like "a sawed-off stump,"[35] dreaming of the "leg play" of his West African boyhood, and anxiously musing on the way forward.) Resembling Gibson's case, defense lawyers for "the company"— an anonymous substitute for Di Giorgio, Inc., the owners of the *Princess May*—argue that Lafala came aboard with diseased feet. Crucially, in distinction to the original litigation, McKay's stowaway collects all he asks, and more, when challenging his fate. Lafala pockets his share of $100,000 in damages, exactly, from the steamship company, reaps the affection of a fellow black stowaway and of his previously untrustworthy North African lover, and acquires the means to cross the Atlantic and eventually return to Africa on a first-class ticket. When his trial is done, Lafala's loss of bodily mobility has incongruously led to greater freedom of movement and an enhanced pursuit of happiness. By the final chapters of *Romance*, arrest, isolation, conspiracy, and murder shadow Lafala's windfall, altering its meaning, but the novel begins with a stowaway fairy tale, a semi-utopian granting of back pay to an African whose wings are clipped but who flies away along a route once bloodied by the transatlantic slave trade. Call Lafala's hard-earned jackpot reparations for slavery, if you like, in imaginative miniature.

The sweep of Lafala's courtroom victory stems in no small part from the good legal fortune of Nelson Simeon Dede. As we have seen, the immediate prototype for *Romance in Mar-*

seille's leading man was not Gibson, thwarted by the real Judge Moscowitz, but this luckier Nigerian stowaway McKay had befriended in France. Over the course of his February 1928 letter to literary agent William Aspenwall Bradley, McKay recounts that Dede hid in the hold of a Fabre Company steamer bound for New York in 1926, the same year as Gibson's trip on the *Princess May*. He was found out by a ship's officer and, like Lafala after him, locked in a frigid water closet for the rest of the voyage. Dede's protests that the WC was an icebox were ignored, and, after the steamer docked, both he and the French shipping line learned that his feet were frostbitten. Sometime during American immigration processing, Dede's legs were amputated below the knees, apparently at the Ellis Island Immigrant Hospital, the first public health hospital in the United States and the site of Jonathan Gibson's medical detention. He recovered his will in time to hire what McKay stereotypes as "one of those Jewish accident lawyers."[36] Paving the way to Lafala's effective Jewish attorney in *Romance*, Dede's lawyer won the day in a New York courtroom, bringing home a $17,000 settlement.[37] He took a $5,000 cut, notes McKay, while Dede, armed with his $12,000 portion, far less than Gibson's hoped-for pile, set sail for Nigeria fitted with prostheses. On the way to West Africa, Dede was waylaid and imprisoned once more. When his ship stopped over in Marseille, the Fabre line arranged for French authorities to incarcerate him for "clandestine embarkation":[38] in other words, for the offense of stowing away on a Fabre ship two years earlier. The loss of Dede's lower legs, the French company apparently decided, was not sentence enough. What stowaway, whatever the absurdities of American justice, deserved to be paid for his crime?

Confirmation of the details of Dede's case outside of McKay's correspondence is thin; it is the odd striking stowaway story of the era that is difficult to find in the black press. But a reason for the lack of journalism on Dede is not hard to discover. The absence of coverage presumably reflects the likelihood that his grievance never went to trial. Dede's lawyer negotiated and settled out of court, McKay suggests, and the arrangement in this circumstance almost certainly included an agreement not to spread the story to journalists black, white, or sensationally "yellow." It would have been in the interest of all parties—Dede, his lawyer, and especially the Fabre line— to keep the strange facts under wraps.

In *Romance in Marseille*, by contrast, the story of Lafala's amputation and lawsuit is splashed all over the popular press. Parodic counterfeits of actual African American newspapers scream with headlines hyping the exchange of limbs for cash at the core of the case (and at the core of racial capitalism more broadly). The *United Negro*, for example, a send-up of the Garvey movement's *Negro World*, runs with the banner "AFRICAN LEGS BRING ONE HUNDRED THOUSAND DOLLARS."[39] The onetime owner of these African legs, sums up McKay, "had conquered Aframerica with a whoop. Very literary were the days that ensued for Lafala."[40] Putting Dede's example aside, McKay no doubt drew on the Jonathan Gibson trial, and its lurid life in newsprint, when riffing on the translation of Lafala's disability into "[v]ery literary" fame. The ensuing satire of black American journalism—just one of the "Aframerican" institutions McKay delighted in skewering—helps to explain a puzzling remark of the author on *Romance*'s debt to a "[f]unny case."[41] Offsetting its veins of romance and tragedy, elements of the novel are intended as grotesque social satire, something like the politicized grim humor of George Grosz's caricatures of disfigured veterans amid Berlin prostitutes and profiteers, drawings McKay honored as "rare and iconoclastic" art.[42] More specifically, *Romance*'s breed of black comedy targets the grinding of black flesh and bones through the mechanisms of a capitalist culture industry in league with the shipping industry. The sensational drifting of Lafala's detached legs across the banner section of the front pages is more historically momentous, McKay reckons, than the unrecorded burial of Dede's feet in a potter's field outside the immigration hospital. Like Gibson, Lafala dearly purchases a flash of mass-market fame and therefore takes on an archetypal significance. He becomes a public figure of the black body both supplemented and truncated by modern technologies of rapid transportation and instant mass myth-making.

Dede's explicable absence from the tabloids and other journalistic sources is not duplicated in McKay's own archive. Thanks to McKay's record-keeping, less casual than usual in this instance, we know with some assurance that the author of *Romance in Marseille* intervened directly on Dede's behalf with the "Directeur en Chef" of the Fabre Line. A copy of a carefully typed letter to this effect, addressed from Marseille in January 1928, now sits among McKay's papers at Yale University's Beinecke Rare Book and Manuscript Library.[43] McKay begins this letter to the Fabre honcho with flattery and pathos: "By a happy chance I discovered today that you were Consul for Liberia, whose President, Mr. King, I happened to meet some years ago. . . . May I therefore, [sic] bring to your attention the case of a poor West African boy from Nigeria who stowed away last winter on one of your boats going to New York and had the dreadful misfortune of having his feet frozen in the place where he was locked up, so that they had to be amputated in the immigration hospital in New York?"[44]

Dede, that poor West African boy, no longer required compensation for his lost limbs, states McKay. His lawyer had "negotiated a settlement with the Fabre Line in New York, and the boy received a certain sum that was paid to him through the British Consul in New York."[45] What was still needed was Fabre's intercession to withdraw the charge of clandestine embarkation. In return, Dede was willing to refund the full cost of his stolen 1926 passage, "aller et retour, Marseille–New York,"[46] in order to "get out of prison (where he is very miserable, after having gone through a whole year of sickness and suffering) and get home to Nigeria, Africa, as soon as possible."[47] In his corner, McKay was willing to pledge that his novel showcasing Dede—the brewing *Romance in Marseille*—would treat Fabre more generously if the director's assistance was given. Dede "was one of the liveliest of the stranded black seaman and the best dancer of the Charleston and the Black Bottom, for which he was much admired by the girls of Vieux Port quarter. Now he will never dance again!"[48] For all these losses, "a happy story" based on his life "was still possible," McKay promised, one "showing that the Compagnie Fabre stood honorably by Dede after his accident."[49] Dangling the possibility that Fabre would be cast not as a corporate

villain but as an enlightened hero of race-blind French civilization, McKay did not hesitate to employ the prospect of
Romance as textual blackmail. If the novel to be written
allowed him to act the part of Jonathan Gibson's second judge,
reversing the negative decision of the U.S. District Court in
Brooklyn, it also permitted him to outdo Dede's official lawyer. And if effective representation of his Nigerian client would
require him to make Fabre's director a virtual coauthor—the
comic or tragic destination of *Romance* was seemingly up to
him—it was a loss of aesthetic autonomy McKay was willing
to contemplate.

McKay's letter to Bradley implies that Fabre's director in
chief considered his offer one he could not refuse. "We got
[Dede] out two weeks ago,"[50] McKay boasts in the key of the
royal "we." The polished text of *Romance in Marseille* signals
the same favorable result. McKay's closest self-reflection in the
novel, the Caribbean radical Etienne St. Dominique, once
"hailed as the dark star rising in the European literary horizon,"[51] does his best to spring Lafala from a second imprisonment by flashing a press clipping and other literary credentials.
An executive of the offending steamship company, promising
Lafala's release, says "to St. Dominique with a smile 'Now
don't go away and write anything bad about the company.' 'I
couldn't now,'" replies St. Dominique, "smiling back."[52] For as
long as it takes to free Lafala, McKay relaxes his characteristic
disgust for the art-appreciating liberal idealism associated
with the graying ambassadors of the Harlem Renaissance.
Ironically enough, in fact, he creates a literal-minded dramati-
zation of "civil rights by copyright,"[53] historian David Levering Lewis's skeptical label for elite Harlem's wager that black
art could secure the full citizenship unsecured by political pro-
test. In the parable of the dark literary star and the pale shipping executive, black artistic capacity (St. Dominique's ability
to achieve copyright) neatly routs the racist distortion of the
law (the suspension of Lafala's *droits civil*).

What McKay does not create in his finished *Romance*, however, is a novel in which black art's sway over white power
safeguards a finally "*happy*" story." Neither reparations for
Lafala's pilfered limbs—an emblem of racial and wage slavery

repaid—nor a second rare visitation of justice arranged by St. Dominique prevents McKay's protagonist from returning to Africa all alone, troubled by forged word of Aslima's renewed disloyalty. (The would-be climactic scene of Lafala shoving off from Marseille for his African birthplace indeed takes place offstage, and is cause for only secondhand celebration.) Symbolizing the joint redemption of North and West, Islamic and Christianized Africa, the increasingly true love of the Moroccan Aslima for the West African Lafala cannot save her from her French Corsican pimp. *Romance*'s hard-boiled final sentences capture Aslima throwing "up her hands like a bird of prey," her jealous European handler "cursing and calling upon hell to swallow her soul."[54] The hurdles that Lafala and Aslima confront in sealing a trans-African love match, and in giving birth to a generically comic (as opposed to darkly humorous) novel, disclose more than the limits of McKay's bargain with Fabre's director in chief. McKay's *Banjo* ends with a Huck and Jim–style black male pair escaping from civilized feminine influence, their vagabond story poised to continue in territories "a long ways from here."[55] Written from another country, the furious, plot-stopping conclusion of *Romance*, a more expansively queer novel by a nautical mile, insists on the importance of black women in the rebinding of the black world. *Romance in Marseille*, which opens as a male stowaway fantasy, closes as a warning of the tragedy that haunts male-only strategies for universal Negro improvement.

Despite its eighty-seven years of near-invisibility, *Romance in Marseille* has never been a lost book. *Amiable with Big Teeth*, the McKay novel of the Italo-Ethiopian War unearthed by Jean-Christophe Cloutier in 2009, was as unknown as it was unpublished before its appearance as a Penguin Classic in 2017. *Romance in Marseille*, on the other hand, has been known to a handful of McKay scholars with travel budgets, if to virtually no one else, prior to this Penguin edition. Since the 1940s, first one, then two hand-corrected typescript versions of the novel have been hiding in plain sight in two of the world's richest archives of Afro-Americana: the James Weldon Johnson Collection at the Beinecke Rare Book and Manuscript Library in

New Haven and the New York Public Library's Schomburg Center for Research in Black Culture in Harlem.[56] Why, then, has this obscure but not secret book by a major modern author, Langston Hughes's pick as the "best of the colored poets"[57] and a recognized pioneer of both the Harlem Renaissance and the Francophone Négritude movement, so long evaded print? The reasons are diverse—we discuss the matter in greater detail in "A Note on the Text"—but they begin with the unease of agents, editors, and fellow writers presented with its seeming obscenity and genuinely undissembled treatment of gay and lesbian life. They continue with the existential trials McKay faced during his half decade of on-and-off work on the text. Disabling illness, ungenteel poverty, and French and British government harassment destabilized not only the writing process but also his confidence in promoting its final result. Mislaid plans, copyright limbo, and occasionally sketchy behavior by aspiring rescuers frustrated several efforts to expose the book in the decades after McKay's death. This first publication of *Romance in Marseille* thus marks not so much the unexpected discovery of a valuable novel as the long-overdue freeing of one, the amplifying of entertaining and historically significant voices previously trapped in an archival vacuum.

But why and how did McKay begin *Romance in Marseille* in the first place? What in addition to the fates of Jonathan Gibson and Nelson Simeon Dede and the stowaway era in black cultural life fueled and shaped the book? After the success of *Home to Harlem* in 1928, his only large literary payday, McKay was disappointed when *Banjo*, his *Marseillais* novel of 1929, sold sluggishly.[58] Rallying his pride, however, McKay was seized by the idea of a second novel set mostly in the Vieux Port, believing he had something to add on the subject of the international guild of black sailors and dockworkers gathered in France's second city. "The Jungle and the Bottoms," as it was first called, was conceived as another diffuse Marseille bouillabaisse, and it initially reworked material once intended for *Banjo*. But McKay then found himself aspiring to a narrative style different from either of his two previous novels. In *Banjo* and *Home to Harlem*, he had spun discursive and digressive yarns, wheeling characters in to argue, sometimes at chapter length, from assorted national and ideo-logical perspectives. In both of these novels, in fact, the persona of Ray, a Wordsworth-quoting Haitian political exile, spoke transparently for his Jamaican émigré creator. In "The Jungle and the Bottoms," McKay would fashion an intellectually provocative but less talky and idea-driven narrative, pointing a brighter spotlight at the actions and psychology of the restless black men he had encountered in Marseille. At the same time, he would venture beyond the spontaneous black male communities of his first two novels to envision Aslima along with her complex black lesbian counterpart, La Fleur, and the compelling white longshoreman, Big Blonde. Most unusually, McKay parted from the effortless ramblers of his earlier fiction to flesh out a protagonist who confronts a serious bodily disability. Reversing *Banjo*'s subtitle, "The Jungle and the Bottoms" would be a love story including a plot, a fully peopled, dramatically sequenced romance steered by a physically challenged African hero and his wholehearted "burning brown"[59] mistress.

Stopping in Barcelona in September 1929, McKay wrote the novel's first words, and by December he had enough pages to solicit the opinion of his eminent literary agent.[60] William Aspenwall Bradley, praised by Gertrude Stein as the foremost "friend and comforter of Paris writers,"[61] responded with reservations, most of all about the supposedly unsympathetic treatment of the protagonist, at that time still called Taloufa. Essentially agreeing with Bradley's concern that the new novel replicated *Banjo*'s discursive style, McKay replied in turn by emphasizing his intent to "tackle Taloufa's story in another form"[62] and "make a difficult thing of it,"[63] adding greater suspense and intricacy. McKay also assured Bradley that the novel would be notably different from the two that came before it. For one thing, he would dispense with an obvious alter ego, eventually landing on the better-disguised mouthpiece of Etienne St. Dominique, his last name evoking Saint-Domingue, the French colony that became the black republic of Haiti, and thus a reminder of the long, not-just-personal history of black revolution. "You see there is [not] and won't be any Ray in the tale," McKay guaranteed, since he "realized that the form was very awkward and that some of my best scenes, the love ones for instance, would be stifled by it."[64] St. Dominique's divergence from Ray/McKay is reinforced by his resemblance to another historical figure, the Senegalese Communist and black nationalist Lamine Senghor (1889–1927). McKay's *A Long Way from Home* cordially recalls his friendship with this founder of the radical *Comité de Défense de la Race Nègre*—and distinguishes him from the better-remembered Négritude poet and Senegalese politician Léopold Sédar Senghor. "This Senghor," McKay clarifies, "was a tall, lean intelligent Senegalese and his ideas were a mixture of African nationalism and international Communism. Senghor was interested in my writing and said he wished I would write the truth about the Negroes in Marseilles. I promised him I would some day [sic]."[65] "The Jungle and the Bottoms," McKay's second crack at fulfilling this promise, sprinkles Lamine Senghor's left-nationalist opinions into its comparatively unforced political dialogue. It also memorializes his patronage of Marseille's Communist-sponsored "International Seamen's Building,"[66] renamed the "Seamen's Club" in *Romance*'s final draft.[67]

McKay took much less kindly to his agent's recommendation that he show his novel's disabled protagonist in a more pitying light. "Primarily I am not writing a sentimental story about Taloufa," he instructed Bradley. His hero was no Dickensian puppet of lamed innocence, and to make him "extremely acceptable I should have to write a real sob-sister story and that I just cannot do."[68] Softening the tenor and language of Taloufa's less-than-angelic reactions to his disability would betray not only the character's humanity, but also the novel's racial distinctiveness, McKay suggested, which he meant to present without special pleading. Implicitly tangling with Du Bois, a sworn enemy of *Home to Harlem*'s "filth"[69] who controversially preached that "all Art is propaganda and ever must be,"[70] McKay insisted on the naturalness and political ingenuousness of Taloufa's racy speech. Of that and other frankly "racial stuff in the story,"[71] McKay told Bradley, "I felt that that came naturally as the talk and thought of the Negroes, giving a peculiar and definite color to the human story. I never thought of it as propaganda nor felt even the happy-go-lucky Negro does not think and feel and talk that way."

Interestingly, McKay's response to Bradley's letter also lays out his blueprint for shaping Taloufa's trajectory into a "problem novel." As McKay understood the genre, such a novel would be less a muckraking exposé of a social crisis than an articulate study of socially molded intellectual and psychological tensions. "I don't think a good problem novel of Negro life should not be written," McKay enjoined. "I will admit that perhaps Taloufa's state of mind and my analysis of it do not go with the picaresque story—but if I am to go on as a writer my characters beside acting must think and talk some sense. . . ."[72] In this way, diving deep into Taloufa's motivations, some of them less than noble, the novel could air both the racial particularity and interracial universality of his unstable experience. Taloufa's "character is changed by his fortune—but that is also a common human thing. [He] excuses himself because he has been amputated but that is also the common human trick."[73] His protagonist's tricky human psychology, moreover, would not crowd out a vivid storyline. McKay repeatedly warned himself off a shaggy narrative, instead diagramming arcs and plot points: "The climax comes when Taloufa is arrested just when he was about to slip away" and his comrades "have to try to get him freed."[74] In another, June 1930 letter to longtime friend and mentor Max Eastman, McKay distinguished "The Jungle and the Bottoms" as "a real story with something of a plot, involving a West African young man (who had lost his legs stowing away and received good compensation through the efforts of an ambulance chaser) and a North African Negroid girl. They two represent the 'jungle' in the 'bottoms' that the girl, who is a whore there, wants to leave to go back to Africa with the man."[75]

McKay's apologia for his infant novel was extensive, foreshadowing the many obstacles it would confront on the way to completion. Nine months after his initial letter vindicating "The Jungle and the Bottoms" to Bradley, he was back at its defense, answering his agent's persistent worry that it was *Banjo* redux. This time out, McKay pledged to Bradley that he was structuring a narrative "very different in style and

mood,"[76] with characters "more fully realized"[77] than any he
had conceived previously. "As the book is a more serious
attempt than the others and will set the tone for future work,"
McKay maintained, "I should like to make it as perfect as I
can."[78] Making it perfect, at this stage of the game, involved
veiling pieces of its unmistakable Marseille scenery. The final
draft of "The Jungle and the Bottoms" refers to the city as
"Dreamport,"[79] and the Vieux Port, the culturally subterra-
nean precinct of Marseille where his characters roam and
clash, as the "Bottoms." A candid explanation of the Dreamport contrivance appears in McKay's June 1930 letter to Eastman: "The scene is the same as 'Banjo,' but I call the town
Dreamport as it might have been any of six European ports."[80]

Though insincere about his setting, McKay was in earnest
about the fuller realization of his characters. For the first time,
his fiction regularly turned to focus on well-rounded though
hypersexualized female actors. La Fleur Noire enters "The
Jungle and the Bottoms" as the most-desired and most-fêted
black escort in Marseille. She is equally "small and straight"[81]
and strong-willed, autonomous enough to carve a path without a pimp despite her likeness to "a new-fangled doll done in
dark-brown wax."[82] La Fleur's defining enemy, Aslima, nicknamed "the Tigress," is a Quayside prostitute who learns to
love Taloufa/Lafala without mercenary reservation. Glow-
ingly "stout and full of an abundance of earthly sap and compact of inexhaustible energy in spite of the grinding waste of
it,"[83] her appearance cleanly divides her from La Fleur while
sounding a related note of three-dimensional self-contradiction.
Laboring on his initial draft, an animated McKay notified
Bradley that Aslima ("Zhima" in a now-lost, initial version)
was flourishing of her own accord and taking control of the
narrative, its author included: "the Arab girl is growing bigger
than I ever dreamed and running away with the book and
me."[84] Further down the road of composition, Aslima took
possession of the book's final chapter, scene, and paragraph,
her martyrdom reorienting the meaning of Lafala's rags-to-
riches return to Africa, at last glance a kind of solo Garveyism
purchased at an excessive price.

Another sign of the complexity of La Fleur's character is her unashamed lesbianism. When it comes to the business of sex, and the points of pride derived from it, La Fleur and Aslima vie for Lafala's trade and devotion, forming a prototypical novelistic love triangle. In a not-uncommon eroticizing of disability, the two *desmoiselles de Marseille* echo a team of Harlem working girls introduced earlier in the novel and compete to transform Lafala's figuratively castrated legs into potent "honeysticks."[85] When it comes to La Fleur's unpurchased affections, however, her desires are same-sex. As Aslima explains, her rival is "different from most of us. She doesn't go crazy over men. She hates men and goes with them only to make money."[86] Dissecting the sexual politics of modern prostitution with unusual realism and a creative dose of Charles Baudelaire's *Les Fleurs du Mal* (1857), the novel clarifies that La Fleur's authentic love and trusted partner is no male procurer but a "Greek girl."[87] In *Home to Harlem*, McKay's spokesman Ray praises the ancient lyricist Sappho as "a wonderful woman, a great Greek poet," whose life gave "two lovely words to modern language," "Sapphic" and "lesbian."[88] In *Romance in Marseille*, these words spring into modern life in the person of La Fleur's girlfriend, a young woman from Sappho's part of the world. And they are underlined by La Fleur's last interaction with Aslima, which hints that her antipathy to the Tigress has been the other side of craving. La Fleur fights to save her adversary from her pimp's vengeance, pulling at her on her couch and breaking down in tears, vowing that "she was sorry"[89] she had ever been cruel. The Tigress neither reciprocates nor acts on La Fleur's warning, but McKay succeeds in planting the prospect that Lafala has been the odd one out in the triangle, from one angle the empowered subject of Aslima's maturing love and from another the token object of a charged emotional exchange between women. None of this last-minute retouching erases the novel's displays of nonchalant misogyny. Lafala righteously gut-punches La Fleur with his remanded "stump,"[90] for example, and affections between men on McKay's Marseille docks are readily cemented through common enjoyment of a woman's humiliation. For its part, Du Bois's NAACP comes in for a nasty sexist insult as "C.U.N.T.," the "Christian Unity of Negro Tribes."[91] Even so, the late-arriving evidence of La Fleur's hunger for Aslima reveals that more than one formidable, plot-moving female character promised to grab the book before McKay let it go.

"The Jungle and the Bottoms," the first step toward *Romance in Marseille*, opened new paths for McKay when depicting women and same-sex desire. "The Jungle" would not only bring male queer figures out of the shadows, it would also portray flawed but sympathetic lesbians. Wayne F. Cooper's excellent, still-standard 1987 biography of McKay observes that in "The Jungle and the Bottoms," the author "frankly and sympathetically discussed for the first time the plight of homosexuals in Western society."[92] Cooper's praise overstates the book's qualifications as a landmark LGBTQ manifesto, since it misses the fact that it refrains from picturing homosexuality as much of a plight to begin with. But Cooper's accent on the candor and compassion of McKay's portraiture points to one reason behind the hesitation of potential publishers. McKay's editor at Harper & Brothers beginning with *Home to Harlem*, Eugene Saxton, apparently winced at the comfortably queer characters of "The Jungle," wondering if they "would be accepted by the American reading public."[93] Saxton's push to renovate and liberalize Harper led him to court such pagan moderns as Edna St. Vincent Millay, but his plans to publish the new did not eliminate every trace of his editorial squeamishness. As *Banjo* made its way to press, he had supervised Harper's removal of the novel's most graphic "vernacular phrasing."[94] He surrendered to McKay's pleas to return his original language only at the author's own expense, reasoning that "the book was already in proofs."[95] The bald-faced take on the queer vernacular in McKay's "Jungle" was a bridge too far for Saxton, it seems, beyond the reach of even such a one-sided bargain.

Unease with a novel's open and flexible sexuality was a familiar complication for the bisexual McKay, like Millay a veteran of Harlem and Greenwich Village bohemias in the "Lyrical Left" era of hybrid erotic and political radicalisms. Following the critical yet not financial success of *Harlem Shadows*,[96] an epochal addition to black world poetry including the now-canonical sonnets "If We Must Die" and "America," McKay decided he should try his luck in a more popular mode. Settling in Paris with the support of a Garland Fund[97] grant from 1923 to 1925, he took his first stab at a novel. The result was "Color Scheme," an effort to narrow the gap between Harlem's official renaissance and its everyday black folk, to McKay's mind a people of unprompted creativity who expressed themselves "with a zest as yet to be depicted by a true artist."[98] His inaugural novel would hew "hard to the line" of their lively sincerity, McKay affirmed, and compose "a realistic comedy of life as I saw it among Negroes."[99] A sexual passage or two might need masking in French phrases, he conceded, but the truth of humanly messy black desire would for once be told without regard for the consequences. "I make my Negro characters yarn and backbite and fuck like people the world over,"[100] McKay swanked to Arthur Schomburg, the Puerto Rican bibliophile whose collection grew to include the final, finished typescript of *Romance in Marseille*.

McKay's design for "Color Scheme," an anticipatory salvo against the slightly later Du Boisian case for art as racial propaganda, prefigured the impetus behind the stories, poems, and plays of *Fire!!* (1926), the little magazine that sent the biggest shockwaves through Harlem's renaissance. Edited by Wallace Thurman and with contributions from "Younger Negro Artists" including Langston Hughes, Countee Cullen, Zora Neale Hurston, Gwendolyn Bennett, and Richard Bruce Nugent, *Fire!!* was intended "to burn up a lot of the old, dead conventional Negro-white ideas of the past"[101] and to scandalize black bourgeois tastes in particular. It emphatically accomplished the second task. The reaction of the bourgeois critic at the *Afro-American*, who owned up to tossing "the first issue of *Fire!!* into the fire,"[102] was typical. Had it been published, McKay's "Color Scheme" would have come in for similarly spirited reactions. More important, it would have antedated the first starkly queer prose fiction of the Harlem Renaissance, Nugent's most daring addition to *Fire!!*, the elliptical, genre-bending New Negro roll call "Smoke, Lilies and Jade,"[103] now considered the font of black queer writing. All that can be known for sure about the contents of McKay's first pass at a novel, however, are references to the text in correspondence. Alfred A. Knopf, Hughes's innovative highbrow publisher, rejected "Color Scheme" in July 1925, citing its unevenness and the minor snag that "should it ever appear in print its explicit sexual references would almost certainly be judged obscene by the courts."[104] McKay avoided a chancy future as a modernist cause célèbre by burning his single copy of the novel, beating every reviewer to the bonfire.

Romance in Marseille provides our best guess as to what "Color Scheme" would have done with its "explicit sexual references." Both *Home to Harlem* and to a lesser extent *Banjo* contain recognizably gay characters, but they are generally surveyed from a distance as urban subcultural types, quick-drawn baby-doll "fairies" or broadly comic butches as in Billy Biasse, a *Home to Harlem* sidekick nicknamed "the Wolf" because "he eats his own kind."[105] A lone three-dimensional queer character, the authorial stand-in Ray, offers learned color commentary on sexual diversity in both novels, but (unlike McKay) suffers from a debilitating Freudian latency and alienation. In the less inhibited universe of *Romance*, same-sex love is consciously normal, customarily accepted behavior. A character called Babel, a stowaway companion of Lafala, ironically speaks in the queer-friendly lingua franca of McKay's Vieux Port. When stealing a dance with Big Blonde, the equally king-size Babel declares that if sex is madness, then he is "crazy all ways bar none."[106] Big Blonde and other more exclusively gay characters are presented as pillars of the Quayside community, personifying neither the neurotic costs of the closet nor a desublimated Jazz Age liberation. Like *Romance*'s straighter figures, they naturalistically navigate the Marseille waterfront and supply plotlines along with titillating atmosphere. The lesbian La Fleur, for example, injects a louche Baudelairean note while playing a vital role in the unraveling of events involving Lafala and Aslima. Her interactions with both of these lovers underscore the ethic of sexual pleasure that McKay introduces in company with his queer characters. Lafala's road to restored wholeness is divided between the private satisfactions of his bank account and the mutual joys of sleeping with Aslima, who refuses payment for sex and quickly refutes his worry that "'I can't be as piggish as in my able-bodied days.'" "'Pigskin!'" she exclaims. "'Forget about your feet now and thank God it wasn't something worse that was cut off.'"[107] Taking leave from Jake Barnes, the impotent hero of Ernest Hemingway's modern classic *The Sun Also Rises* (1926), Lafala has the option of loving his way past his injury and trauma. "'[W]ith you I don't feel that it's just a mud bath,'" Aslima offers, "'I feel like we're clean pigs.'"[108] His culminating choice of dirty money over purifying lust makes for *Romance*'s saddest tragedy. The waning of compulsory heterosexuality, the novel submits, might relax compulsory able-bodiedness inside and outside the bedroom. As the novel's last ship sails, however, McKay's disabled protagonist has elected the less sensuous, less virtuous path.

Fortunately, McKay did not destroy "The Jungle and the Bottoms," though he did wrestle with aspects of its cleanly piggish erotic scenes.[109] First and foremost, he faced the challenge of devising a romantic lead whose disability was based on one or more cases well-known to him while remote from his own bodily history. In 1923, McKay had spent six weeks in a Paris clinic under treatment for syphilis, and his bedridden convalescence there informs the opening hospital chapters of "The Jungle and the Bottoms." Slow-boiling health problems derived from his venereal disease, exacerbated by its debilitating treatment with mercury, mounted as McKay pursued the novel, and forced him in 1930 into painful spinal tap surgery in Berlin.[110] Lafala's infirmity was of a different order and location than his own, however, and McKay was at times unsure of his ability to give it life. An "amputated man" was a full-blown departure from Jake Brown, the footloose hero of *Home to Harlem*, and from practically the whole vagabond society of *Banjo*'s black "beach boys." McKay was among the New Negro authors most identified with black male vitality, his early fiction elevating a still-primal black manhood above an emasculating West to overturn the venerable racist opposition between the civilized and the primitive. Léopold Senghor, Aimé Césaire, and other originators of Négritude were not alone in memorizing *Banjo*'s hymns to the superior vital force of black men.[111] Yet in "The Jungle and the Bottoms," McKay asked himself to inhabit a demobilized black male body, one whose taxing prosthetic travels would illuminate ableisms of race and sex, labor and capital, international imperialism and transatlantic black resistance. What Lennard J. Davis, one of the creators of disability studies, describes as the moral of "dismodernism" also summarizes a lesson that "The Jungle" intuited but rather struggled to express: "Impairment is the rule, and normalcy is the fantasy. Dependence is the reality, and independence grandiose thinking."[112]

When McKay first put aside "The Jungle and the Bottoms" in June 1930, the impairing effects of syphilis were one culprit. (His disease and its dire treatment, he wrote his agent, had become "something terribly real."[113]) Another reason for quitting the book was Harper editor Eugene Saxton's ongoing doubt, which led McKay to sift through "the novel again more critically," and decide "that the whole second half"[114] needed work. The self-imposed distraction of a book of short stories, what became McKay's 1932 collection *Gingertown*, was the final straw. *Gingertown*'s exploration of another prose genre, McKay wrote to William Aspenwall Bradley, would show "that I am a writer of many moods and open the way for any book on any theme I may choose to write."[115] Attempting to persuade McKay to return to "The Jungle and the Bottoms," judging it flawed but still viable, Bradley warned that short story collections rarely sold.[116] But an obstinately freelance writer, most headstrong when cornered, failed to take his agent's advice. As both Saxton and Bradley predicted, *Gingertown* was a commercial failure, earning nothing for either Harper or its author.[117] Though the book did better with the critics, some important reviews slighted McKay as démodé. Writing in the *New York Herald Tribune Books* supplement, the witty Harlem novelist Rudolph Fisher implied that the long-absent Jamaican had lost touch with black New York's evolving modernisms. The "robust vigor" of *Home to Harlem* and *Banjo* was still there in quantity, Fisher allowed, but the collection's suite of Harlem stories was set in a New York in name only, an illusory place where "strange West-Indianisms" were placed in the "mouths of American blacks."[118] In short, the collection suffered from making Black Manhattan another version of McKay's multilingual Black Marseille.

As the *Gingertown* disappointment swelled, McKay took

his character Lafala's cue and pursued his favorite remedy for disenchantment: migration. He returned to Tangier, Morocco, and, flouting the French colonizer's rules on the habitation of non-Moroccans, moved into a small house outside the intensely watched International Zone. Transforming the place from an "old barn without doors" into a "very habitable" home took time and "the best part"[119] of his remaining assets, McKay reported. A unified, pot-boiling novel—not stories of many moods—was thus required if he was to maintain his new dwelling with "a most lovely view of the sea."[120]

Rather than taking the simplest step (seldom McKay's first move) and returning to his shelved Marseille manuscript, however, he launched a new novel set in Jamaica, eventually published by Harper & Row in 1933. This novel's title, *Banana Bottom*, obviously borrows from that of "The Jungle and the Bottoms." Less plainly, McKay's unanticipated fascination with Aslima, depicted as a former child prostitute in "The Jungle," factored into his decision to focus on a sexually abused female protagonist, Bita Plant. Invisible to most every reader of *Banana Bottom* was the stress added to McKay's writing life by surveillance from French intelligence agents and British operatives, a bitter encore of earlier harassment from the American FBI. During the worst of the scrutiny, McKay's old house was burglarized, and his passport taken, in dodgy circumstances. By the time he received a new passport, biographer Wayne F. Cooper tells us, "the chief English consul in Tangier had removed from it his right to travel in the territories of the British Empire."[121] McKay could thus go home to Harlem, as he did in 1934, but never again to the Jamaican birthplace in which he situated Bita Plant's life story.

Soon after New Year's Day, 1933, awaiting news of sales and reviews of *Banana Bottom*, McKay at last resumed work on "The Jungle and the Bottoms." Recognizing that he should avoid a duplication of *Banana Bottom*'s "bottom" in the title, he renamed the book "Savage Loving." And, following through, the name of his Marseille neighborhood—the "Bottoms," in the previous draft—became "Quayside." The spicy "Savage Loving" was also chosen to make a marketable impression. McKay had a new representative, moreover, to peddle his newly titled novel. Resentful of Bradley's lack of enthusiasm for *Gingertown*, he had replaced him with John Trounstine, a New York–based literary agent McKay met in Tangier with Paul Bowles in 1932.[122] One of Trounstine's first duties, unfortunately, was to deliver a "knock-out blow"[123] to his client, news that *Banana Bottom* had fared no better than *Gingertown*. "Evidently my readers prefer my realism of rough slum life [over that] of rural life," McKay groused in a letter to Max Eastman. Again lifting himself off the canvas, McKay concluded that he had no choice but to "supply the need"[124] for his rugged urban realism. Here, then, was further reason to bury the title "The Jungle and the Bottoms." "Savage Loving" was both more suggestive and less primitively pastoral.

One of the weightiest revisions McKay tackled on "Savage Loving" was the addition of Big Blonde. As his name underscores, this "firm-footed, broad-shouldered," and "splendidly built"[125] specimen is larger than life, a specifically working-class American émigré whose status as a socialist colossus is barely undercut by his lack of "interest in the workers' unions."[126] An oversized propaganda drawing in the novel's Communist Seamen's Club, hung under smaller photographs of Marx and Lenin, mirrors Big Blonde's heroic proletarian heft and easy intimacy with black working men. In the drawing, a pair of "terrible giants, one white, the other black," braced "themselves to break the chains that bound them. And under the drawing was an exhortation: 'Workers of the World, Unite to Break Your Chains!'"[127] Big Blonde can be said to take this famous exhortation, a popularization of the final lines of *The Communist Manifesto*, as literal writ. He enters McKay's novel just in time to free his black radical pal St. Dominique from the clutches of an enraged mob. And he does such chain-breaking work in full ownership of the feminizing *e* at the end of his name. McKay's character tips his hat to the less intrepid female heroine of Dorothy Parker's story "Big Blonde," not coincidentally published in 1929. Parker appreciated McKay's fiction, praising *Home to Harlem* for "putting even further in their place the writings of Mr. Carl Van Vechten,"[128] above all the white Negro's cluelessly titled novel *Nigger Heaven* (1926). McKay returned the favor in *Romance*, whose Big Blonde seconds Parker's in savoring the power to incite "some men when they use the word 'blonde' to click their tongues and wag their heads roguishly."[129] With his variation on a Big Blonde theme, McKay makes a fearless butch-femme out of the socialist-realist ideal of the hammer-swinging male proletarian.

During the "Savage Loving" stage of revision, McKay also pressed forward on the scheme he had laid out in his December 1929 letter to Bradley. For a change, he would compose a Marseille novel *avec* plot. Political allegories attached to Big Blonde and St. Dominique would not be pinned to a merely episodic arrangement, McKay ensured, adding more than ten new chapters that kept the story flowing. A willing publisher still proved a hard target, however. After the failure of *Banana Bottom*, Harper & Brothers refused to sign another contract with him.[130] Alfred A. Knopf agreed to consider the novel, but from their perspective, perhaps tainted by considering "Color Scheme" almost a decade prior, "Savage Loving" appeared "crudely thrown together and strangely dated in depression-ridden New Deal America."[131] Closer to the end of his rope, McKay once more wrote to Max Eastman for advice. Unsure of his ability to approximate the tastes of contemporary publishers, McKay's oldest sounding board punted the task to Clifton Fadiman, an experienced reader for Simon & Schuster. The result was the opposite of encouraging. Fadiman intensely disliked "Savage Loving," judging that "McKay is trying to work a Hemingway on material to which Hemingway is not adapted."[132] *The Sun Also Rises*, it seems, had better framed the scene of Lost Generation refugees trapped between alcoholic hilarity and primal struggles over love and loss. In the most crushing blow, Fadiman demeaned McKay's novel as "sex hash" without redeeming literary merit.[133]

While we tend to think of the Lost Generation and the Harlem Renaissance as discrete, even antagonistic schools of interwar literature, Fadiman's detection of Hemingway's imprint on "Savage Loving" in fact was warranted. Like the Papa of American minimalism, McKay lived and wrote as an expatriate, primarily in Paris, during most of the 1920s. While it is unknown if the two modernists' paths crossed on the Left Bank, McKay certainly respected the Hemingway style. In his

1937 memoir, *A Long Way from Home*, McKay confessed to
"a vast admiration for Ernest Hemingway as a writer."[134] His
comments on Hemingway's *In Our Time* (1925), "that thin
rare book of miniature short stories," include the cherished
memory of receiving as a gift a first edition at the Café du
Dôme: "My hand trembled to take it. . . . I have it still. It
became so valuable that I once consigned it for a loan. But I
redeemed it, and, excepting my typewriter, I hardly ever trouble to redeem the things I own."[135] When he speaks of *The Sun
Also Rises*, McKay unwraps a metaphor that echoes Hemingway's stylistic pugilism: "When Hemingway wrote *The Sun
Also Rises*, he shot a fist in the face of the false romantic-
realists and said, 'You can't fake about life like that.'"[136] None-
theless, *A Long Way from Home* takes the trouble of rejecting
Fadiman's charges that McKay was a Hemingway mimic:
"Some of my critics thought that I was imitating him. But I am
also a critic of myself. And I fail to find any relationship
between my loose manner and subjective feeling in writing
and Hemingway's objective and carefully stylized form."[137]

If Fadiman missed the measure of literary value in "Savage
Loving," he was onto something respecting Hemingway's
imprint on the novel. The McKay prose that grew into
Romance in Marseille is in fact some of his least "loose" and
most Hemingwayesque. Its third-person narration swells into
a number of figurative dream sequences in free-indirect style,
but elsewhere favors a brisk, "objective" concision. Tight,
tough talk in relatively short, declarative sentences—the voice
of the Black Renaissance gone proto-noir—is a *Romance* rule
less scrupulously observed in *Banjo* or *Home to Harlem*.
"'There'll be lots of people trying to get on to you,' said the
nurse," runs a typical exchange. "'They won't find me easy
though,' said Lafala. 'I've lost my legs but not my head.'"[138]
Pile-ups of unadorned *said*s suggest another Hemingway nod.
Beyond the similarities in prose style, Lafala's symbolically
rich amputation is of course a cousin to Jake Barnes's Great
War castration. Like *The Sun Also Rises*, *Romance*'s narrative
stems from a modern male body shorn of vital parts. Along
with the indelible character of Porgy, the lovesick African
American beggar with "inadequate nether extremities"[139]

introduced in DuBose Heyward's 1925 novel of the same
name, Hemingway's hero is Lafala's most important fictional
predecessor.

Fadiman's ungenerous remarks on "Savage Loving" also
accurately warned of New York publishing's continued wari-
ness of modernist obscenity, real and imputed. His dismissal
of the novel's "sex hash" must have reminded McKay of
Eugene Saxton's suspicion that "The Jungle and the Bottoms"
was, as Gertrude Stein deemed Hemingway's short story "Up
in Michigan," "*inaccrochable*"[140]: unmarketable due to its
ostensible indecency. McKay knew the high stakes of American obscenity law as a book buyer as well as a book writer. In
1927, Harold Jackman, the chic companion of the Harlem
poet Countee Cullen, wrote McKay in Paris, hoping that he
might send back a copy of James Joyce's *Ulysses*, then banned
in the United States. Jackman mailed McKay a money order
and instructions on how to ship the book, a "stunt" he had
learned from mutual friend Gwendolyn Bennett. While living
in Paris on scholarship during the mid-1920s, Bennett had
smuggled a disguised edition to her U.S. home address. The
best method, she advised Jackman and Jackman advised
McKay, was to remove the novel's cover and first two pages. A
"dummy" cover could then be attached, ensuring that U.S.
customs agents were none the wiser. The detached book jacket
and title pages would arrive in a separate package, and *Ulysses*
could be reassembled.[141]

The liberation of Joyce's mega-novel from such minor plots
would come in December 1933, when District Judge John M.
Woolsey decided in favor of its "serious experiment"[142] in the
celebrated case of *United States v. One Book Called Ulysses*.
But Woolsey's blow for free expression did not arrive in time
to keep Countee Cullen from advising, long-distance, that
"Savage Loving" was burdened by a risqué title begging for
censorship. In June 1933, McKay complained to Eastman that
Cullen had convinced Trounstine, McKay's new agent, that
his book-in-progress "sounded obscene."[143] An aging New
Negro prodigy whom McKay condemned as "that little
prig"[144] thus provoked his novel's final name change. During
the summer of 1933, or soon after, "Savage Loving" went

undercover as *Romance in Marseille*, and Cullen effectively had the last word on the title of McKay's last expatriate fiction.

The new and less dangerous title was insufficient to convince McKay that he would make a success of *Romance in Marseille*. His final year in Morocco was plagued by colonial authorities and mounting health problems, and little in the reaction to his developing novel argued that it would ease his financial distress. In August 1933, he lost the lease on his seafront home outside the French-policed International Zone, and was forced to sell his furnishings in Tangier's "native market."[145] "I won't be able to carry on [writing] with a sure hand," McKay wrote Eastman, "until I hear from you or some other good critic that I am on the right track."[146] No encouraging word arrived, and by October, McKay was without "a sou"[147] and close to collapse. "Aframerica" called out to him for the first time in more than a decade, principally because Alain Locke, James Weldon Johnson, and other patrons of the Depression-slowed Harlem Renaissance promised to raise money for his ticket to New York. "New York is your market," Johnson assured him, "and the United States is your field. Furthermore, we, the Negro writers, need you here."[148] The odds are that McKay put his final stamp on the completed typescript of *Romance in Marseille* in the late fall or early winter of 1933, rushing to beat a boat to the United States he boarded in January 1934—legally embarking on the ocean crossing his character Lafala had taken illicitly but just as necessarily.

McKay seems to have put *Romance* out of mind as soon as he sailed for New York, and not much changed for it during his first years back in the city. The single, easily overlooked reference to the novel in his 1937 memoir comes as part of an excuse for why he reluctantly, and later regretfully, contributed to Nancy Cunard's *Negro: An Anthology* (1934): "Meanwhile I had come to the point of a breakdown while working on my novel in Morocco; and besides I was in pecuniary difficulties."[149] No identifying title of this novel, neither "The Jungle and the Bottoms" nor "Savage Loving" nor *Romance in Marseille*, is thought worth providing. *A Long Way from Home* abounds with wordy impressions of McKay's rootless life, first as a newly arrived American poet moonlighting on the Pennsylvania Railroad, then as an editor of *The Liberator* and a draftsman of the Harlem Renaissance, and finally as an elective exile in France, Spain, England, Russia, Germany, and Morocco. It is peppered with hundreds of texts, incidents, and observations, from exchanges with prominent artists and underground revolutionaries, to whole poems and stories of cities across Europe and Africa. The memoir's single, cursory reference to a Marseille novel McKay had given five recent years indicates how little he wanted to remember it by 1937, a sign of his bitterness over its long, laborious road. This first publication of *Romance in Marseille* testifies that *A Long Way from Home* buried a worthy book. In the case of Lafala and his stowaway crew, a hard-pressed self-critic proved too mistrustful of his own work, and foreshortened what should have been one of the bravest and liveliest extensions of his legacy.

GARY EDWARD HOLCOMB *and* WILLIAM J. MAXWELL

A Note on the Text

The story of the provenance and absence of *Romance in Marseille* over the past eighty-seven years may be as interesting as the novel itself. To begin with, it should be noted that *Romance* is not a long-lost, now-recovered text, since access to the novel has been possible to some degree since the 1940s. As the introduction describes, the title Claude McKay applied to the novel from 1929 to 1930 was "The Jungle and the Bottoms," and then during the early 1930s, the title became "Savage Loving." For related reasons, two hand-corrected typescript versions of *Romance* have been available to researchers. A truncated draft of the novel is kept in the collection of the Beinecke Rare Book and Manuscript Library at Yale University, while the lengthier, complete, and final version is held at the Schomburg Center for Research in Black Culture in Harlem.[1] How the two versions came to be, and how they came to rest in two historic African American archives, makes for another significant chapter of *Romance in Marseille*.

Distracted by temperament and circumstance, McKay more than once forgot about long writing projects he had left behind, and this is the case with *Romance in Marseille*.[2] By the time he published his 1937 memoir, *A Long Way from Home*, McKay recollected the Marseille-set novel only in passing, and somewhat mysteriously did not call it by any of its several names. A mere four years later, he claimed to have forgotten about it entirely.[3] In 1941, the same year that McKay completed the recently rediscovered novel *Amiable with Big Teeth* (2017),[4] Harlem Renaissance enthusiast Carl Van Vechten asked McKay to donate his manuscripts to the new James Weldon Johnson collection.[5] The collection was under assembly with help from Yale, and was then housed in the university's Gothic Revival Sterling Library (the translucent granite modernist structure now synonymous with the Beinecke would not be built until the 1960s). Habitually itinerant, McKay had lost track of several of his own typescripts over the years, so he reacted positively to the chance to have Van Vechten and Yale do the work of retrieving his missing manuscripts for him.[6] Yale librarian Bernhard Knollenberg contacted McKay's publishers and requested the manuscripts, and all complied.[7] Lee Furman passed along the master copy of the lively *A Long Way from Home*. Dutton sent the manuscript of the Federal Writers' Project–sponsored study *Harlem: Negro Metropolis* (1940). And Harper and Brothers dispatched the original typescript of the last McKay novel published in his lifetime, *Banana Bottom* (1933).

During the acquisition process, however, a phantom document turned up. While looking through his files, a Harper editor found "a shorter typescript of 88 pages which was attached to" the typescript of *Banana Bottom*.[8] "These unnamed scripts had been stored in my files for some time," the editor recounted, "and I should have been unaware of their presence had word not come to me from you of Mr. McKay's wishes." Though the editor does not specify the typescript, he does include the useful information that on the top page is the ink stamp of "W. A. Bradley, the Paris agent who was handling the matter for McKay." In a postscript to Knollenberg, the Harper editor also notes he once had worked with McKay. The identity of the Harper editor, John B. Turner, marks an iconic turn in *Romance*'s provenance, since the man in question was none other than John Trounstine, McKay's literary agent after Bradley. Trounstine's P.S. includes the tidbit that he had legally changed his name to Turner. In the early 1930s, McKay had met Trounstine in Tangier. Having abruptly parted with William Aspenwall Bradley, his astute "Yankee" representative, in part over the fate of "The Jungle and the Bottoms," McKay asked Trounstine to be his literary agent.[9] In 1933, Trounstine sent McKay the demoralizing news that *Banana Bottom* had washed out. To McKay's vexation and eventual wrath, his new agent was then unsuccessful in securing a publisher for the renamed "Savage Loving."[10]

Another curious detail is that participants in the correspondence—including McKay—allude to the *Romance* manuscript not by one of its sundry official titles but as "Lafala." Because no title appeared on the document attached to *Banana Bottom*, Knollenberg and Van Vechten abstracted the name of the protagonist, and McKay likely rolled with "Lafala" in order to expedite his plan. Yale justifiably wanted all the McKay literary documents it could get, including "Lafala." But when McKay learned of the full situation, he wrote back to Van Vechten in a temper, demanding that he be sent all of the scripts with the exception of the just-published *Harlem: Negro Metropolis*: "I especially want to have back Banana Bottom and the unfinished manuscript of Lafala, which I had forgotten about and don't want to be in any collection."[11] A shrewd Van Vechten wrote to Knollenberg forthwith, requesting that he return "Lafala" to McKay, suggesting that the down-and-out author might hope that a benefactor would buy the manuscript from him to donate to the burgeoning James Weldon Johnson collection.[12]

What is now an eighty-seven-page version of the novel at the Beinecke, with Bradley's name and address stamped on the title page, is most likely "The Jungle and the Bottoms," the initial draft that McKay discussed in correspondence with his then-agent William Bradley in 1929 and 1930. Since McKay himself referred to the novel as "unfinished," we are convinced that the Beinecke version is not simply a stray fragment but the honed if uncompleted version that McKay composed before deciding to expand the novel. Near-conclusive evidence suggesting that the eighty-seven-page manuscript is the original version can be found in the fact that Marseille is still referred to as "Dreamport," the code name for the Mediterranean city that McKay decided on while originally outlining the narrative.[13] Moreover, the name "Lafala" is handwritten over the redacted name "Taloufa" eight times in the document, showing that McKay was still in the early stages of changing the protagonist's name. A both helpful and hindering fact is that

on what passes for the cover page of the Beinecke typescript is
the hand-printed name "Mac Kay," misspelled and complete
with a mistaken space between the syllables. Below the name,
in quotation marks, are the words "New Novel," with no
title following, authorizing the three correspondents to refer to
the untitled manuscript as "Lafala" in the early 1940s. While
no title appears on the typescript, the Beinecke manuscript is
catalogued as "Romance in Marseille," with no Anglicizing
final *s*. The "New Novel" label was likely the result of an editor creating a top page for easier filing, which would also
account for the error in McKay's surname. In view of all of the
above, we consider the eighty-seven-page Beinecke manuscript
to be the draft of the novel that McKay produced from 1929 to
1930, known during the time of its creation as "The Jungle
and the Bottoms."

Significantly, rather than intending to find a buyer for "The
Jungle"/"Lafala" with a view toward donation, as Van Vechten guessed, McKay likely planned to try to publish it once
more. Two years after the Van Vechten-Knollenberg-McKay
exchanges, Ivie Jackman, the sister of McKay's friend Harold,
contacted the author to request material for what would
become the Countee Cullen–Harold Jackman Memorial Collection at Atlanta University. McKay replied that aside from a
number of valuable letters from James Weldon Johnson, "the
only other thing I have here is a novel which I was to work
over some day and this is the only copy."[14] McKay is almost
certainly referring to his single copy of "The Jungle"/"Lafala."
The author has apparently regained some of his enthusiasm,
and is thinking of restoring the novel with the final chapters
and dramatic ending that appear in the longer "Savage Loving," ultimately titled *Romance in Marseille*.

The 172-page Schomburg typescript of *Romance* is therefore
in all likelihood the final, complete draft, produced from 1932
to 1933 in Tangier. It is the result of McKay's plan to go through
the novel "again more critically," as he had written to Max
Eastman in December 1930, resolving in particular "that the
whole second half could be rearranged for the better."[15] Typed
on the Schomburg version's title page is "ROMANCE IN
MARSEILLES," and beneath that "BY CLAUDE McKAY."

The added *s* in Marseille might complicate matters except that the title page is the only portion of the document where an *s* is appended. Throughout the remainder of the text, as in the Beinecke version, "Marseille" appears in its shorter spelling. When McKay requested that "Lafala" be returned to him, planning to flog the novel to additional publishers, he likely hoped it was the full, complete version (the Schomburg document) rather than the shorter Yale typescript. We believe, moreover, that McKay never recovered the finished 172-page copy of the manuscript now archived in Harlem.

Among the most compelling evidence that the 172-page typescript is the final version is the fact that throughout the document the urban setting is identified as "Marseille," with no use of the veiled "Dreamport." What is more, McKay changes the name of the neighborhood of the city where most of the narrative takes place. The actual historical name of the Marseille quarter where most of the novel's action occurs is *le Panier*: "the Basket." It's logical, then, given the shape of the Basket, that in the earlier version McKay gives the district the fictional name of "the Bottoms."[16] In the Beinecke version, ~~Taloufa~~/ Lafala is even referred to as a "Bottomist."[17] In the later, longer version, the Bottoms becomes "Quayside," probably owing to the 1933 publication of McKay's novel *Banana Bottom* and the need to avoid another use of the nether term.

When the eighty-seven-page typescript of *Romance* is compared to the 172-page document, the major and obvious distinction between the two is their length. And the difference in size between the two texts is more than their respective page counts would indicate. The Beinecke manuscript comes to about 24,000 words, while the Schomburg version adds up to more than 40,000.[18] The Beinecke draft ends in modernist ambiguity, as a distressed Lafala eludes the "political police" and vanishes back into the obscure backstreets of the Bottoms, just as McKay describes the plot in his December 1929 letter to Bradley.

Revising the novel in 1932, McKay dynamically expanded his earlier draft, adding eleven more chapters to the original. The later version also adds two memorable white characters who play key roles in the plot, Big Blonde and Petit Frère. The

Schomburg version's more recognizably plotted storyline is the most persuasive reason to conclude that it is the finished novel. The narrative's final passages follow the ascent and descent of the classic Freytag pyramid, as the climax-dénouement stages the Aslima-Titin love-hate tango. The wretched La Fleur Noire stands by powerless to prevent the bloodshed as the prostitute and pimp rehearse their variation on the fatal final scene from *Carmen*. Yet this ending, too, tosses in a dash of modern irony, as the reader has learned that Lafala, under threat from the French penal system, has safely embarked for his West African homeland. The extended Schomburg version of *Romance* thereby lives up to the generic "romance" promised in its title— among other, more novelistic things, it is a French-inflected *roman* in which chivalry is dead, but love remains a life-and-death adventure.

While the Schomburg version is complete, the story of how the Schomburg Center came to acquire it is somewhat obscure. Hope Virtue McKay, McKay's only child, was in possession of the 172-page typescript in March 1953, as she loaned it to the Schomburg for an exhibition. The library later returned the manuscript to Carl Cowl, McKay's last literary agent and executor.[19] In the early 1970s, an eager Cowl then sold the typescript to Harvey and Linda Tucker of the firm Black Sun Inc. The Schomburg finding aid indicates that *Romance in Marseille* was acquired permanently as part of a 1974 purchase from Black Sun, a highly regarded dealer in modern rare books and manuscripts.[20]

Tracking down precisely how "Savage Loving" became *Romance in Marseille* has been somewhat less conclusive. McKay produced no known letter or other document that refers to *Romance in Marseille* with or without the *s*. The primary sources we have for trusting that McKay eventually settled on this title are the two typescripts: the Beinecke's finding aid and the Schomburg's title page both list *Romance in Marseille*. In addition, Cowl refers to the novel in his correspondence by this title on several occasions.

One more intriguing detail informs the question of the final title. While frantically searching for a publisher for the novel in

1933, McKay was surprised—and disgusted—to discover that the name "Savage Loving" had provoked a negative reaction from a Harlem Renaissance luminary: his fellow poet Countee Cullen. Writing to Max Eastman from Tangier on June 28, 1933, McKay fumes yet again about his ineffectual, "sissy" agent John Trounstine: "He writes that he was discussing the title of the book with Countee Cullen who thought it sounded obscene. Can't understand why he would consider the opinion of that little prig important and also give out the title of the book in Harlem before it has found a publisher. Next thing he will be showing them the manuscript up there."[21] Given McKay's history of second-guessing himself, it nevertheless seems sure that he allowed "that little prig" to inspire a change in the book's title. It would not have taken long to hear the carillons set off by the word "obscene." The same rhetoric was used to suppress Joyce's *Ulysses* (1922) and Lawrence's *Lady Chatterley's Lover* (1928), two of the modern novels McKay prized the most. McKay also knew all too well the violent reaction to Carl Van Vechten's *Nigger Heaven* (1926). Such hostility, Langston Hughes reports in *The Big Sea* (1940), was due to black readers' abhorrence for the offensive, sensational title.[22] McKay would also have recognized Cullen's relative shrewdness when measuring the mood of critics and consumers on both sides of the color line, the wide range where McKay intended to target his book.[23] Practically begging for scraps, the Jamaican author was in no position to risk further rejection simply because of a title. At some point, likely in late 1933, he changed the novel's name to the picturesque and less provocative *Romance in Marseille*.

Why *Romance in Marseille* has remained out of print for the past several decades marks a final, frustrating chapter in the novel's history. During the 1990s, Carl Cowl initiated an arrangement to allow the University of Exeter Press to publish *Romance in Marseille* along with three stories from *Gingertown*. Premature listings to the contrary, however, the book was never finalized for publication. Eventually, the Schomburg Center, then representing McKay's estate, intervened with the UK press, noting the termination clause entailed in the contract:

xlviii   A NOTE ON THE TEXT

"If at any time before or after publication of the Work . . . [it]
is not listed in the Publishers['] catalogue of books in print,
and this condition continues for more than 6 months, . . .
[this] Agreement will terminate immediately, and all the Publishers' rights to the Work herein granted shall immediately
revert to the Proprietor."²⁴ Despite the flurry of promise,
Romance thus lingered in the archives, a dream of republica-
tion deferred.

This first-ever published text of *Romance in Marseille* is
based closely and faithfully on the longer, final Schomburg
version of the novel. (Our thanks to Shannon Davis of the
Olin Library at Washington University in St. Louis for her
assistance in scanning the typescript.) We have edited the book
with a light touch, doing as we imagine McKay's Harper editor Eugene Saxton would have done had he been less wary of
raw language and queer themes. We have refrained from any
major changes to McKay's sentences, correcting negligible
spelling and typographical errors and supplying a handful of
obviously missing words. More consistently than in the original typescript, we employ American spellings, regularize
punctuation and some references to people and places, and
respect undraconian modern conventions for representing dialogue. Dedicated readers may of course check the results
against the available Schomburg source. We have also added
explanatory notes that follow the main text, most of which
illuminate the novel's wide-ranging and often learned political, musical, and literary intertexts or which translate French
terms left untranslated by McKay. The reader is invited to use
or ignore the notes as she or he likes, since our intention is to
add to firsthand engagements with McKay's work only as
much as desired. We of course hope that every reader enjoys
Romance in Marseille's never shy, at times eccentric, and thoroughly distinctive contribution to modern black fiction.

1. Claude McKay, "Romance in Marseille" ("Mac Kay, 'New
    Novel'"), Claude McKay Papers, James Weldon Johnson Collec-
    tion, Beinecke Rare Book and Manuscript Library, Yale Univer-
    sity, New Haven; and Claude McKay, "Romance in Marseilles,"

Claude McKay Letters and Manuscripts, Schomburg Center for Research in Black Culture, The New York Public Library, New York. The pagination of both manuscripts is at times unstable. The Beinecke manuscript ends with page 88, but is actually 87 typed pages, since the document has no page 25. An unknown person, perhaps McKay himself, attempted to correct the problem. Written over the 5 on the typed 25 is a "6," thereby identifying the leaf as page 26. Over the 6 (on p. 26) is a "7," indicating that the sheet is meant to be page 27. Meanwhile, pages 28 to 88 show no signs of attempted correction. In contrast, the Schomburg manuscript ends at page 171, but actually numbers 172 pages, since it contains two page 99s, the second marked, "99a."

2. See Jean-Christophe Cloutier and Brent Hayes Edwards, "Introduction," *Amiable with Big Teeth: A Novel of the Love Affair Between the Communists and the Poor Black Sheep of Harlem,* by Claude McKay, New York: Penguin, 2017, ix.

3. Claude McKay, *A Long Way from Home,* ed. with introduction, Gene Andrew Jarrett, New Brunswick, NJ: Rutgers University Press, 2007, 261.

4. Jean-Christophe Cloutier and Brent Hayes Edwards, eds., "Introduction," ix–xxxviii, xliii.

5. Claude McKay, letter to Carl Van Vechten, Sept. 11, 1941, Carl Van Vechten Papers, Manuscripts and Archives Division, The New York Public Library, New York.

6. Claude McKay, letter to Carl Van Vechten, Oct. 26, 1941, Carl Van Vechten Papers, Manuscripts and Archives Division, The New York Public Library, New York.

7. Bernhard Knollenberg, letter to Claude McKay, Oct. 10, 1941, Carl Van Vechten Papers, Manuscripts and Archives Division, The New York Public Library, New York.

8. John B. Turner (a.k.a. John Trounstine), letter to Bernhard Knollenberg, Oct. 3, 1941, Carl Van Vechten Papers, Manuscripts and Archives Division, The New York Public Library, New York.

9. Claude McKay, letter to Max Eastman, likely May 1933, Claude McKay Papers, Lilly Library Manuscripts Collection, Indiana University, Bloomington.

10. Claude McKay, letter to Max Eastman, April 21, 1933, Claude McKay Papers, Lilly Library Manuscripts Collection, Indiana University, Bloomington.

11. Claude McKay, letter to Carl Van Vechten, Oct. 26, 1941, Carl Van Vechten Papers, Manuscripts and Archives Division, The New York Public Library, New York.

12. Carl Van Vechten, letter to Bernhard Knollenberg, Oct. 27, 1941, Carl Van Vechten Papers, Manuscripts and Archives Division, The New York Public Library, New York.

13. Claude McKay, letter to Max Eastman, June 27, 1930, Claude McKay Papers, Lilly Library Manuscripts Collection, Indiana University, Bloomington.

14. Claude McKay, letter to Ivie Jackman, Sept. 15, 1943, Countee Cullen-Harold Jackman Memorial Collection, Robert W. Woodruff Library, Atlanta University. Our sincere thanks to Jean-Christophe Cloutier for suggesting that in the letter to Ivie Jackman, McKay may be referring to *Romance in Marseille*. The editors of *Amiable with Big Teeth*, Cloutier and Brent Hayes Edwards, note McKay's letter to Ivie Jackman in their introduction, speculating that the manuscript McKay may have been referring to in 1943 was "Amiable with Big Teeth." See Cloutier and Edwards, "Introduction," *Amiable,* xxxviii, and n104, 285. But in an email to the editors dated September 19, 2018, Cloutier states that, on reflection, he suspects that the typescript McKay is referring to is "Lafala," or *Romance in Marseille*, given that McKay was likely not in possession of the "Amiable with Big Teeth" manuscript when he wrote the letter. In 1943, the sole copy of "Amiable with Big Teeth" was almost certainly in the hands of Samuel Roth, the publisher who acquired the manuscript, among whose papers "Amiable with Big Teeth" was found.

15. Claude McKay, letter to Max Eastman, Dec. 1, 1930, Claude McKay Papers, Lilly Library Manuscripts Collection, Indiana University, Bloomington.

16. Many thanks to Brooks Hefner of James Madison University for pointing out that the real Bottoms (or Quayside) is *le Panier*.

17. "Mac Kay, New Novel," Beinecke Rare Book and Manuscript Library, 7.

18. The word count of the Schomburg version is approximate due to the fact that the document contains cross-outs, redactions, insertions, and other mechanical and handwritten effects that render an absolute count difficult.

19. Diana Lachatanere, email to Gary Edward Holcomb, Oct. 6, 2018.

20. The editors are again indebted to Professor Cloutier for sharing information about Black Sun Books. See Cloutier email to editors, Sept. 19, 2018.

21. Claude McKay, letter to Max Eastman, June 28, 1933, Claude McKay Papers, Lilly Library Manuscripts Collection, Indiana University, Bloomington.

22. Langston Hughes, *The Big Sea* (1940), New York: Hill and Wang, 1993, 270.
23. See Charles Molesworth, *And Bid Him Sing: A Biography of Countée Cullen*, Chicago: University of Chicago Press, 2012.
24. Diana Lachatanere, email to Gary Edward Holcomb, July 1, 2019.

And now it developed that there were many formalities to go through before the lawyer could touch the money.

Lafala had to be represented by some official. He did not belong to any of the two or three dependent free states that remain of the vast strange African land; he belonged to one of the parcels and was therefore either a colonial subject or a protected person. Some important white person in the big city was entitled to represent Lafala ~~Taloufa~~ formally. Meanwhile the company had informed the official of the impending payment to Lafala and asked that it should be officially witnessed. A duplicate of the documents concerning the case was sent to the official office.

The day arrived when was taken to the city to receive his payment officially from the lawyer. The official was a rather tall suave ready-made impressive type. He received the lawyer coldly and in the manner of an elder unbending to a child.

The lawyer had his papers and Lafala's payment ready. Lafala's share was about twenty thousand dollars. The lawyer laid a cheque on the table. The official picked it up but stopped the signing of the papers. In drawing up the papers the company's lawyers had put down a round sum amouting to about a quarter of the payment, for the lawyer's fee, the rest of the money going to Lafala. The lawyer had accepted it. It was a catch for him and he did not relish the idea of prolonged negotiation over that particular point. There was the contract with Lafala ~~Taloufa~~ for the final settlement between them. But now the official raised an objection to that.

Page 26 from the typescript of "The Jungle and the Bottoms" version of *Romance in Marseille*, produced circa 1929–1930, and held in the James Weldon Johnson Collection at Yale University's Beinecke Rare Book and Manuscript Library in New Haven. The page shows that McKay crossed out the original name of the novel's protagonist, Taloufa, and wrote above it "Lafala," the name he would use for the longer, completed version.

There they discussed Lafala while drinking.~~xxxxx~~ Babel related how they had stowed away together and that he had seen
Lafala being taken off the ship to the hospital. He omitted
to tell, however, that he had escaped as a stowaway prisoner
                    Marseille.   told them of
on his return to ~~xxxxxxxxxxx~~ St. Dominique ~~xxxxxxxxxxxxxxxxxx~~
                                      Seamen's Club , St Dominique
the afternoon with Lafala at the ~~xxxxxxxxxxxxxxxxxxxx~~ said
he was sorry he did allow Lafala to get out of the taxicab
                              But he and his West African
alone when he said he was being followed. ~~xxxxxxxxxxxxxxxxxxx~~
friend had not taken the matter seriously, as they felt convinced
~~xxxxxxxxxxxxxxxxxxxxxxxxxxxxxxxxxxxxxxxxxxxxxxxxxxx~~
that the men of whom Lafala was afraid were
political secret police. Big Blonde felt certain that Lafala
would turn up all right.

From the wine cellar they went to La Creole. La Creole
was one of the most popular of the loving houses of Quayside.
It was Big Blonde's favorite as his little friend worked there.
It was much frequented and touted by the colored Quaysiders
and they always recommended it to colored newcomers. Madam,
the proprietress a European, had a partiality for colored folk.
Aslima was once engaged there and was a good attraction. But
she was too savage and Madam couldn't hold her in check and had
to let her go regretfully.

There were seven girls in the place, among them a tall
mulatress who claimed to be an Egyptian. St. Dominique was
surprised to recognize in the assistant mistress a gay girl
                                   Seamen's Club
he used to know at a bal musette near the ~~xxxxxxxxxxxxxxxx~~
and who was very popular among the seamen, some of them even
                  dances at the club.
taking her to ~~xxxxxxxxxxxxxxxxxxxxxxxxxxxxxxxxxxxx~~ She whispered to St. Dominique not to gossip to Madam about her former
doings because she had a serious position.

There were not many visitors. A middle-aged man was

Page 124 from the typescript of "Savage Loving" version of *Romance in Marseille*, produced circa 1932–1933, and held in the Claude McKay papers at the New York Public Library's Schomburg Center for Research in Black Culture. This page indicates three key features of the final version of the novel: the setting is identified as "Marseille" (rather than the redacted "Dreamport," as in the Beinecke typescript); the "Seamen's Club" has replaced "Proletarian Hall"; and the character Big Blonde, missing from the earlier typescript, has made his vivid appearance.

Romance in Marseille

FIRST PART

CHAPTER ONE

In the main ward of the great hospital Lafala[1] lay like a sawed-off stump and pondered the loss of his legs. Now more vividly than ever in his life he visualized the glory and the joy of having a handsome pair of legs.

Once again in the native compounds of the bush with naked black youth, he was baptized in a flood of emotion retasting the rare delight the members of his tribe felt always by the sight of fine bodies supported by strong gleaming legs.[2]

The older tribesmen appraised the worth of the young by the shape of their limbs. Long legs and slender made good swimmers. Stout legs and thick, good carriers. Lithe and sinewy were runners' legs. And long swinging monkey arms marked expert climbers of palms and jungle trees.

The lads fancied the girls by the form of their legs, the shape of hips and firmness of thighs in symmetrical motion with coral-covered arms poised at oblique angles steadying burdens on their heads.

Lafala as a boy was proud of his legs, participating in all of childhood's leg play, running and climbing and jumping, and dancing in the moonlight in the village yard. He remembered lying down naked under the moon and stars while his playmates traced his image with pieces of crockery. And when they were finished they all held hands and danced around it singing "The Moonshine Kid."[3] He remembered the fine shock of wading through the tall grass in the cool early morning after the hot night, the heavy dews bathing his naked skin. . . .

As a kid boy, the missionaries brought him from the bush to the town where they lived and taught. His legs were put in pants and soon, soon he learned among other things the new delight of legs. . . . Legs like a quartette of players performing the passionate chamber music of life. Loud notes and soft, notes whispering like a warm breath, a long and noiseless kiss, flutes and harps joined in enchanting adventures, in ritual unison, trembling and climbing together in the high song of life and leaving unforgettable sensations in the blood, in the brain.

Legs of ebony, legs of copper, legs of ivory moving pell-mell in columns against his imagination. . . . Dancing on the toes, dancing on the heels, dancing flat-footed. Lafala's dancing legs had carried him from Africa to Europe, from Europe to America.[4]

Legs. . . . Feet that were accustomed to dig themselves into the native soil, into lovely heaps of leaves, and affectionate tufts of grass, were now introduced to luxuries of socks and shoes and beds of iron.

Lafala had gone on wandering impressionably from change to change like a heedless young pilgrim with nothing but his staff in his hand and playing variations on the march of legs. Come trouble, come worry, blue days without a job, without food, without love. . . . Dance away. . . . Think not of age, of accident, the festering and mortification of youth and poisoned worms corroding through the firm young flesh to the sepulchral skeleton. His dancing legs would carry him over all.

Suddenly they were jerked off and there he lay helpless.

On an impulse of self-disgust Lafala had stowed away from Marseille leaving at Quayside pals and wenches, frustrated feelings and dark desire. For there he had met the Negroid wench Aslima, a burning brown mixed of Arab and Negro and other wanton bloods perhaps that had created her a barbaric creature.

It was a time of universal excitement after the war and even among Negroes there were signs of a stirring and from the New World a dark cry of "Back to Africa" came over the air.[5]

Lafala was a child of black bush Africa. The missionaries had brought him out of the bush to educate in the mission school of the town. But Lafala had not remained a missionary credit. He left the school to ship as a sailor boy. He reached the land of the missionaries and stayed there, spending himself in the low-down places of many ports.

There Lafala heard the other Negroes discussing the Back-to-Africa news and wondering what would become of it. Lafala listened and was stirred too. Return. . . . Return. . . . Turn away from strange scenes and false gods to find salvation in native things. . . .

Then Lafala met Aslima, a near-native thing, and there found a way to go back too, he thought, if he could ever wrench free from the fascinating new idols native to go again. Aslima was a striking girl with a face that looked as if it was hewn out of hard brown wood into beauty. And like a magnet she drew Lafala to herself. Day and night they spent together, eating, drinking and sleeping together. Dancing together in the bars down at Quayside. Going boating together in the bay, their faces moistened by the salty spray, happy little brown and black birds together.

Ah! It was the happy meaning of a dream. Aslima was the real thing, Lafala thought. Not just a transient piece of luck of a moment only. But alas he awoke one morning to find that Aslima had snatched all his material assets and left him with the dream.

An object of ridicule and an object of pity at Quayside, Lafala had no desire to remain there and join the gang of dark drifters until his only suit was worn to rags. And so, disgusted and chagrined, he had stowed away as soon as he found an accessible ship.

Being very black, Lafala had hoped to escape detection in the gloominess of the bunker. But they found him. He was locked up in a miserable place. It was very cold crossing the Atlantic. When the mess boy brought him food, Lafala tried to explain that he was freezing to death. But they could not understand each other. It was a foreign ship and the mess boy did not think that Lafala's signs were serious enough to call an officer.

By the time the ship docked, Lafala's legs were frozen stiff. From the ship he was taken to the immigration hospital. There the doctors told him that they could save his life only by cutting off his legs.

Lafala passed out from hearing or feeling anything. He had a confused vision of childish impressions of the bush country and then all was blank. When he came back to the reality of himself and his environment, his dependable feet were gone.

Oh, that he had not been brought back from the state of oblivion! In a strange land, without home, without friends, without resources, without his greatest asset—his faithful feet! Why had the doctors saved him? He had often heard his ignorant companions say that hospitals were the final passage to the grave for poor and unknown persons. The black drifters were superstitiously afraid of hospitals. They said the doctors never had enough corpses for laboratory work and would not worry about the life of a poor unknown beggar when a body was wanted for dissection.

All that talk was just so much bunk, he mused now. The doctors had been so assiduous attending to him, the nurses so kind. Terrible attention and kindness, for what was he going to do with himself when he was better and discharged? With the crutches in his armpits would he have to squat down on the hard-hearted city pavement and beg, he who had gone so headlong proud through life?

Better he had not come back to this reality. Life was now behind him. In the future there was no hope. Peering, exploring, the world that he saw was a ball heavy with mist with no light or warmth.

Oh, God! He whinnied like a sick pony in a paddock and buried his face in the pillow, his stump of a body twitching under the long white nightshirt.

Lafala was in heaven. There were no black things there. The terraces were paved with gold and beautiful flowers of every hue spilled their scents everywhere. There were pretty woodlands with spotless pools where birds of the richest tropical colors nested and were ever singing. The palaces were wonderful creations of marble and crystal and rarest glass reflecting white the saints and angels in attitudes of heavenly voluptuousness. Lafala was transfigured beyond remembering what complexion he was, but his legs were all right there, prancing to the lascivious music of heavenly jazz.

Oh, what a welcome there. . . . All the jazz hounds who

raised hell in the mighty cities of earth were summoned here by the Almighty to welcome him. All the saints were strutting their stuff and the angels fluttering their wings for him, the center of attraction. A beautiful angel child was floating toward him. What magnificent wings! Many were the birds that Lafala had known on earth, but none with wings like this argent gorgeousness. The angel child was certainly coming to take him to the Prince of Heaven, to the throne above all thrones in the Holiest of the holy places.

The wings were enveloping him. He was lifted up. The music now far away reached him as from a celestial broadcasting station. On, on through heavenly space!

Angel wings! Salvation. How comforting to be warmly folded.

A sudden stop. Arrival. Was that the Prince of Heaven bending down to welcome him?

Lafala opened his eyes and saw a huge black face, yellow teeth in a badly-molded mouth, bending over him. Black things in heaven! Good God! And he was black in hell. A block of blackness in a hospital shirt. Why was he dumped down so violently upon the fact of himself and what did this other black want fooling over him?

Lafala had never liked him although they were the only two Negroes in the ward. The other black patient irritated him.

It seemed to Lafala that he was jealous of him because he was a favorite among the nurses and even the doctors took more than an ordinary interest in him.

Lafala was really handsome. A shining blue blackness, arresting eyes, a fine protruding forehead topped by a mat of closely-weaved black hair. Sometimes the nurses asked him to say something in his tribal language and one day he sang a little song of his people that they all liked. He was happy that he could do something to please them. Then suddenly he remembered his legs and was sad and tears stole down his face. He was very agitated and shuddered thinking of the future. The nurse that always attended to him patted him gently and Lafala kissed her hand and held it against his cheek. . . .

The other black, whose cot was on the side of the ward

opposite Lafala, observed them with a grin and later in the day when the nurse approached him to do something, he grabbed her hand and kissed it. She gave him a slap and cried "Insolent nigger!" And he became very angry and morose.

What did he want with his objectionable mug hanging over me? thought Lafala.

"I jest want to say bye-bye and good luck, ole fellah, 'cause they done told me I can quit this shop today and although we ain't been no best buddies"—he hesitated a little—"I bin thinking right hard ef I kaint do some'n' on the outside foh you."

"No, nothing. You know they are going to ship me back to the port I stowed away from as soon as I am better," Lafala replied impatiently.

"But it's that there case o' yourn," the American black insisted. "You oughta get some good money with you laigs chopped off and throwed away like trash. I been thinking big about you' case as I done heared it told and I believe theah's good money in it."

"Money," sneered Lafala. "I stowed away on the white man's boat. Do you think they're going to pay me for getting cold feet?"

"We got laws ovah heah can see about that better'n them in the woods you come out of, fellah," the American said with a friendly grin.

He told Lafala that there were lawyers in the mighty city who knew how to squeeze money out of all kinds of accidents. He made Lafala relate all the details of his stowing away, how he was discovered, how he was treated, the kind of cell in which he was locked up. . . .

"It was a toilet," Lafala said.

"You mean a lav'try?"

"No, a real WC."[6]

"But that ain't possible in Gawd's kingdom. They wouldn't do that to a hog."

"They did it to me all right though, and they knew what they were doing too, for after they fed me they didn't even think it was necessary to let me out to take the air."

The American shook his head with a ripe giggle.

"You nevah can tell what a white man will do. But all the same I'm going to take this business a yours to a white lawyer. I don't trust no nigger lawyers. They'll sell you out every time."

Lafala wanted to defend Negro lawyers.

The American Negro grinned. "Race ain't nothing in this heah hoggish scramble[7] to get theah, fellah, wif the black hogs jest that much worser because them is way, ways back behind. Ise gwina get you a go-get-'im-skin-and-scalp-him of a lawyer and take it from me that when him done get through fixing you up youse gwina have you a pair of legs to walk on and good dollars in you pocket."

"You think so?" asked Lafala.

"I done think, I knows it."

Alone, Lafala wondered if anything would come from the talk of Black Angel. It was the first sign of hope for the future that he had seen. He had never before thought of gaining something from such a loss, never dreamed there was the slightest chance. The hospital staff had avoided talking to him about the subject of his future. Doctors and nurses. "Poor boy!" a doctor would ejaculate, passing his cot. Sometimes he noticed a group of visiting doctors and internes and students talking with sympathetic glances towards him. He knew they had been told about his case. The nurses, even his nurse that called him "my boy," could not grant him that essentially feminine word of encouragement that always works such a miracle on the masculine mind. In their eyes, in their silence about his future, he saw only pity, that terrible dumb pity that can sweep the fibers of feeling for a fine man or beast that has fallen from self-sufficiency into a hopeless case.

Now from the thought of the other black whom he had avoided as a fool, he saw himself again facing existence. Suppose the shipping company came across with something! A thousand dollars!

I wonder if they could give that much for a pair of black feet on the shelf. I could go back to one of those ports where all the seamen know me and open up a little grogshop. A kind of seamen's shelter without the chaplain and the hymns. Do something and make something and live again.

How ironical it would be if by the intervention of his ignorant fellow black, whom he had disliked, he should strike the
way to good fortune. But there could be no greater irony now
than his own macabre self in the hands of fate. The surprising
fact of himself was so terribly real, he felt that nothing in life
could ever give him the fine moving shock of surprise again.

CHAPTER TWO

It was early afternoon, three days since the departure of Black Angel. Lafala lay speculating about the future, his thoughts alternating from sugar-sweet to sour, between hope and doubt, when the lawyer appeared to him.

So warmly and heartily he shook Lafala's hand that he pulled him right up off his butt of a self, and before Lafala, confusedly thinking of showing some native warmth himself, was settled again, his visitor had plunged into business.

Lafala had to rake up all his recent past to give precisely the details of his stowing away and he was deftly handled and steered into giving only such details as could form the basis of a lawsuit with favorable results. Lafala, for instance, seemed to have a grievance against some individual of a little importance whom he said he had paid to protect him if he were found.

"How much did you pay?" the lawyer asked.

"About five dollars."

"Five dollars. You expected protection for five dollars? Now listen to me. Don't ever mention that at any time to anybody. What we are after is the company and no individual to spoil the big game. I'm going to tell you what to say and you must never say anything more than that to anybody. Get me? Right. And don't talk too much about your case. You're in *my* hands now."

One hundred thousand dollars was what the lawyer said he intended to sue for. Lafala was struck dumb by the idea of such a sum. The shipping company would either compromise or go to court. In a case like his, the lawyer told Lafala, it wasn't necessary to get the judge and jury to think. It was straight heart stuff. Poor African boy without any relatives taken away from his people when he was so young he did not even remember them, without family, without country even, without legs.

He did not know how much he would get. Maybe not more than ten thousand dollars. All depended on the company's lawyers and the kind of fight they could put up. But it was better to ask for a big sum.

Then the lawyer said that before he touched the case Lafala would have to sign a paper giving him half of whatever he obtained as damages. Frankly he explained that he was not going to handle the case for sympathy only, although he sincerely sympathized with Lafala. He was asking a half of any amount that was paid because he was as much plaintiff as lawyer. Lafala did not have the means nor the influence to procure a lawyer and in all such damage suits lawyers' fees were enormous. He didn't want Lafala to think that he was taking a mean advantage of him. All cases like his were handled on a fifty-fifty basis. He would give Lafala two days to reflect.

When the lawyer was finished, Lafala said "I don't need two days to make up my mind. Just give me that paper and I'll sign it right away."

The lawyer produced the contract stipulating that he should receive as a legal fee one-half of any payment that he obtained from a certain company for the loss of Lafala's legs. Lafala signed. The lawyer produced a little camera, made Lafala pull up his night shirt to show his stumps and photographed him. Lafala had a photograph of himself before the accident and this the lawyer also took.

The lawyer had visited Lafala on a Wednesday. On Saturday morning the nurse approached him smiling with a tabloid in her hand. Lafala had achieved publicity. The tabloid contained an account of his accident, written in pointed modern sentimental sentences, and his two photographs. Under the first was printed "Before"; under the lawyer's snapshot "After."

That same evening another paper carried a pathetic story with the photographs of Lafala.

The next day the lawyer visited Lafala and cautioned him never at any time to talk to anyone about his case unless he was present and that he should refer all interviewers to him.

Thus began a new outlook for Lafala. It was the first time that he had ever appeared in print and that impressed on his mind the assurance that out of his trouble he would win something tangible. His lawyer kept in close touch with him by visits and by correspondence. Twice he was visited by an official of the shipping company, but he refused to talk. Vigilantly his nurse stood by to see that he didn't. The lawyer had shrewdly seen and enlisted her sympathy.

She despised those people who could treat any human being, even a black, like that—locking him up in a water-closet until he was frozen.

One day an official of the shipping company came with the lawyer. The official tried to make out that Lafala might have had some disease of the feet before he stowed away. He couldn't freeze like that if he were in good health, for the ship had a fine heating apparatus.

"What disease you think?" Lafala asked. "I was a dancing fool in the port I came from. You can go there and ask the gang."

The official left. The lawyer stayed for a while to talk with Lafala. He told Lafala that the newspaper stories had stirred up the officials and that they wanted to avoid further publicity and he was going to work them for a handsome compromise. A compromise was better than going to the courts. For a lawsuit of that kind was like a strike. The employers will go their limit to compromise a strike, but once it is on and the works dislocated, they don't care if the workers starve. So the lawyer told Lafala that his business was to work the publicity scare to obtain the best settlement from the company. Better not to go to the courts where the company's big lawyers may start in to wear them down on legal points and a callous judge cut down the damages to nothing.

Lafala listened and thought his lawyer's argument was good.

During the long interval of negotiation a pretty friendship sprung up between Lafala and his lawyer. Lafala's spirit was lifted up and like a feather in space, he felt himself floating in the delightful realm of futurity. A desire for activity seized him again and it found outlet in his nimble hands. He obtained some hemp and varicolored wool and began weaving girdles,[1] the only clothing that his tribeswomen used to wear when he was a boy in the bush. The first one finished he presented to his nurse and she told him it was the nicest gift that she had ever had and it made her happy to be a nurse. Lafala sent the second girdle to his lawyer with a note by the hand of Black Angel who had been to see him.

Lafala wrote "This is the only thing I remember my tribes-women wearing in the bushland when I was a kid. I began making them because I was so nervous wanting to do some-thing. I remembered I could make them and so I got the stuff and set to work. I hope you like it. The wool is my own inven-tion. They used to put the color in with specially dyed straw."

The lawyer replied, "The girdle is very pretty. My wife appropriated it at once. It carried me back to very ancient times. I mean the times when my people were also divided into tribes and wore girdles just as your people do today.

"Our case is progressing nicely. It may seem a long time get-ting done to you, but these legal affairs can't be got through in a hurry. Don't worry. You're going to get all out of that com-pany that I can possibly get for you. So give them time and keep cheerful."

CHAPTER THREE

In the meantime Lafala was pronounced officially better and thus due to leave the hospital. In a sense he was not a patient only, but technically also a prisoner held for deportation to the port that he had left clandestinely.

And one morning an official of the shipping company appeared in the ward and announced to Lafala that he had orders to ship him back to that port.

"And what about my case?" Lafala asked.

"That will be settled on the other side."

"But the immigration officials?"

"They know all about it. You're discharged from the hospital and out of their hands now and we'll be getting into more trouble if we don't take charge of you and take you back where you stowed away from."

It was the international usage. . . .

Lafala said he would like to see his lawyer.

"All right, we'll see about that for you."

His little bundle of clothes was brought. He dressed and was lifted into a waiting taxi-cab and whisked away.

The nurse had stood by in helpless agitation. Frantically now she rushed to the telephone to call the lawyer, only to learn that he knew nothing of Lafala's being sent away. The lawyer got busy in a hurry. He got out an injunction to prevent Lafala's sailing before his case was settled. He looked up which of the company's ships was sailing and likely to take Lafala. He did not telephone the company's office, but sent someone to see, without asking, if Lafala was there. He was not, so the lawyer instituted a search and finally found the helpless black on the company's pier. He snatched him up and the game was won.

"I'll squeeze something more out of the company for this," he said, "or I'll get this straight into the papers. And when I get your money, I'll see that you don't go back to the port you stowed away from, for you never can tell what they might do to you there."

That night Lafala slept in the lawyer's apartment. The following afternoon he was at the lawyer's office when Black Angel walked in.

"See youse looking better," Black Angel said, his features glowing with a large smile.

"Feeling better, too," Lafala grinned back.

"And you'll soon be walking bettah, so that the chippies meeting you in the street will jest think youse got a sprain ankle."

"Why not take him up among your folks tonight and show him a good time? He needs it after so many months in the hospital," the lawyer said with a wink.

The lawyer advanced Lafala some money. But Black Angel had money of his own and it appeared to Lafala that he was very much in the lawyer's confidence. Lafala was curious and Black Angel explained that he was due to get his runner's reward from the lawyer, about five hundred dollars more or less, according to the final amount obtained in damages.

That evening for the first time Lafala had a glimpse of the life of Harlem. In the basement kitchen and dining room of Black Angel's house a woman was preparing a feast for Black Angel and Lafala. It was a big dinner of celery soup, fricassée chicken and mashed potatoes. After the dinner Black Angel gave a party in his room for Lafala.

"Ise got a buddy working for a big bootlegger," he said, "and I'm gwine have him heah tonight wif some good liquor. You can play the phonograph theah, if youse tired waiting befoh I git back."

Lafala cushioned his butt of a body in an old Morris chair[1] and biting off the point of a cigar, he lit it.

Black Angel returned with a brown girl and a bottle of gin. A little later his buddy appeared with two girls, a dark-brown with rouge in her cheeks that gave her an exotic maroon color and a lemon-colored one. He deposited a package on the chiffonier, which contained two bottles of gin and two bottles of wine.

"Gwina make a little cabaret a this heah joint foh you special benefit," Black Angel assured Lafala.

The buddy made a strong punch. Black Angel started the phonograph.

"Don't think no affliction of you'self that you kaint dance as we do," said Black Angel to Lafala. "Ef you kaint dance on the floor, you can dance in the bed."

While they were dancing somebody knocked on the door and another girl entered, a warm satin-skinned mahogany brown.

"One plus, gotta do some figuring," muttered Black Angel. He introduced the girl. And now Lafala had two girls, one on each side entertaining him when the others danced. He was the center of the show, with Black Angel and his buddy replenishing the glasses. He was pitied and praised and beamed upon and his stumps of legs were fondled and caressed as if they were honeysticks. It was a great evening for Lafala. Black Angel had taken care all right that the company should know that there was a fortune in Lafala's misfortune. . . .

Said Black Angel to the lawyer when they met again, "I done gave him a sweet souvenir a high life, boss, and he sho' will remember it all them days that he's gwine spend chasing chimpangees when he scootles back to jungle-land."

CHAPTER FOUR

After his haphazard leave of absence, Lafala returned to his cot in new colors. His nurse welcomed him happily.

"You're lucky to have such a real person for a lawyer," she said. "He's square and working hard for you."

"Sure, but remember it's fifty-fifty," said Lafala, "and the harder he works for me, the more he'll get for himself."

"But there's more to it than that," she maintained, "he's human."

On a fine spring day the rumor ran through the ward that Lafala had been awarded some thousands of dollars. The figure went up to fifty. Lafala had not yet heard directly from the lawyer. But although it was really a big sum, exceeding anything his imagination was capable of, he was less excited than the nurses and his fellow patients. He accepted the godsend with a primitive dignity that appeared like indifference.

His real excitement was reserved for the cork legs that he was to get at the company's expense. He was eager to try himself out in them. How would he look with a girl in the street? He might learn to dance with them and do the things that whole-legged people did.

Lafala was sent to one of the best houses for artificial limbs in New York to fit himself. He surveyed his stilted form in the full-length mirrors and felt good. He shuffled with a stick. He stepped. He felt that with a little more practice he would soon hold his own with other promenaders. Nobody observing him a little halting would think that it was more than a sprain. . . .

At last the Negro newspapers caught up with Lafala and front-paged him with a blast so big and so black that such permanent front-pagers as the pretender to the throne of Africa and his titled entourage and all the other personages of the moment were buried beneath it.

The *Bellows of the Belt*[1] shouted:

AFRICAN DAMAGED FIFTY THOUSAND DOLLARS

But it was outdone by the *United Negro*[2] which ran:

AFRICAN LEGS BRING ONE HUNDRED
THOUSAND DOLLARS

The African had conquered Aframerica with a whoop. Very literary were the days that ensued for Lafala.

He received letters asking individual gifts and detailing pitiful cases of persons who had been badly injured and received no compensation. One letter came from a youth, accompanied by his photograph. He had written a book in which he had shown how the Negro Problem could be eliminated by the Negro himself by means of psychic development.

"It would be wonderfully appropriate," he wrote to Lafala, "if a full-blooded African should be the instrument by which my sublime opus was brought to light."

Another letter was received from C.U.N.T. (Christian Unity of Negro Tribes)[3] asking Lafala to communicate with the association if he needed any spiritual assistance in the handling of his affairs.

Lafala showed some of the letters to the nurse and they had an amusing time reading them.

"There'll be lots of people trying to get on to you," said the nurse.

"They won't find me easy though," said Lafala. "I've lost my legs but not my head."

Lafala had more fun out of the letters when Black Angel visited him. He read a number of them. There was one that made Black Angel exclaim "Hot nuts! Now tha's a wench foh you!"

The letter was from the directress of the Nubian Orphanage,[4] asking a contribution. Black Angel explained to Lafala that it was common knowledge in the Black Belt that black babies were not made welcome in that orphanage. They looked comically at each other and burst out laughing.

"You oughta make a little one just like you self and take it ovah to that theah cullud lady as a contribulation," said Black Angel.

And now it developed that there were many formalities to go through before the lawyer could touch the money.

Lafala had to be represented by some official. He did not belong to any of the two free states that remain of the vast African land; he belonged to one of the parceled regions and was therefore either a colonial subject or a protected person.[5] Some important white person in the big city was entitled to represent Lafala formally. Meanwhile the company had informed the official of the impending payment to Lafala and asked that it should be officially witnessed. A duplicate of the documents concerning the case was sent to the official's office.

The day arrived when Lafala was taken to the city to receive his payment officially from the lawyer. The official was a tall, impressive person. He received the lawyer coldly in the manner of a lord condescending to a vassal.

The lawyer had his papers and Lafala's payment ready. Lafala's share was about twenty-five thousand dollars. The lawyer laid a check on the table. The official picked it up but stopped the signing of the papers. In drawing up the papers the company's lawyers had put down a round sum amounting to about a quarter of the payment for the lawyer's fee, the rest of the money going to Lafala. The lawyer had accepted it. It was a catch for him and he did not relish the idea of prolonged negotiation over that particular point. There was the contract with Lafala for the final settlement between them. But now the official raised an objection to that.

The official said "This man is entitled to more money."

"He's not," said the lawyer. "I made a fair agreement with him before I took the case. Fifty-fifty. Didn't I, Lafala?"

Lafala did not reply. The phrase "entitled to more money" was singing in his ears.

"That was not a fair agreement," said the official. "You had him at an advantage. What else could he do but agree when he was lying on his back crippled?"

"Rather belated pity you're working up for the poor fellow now," the lawyer sneered. "I think he would have been glad to have just a little of that pity before I went to the hospital to see him. I've done for him more than any other lawyer would. I told him he could think it over before he signed the fifty-fifty agreement. I told him there was a Legal Aid Society, only I didn't think it would help him much. I did my utmost for him. Got more money for him from that company than anybody else would."

"That may be so," said the official, "but the company has stipulated a certain sum for the lawyer's fee and you cannot have a half. I am here to protect this man's rights, that's all. That's my duty."

"Protect him? Protect him! Good God! Why didn't you and your protecting kind protect him before he stowed away to get frozen on the boat? Why didn't you find out about him before his legs were sawed off? Why didn't you prevent the company people from kidnapping him away from the hospital? Fine protection you all give to these sort of people!"

"I'm not here to listen to a lecture from you, Mr. Jew. You did wring that money out of the company alright—to get your big share. All I want is that you hand over now the balance of the money that has been allotted to this man."

"I will not! I am entitled to a half. Lafala, we have an agreement between us. If you will stick to it and stand by me, it's okay."

"But I don't think I can interfere now, since I'm in official hands," said Lafala.

"Yes, you can. All you have to say is that you're willing to let our original agreement stand. You know I treated you straight from the very beginning. If you say you're satisfied with our original agreement and sign this paper to that effect, everything will be settled without difficulty. I didn't argue with the company about the lawyer's fees clause because I was convinced you would stand by the fifty-fifty agreement."

But Lafala's mind was fully occupied with the official statement "entitled to more money". . . . More money. That was the slogan of life. Everybody and all the world wanted more money. Those who had none wanted some. And those who had some wanted more. And the more many had the more they wanted. Why should a little contract stand in the way when there was something more to gain which was legally awarded to him? Why should the lawyer appeal to him? The company had granted him more. The official said he was entitled to it. Let the big white men battle it out over him. All he wanted was to come out from under it with what was left of his skin and all he could possibly get.

"Well, Lafala, it's up to you now," said the lawyer.

"It's like this with me," said Lafala. "You are a good lawyer; this gentleman is a big official. I am nothing. I put the case in your hands and you handled it fine. But now you bring me here and put me in the hands of this gentleman as my official representative. I'll have to follow the advice of this gentleman now. If I'm entitled to more money, I want it."

"But I did not bring you here—," began the lawyer.

"Can't you see it's useless arguing anymore," the official interrupted. "The man has made his decision. I am responsible for him now and all I want is that you pay over all his share of the amount the company allotted to him."

The official's voice was cold, smooth and timbreful like tempered old steel. His hands betrayed none of the ungenteel gestures of the lawyer and his eyes were full of the contempt of the aristocrat of a Great Tradition looking down upon the parvenu bounder.

"I refuse to be done out of my share by you," cried the lawyer excitedly.

"Then it simply means that we will have to go to the courts to get it," said the official.

"You! You? You're in with the company against us—against this poor crippled black man," the lawyer leveled his finger at the official. "You can take the case to court. I'll fight it on my original contract. You don't mean this man any good. You couldn't. You're a company man yourself, only the company you work for is bigger than the one that maimed him. But you all belong to the same Big Brotherhood."

The official pointed to the door: "Now get out or I'll have you thrown out, you dirty ambulance-chaser."

"Thank you!" The lawyer bowed sardonically and stalked out.

CHAPTER FIVE

It was four days since Lafala's difference with his lawyer; to be exact, Saturday after the midday meal. The dishes had been gathered from the patients and wheeled away. The cots were straightened out for the visiting hour. Round an unoccupied cot toward the southern end of the ward a group came together to play cards.

Lafala sat on his cot, curiously caressing his corks preliminary to fixing them on for a walk, when Black Angel appeared to him. Black Angel came with a grievance. When he put the lawyer on to Lafala's case, he was made to understand he would receive five-hundred dollars if the suit were successful. But the lawyer had given him two-hundred and fifty dollars only. Black Angel told the lawyer that this was a breach of their gentleman's agreement. The lawyer referred him to Lafala. He would have paid Black Angel the five-hundred dollars if Lafala had not repudiated his contract before his official representative. As it was, he was in trouble. He was worried by the official's threat of a lawsuit and that he would get him suspended. He was going to fight, but he might lose. Black Angel should ask Lafala to pay him the balance.

"I think Ise worf it," Black Angel said, "for all I did. And you all should give it to me."

"I haven't any money, Angel," said Lafala. "The official man is taking care of it."

"Sure but he'll pay me ef you tellum to."

"God! This money business is a bigger pain in the bone than it was sawing off my legs," said Lafala.

"I understand how you feel, fellah," said Black Angel. "Ise a race man and Ise with you alright against the lawyer. But I think I done earned what was promised to me. You oughta put the other half to this heah."

Black Angel laid the lawyer's check for two-hundred and fifty dollars upon the cot.

"Look here, Angel," said Lafala. "You opened up the way to heaven for me alright and I'm aiming to get there, but I got to look out for every step I take. I can't do this thing. I can't start paying out money like that. You got to be contented with what you have."

"But you wouldn't mean to say I ain't worf five-hundred dollars fohal I did?"

"Sure, but oh God! Don't ask *me* to pay, Angel. I'm an amputated man, my feet laid on the shelf and I need all I can get to carry me along."

Black Angel got up, pocketing the lawyer's check. "Alright fellah, Ise going then, but you all ain't done treat me right."

SECOND PART

CHAPTER SIX

The water went green and the water came yellow and indigo, gray, mottled and foaming white. And up and down, over and over, Lafala came and went with the waves. He closed his eyes to shut the ocean outside, but it washed him clean and green inside. The waves roared up and the waves roared down and inside of Lafala. God-oh! Maybe I'm top-heavy, he thought, with my feet gone. No man's ocean ever did get the best of me in my sound feet, footloose days. Let me walk a little to see if I'll feel better. So he raised his trunk from the bunk and adjusted his apparatus. But that merely helped him out on deck to hang on to the railing and whoop pathetically into the undulating sea. The waves roared up and the waves roared down and Lafala, harassed, agitated, turned upside-down again and again, found final refuge in the WC.

Never, for many years seafaring, had Lafala fallen into such a state. He remembered being a little upset the first time he went to sea, but he was soon all right. Since then how many voyages had he made from port to port, crossing and recrossing the Atlantic without ever getting sick? Because in spite of stopover intervals of loose frolicking, his frugal way of living had inured him against the common indispositions of delicate passenger folk.

But now Lafala was a passenger himself, at the company's expense, first class. And he was living up to it. He had decided to make good use of all that the company was paying for. And so thoroughly had he carried out his decision, his long-disciplined body had reacted against the sudden abuse, and his bowels roared resentment against too much first-class food.

Thus, out of tune with the sea and the boat, Lafala, now

completely out of his lawyer's cunning hands, was returning to the dream port of his fortune and misfortune. His official had arranged his sailing back with the same company that owned the boat on which he had stowed away. And like all vain humanity who love to revisit the scenes of their sufferings and defeats after they have conquered their world, Lafala (even though his was a Pyrrhic victory) had been hankering all along for the caves and dens of Marseille with the desire to show himself there again as a personage and especially to Aslima.[1]

CHAPTER SEVEN

Wide open in the shape of an enormous fan splashed with violent colors, Marseille lay bare to the glory of the meridian sun,[1] like a fever consuming the senses, alluring and repelling, full of the unending pageantry of ships and of men.

Magnificent Mediterranean harbor. Port of seamen's dreams and their nightmares. Port of the bums' delight, the enchanted breakwater. Port of innumerable ships, blowing out, booming in, riding the docks, blessing the town with sweaty activity and giving sustenance to worker and boss, peddler and prostitute, pimp and panhandler. Port of the fascinating, forbidding and tumultuous Quayside against which the thick scum of life foams and bubbles and breaks in a syrup of passion and desire.

Down at Quayside there was a colored colony whose complexion was highly emphasized by two of its notorieties who strove in rivalry there. They were the two wenches known as Aslima[2] and La Fleur Noire.[3]

Aslima was nicknamed "the Tigress" and her dominion had been long undisputed at Quayside until the appearance of La Fleur. The resultant clash between the two was inevitable for if Aslima was a strong and restless tigress, La Fleur was something of a wily serpent. Aslima was stout and full of an abundance of earthly sap and compact of inexhaustible energy in spite of the grinding waste of it. La Fleur was small and straight and might have served for an excellent model of a new-fangled doll done in dark-brown wax.

Many legends had sprung up around La Fleur. One of the most unusual was the incident about her and a personage who had gone sightseeing down Quayside way and seen La Fleur promenading on Number One Quay. La Fleur had excited the personage's interest and his guide told him that he could easily arrange a rendezvous.

The guide enlisted the aid of the mistress of a sumptuous rendezvous house in the high-up part of the town and a champagne dinner was organized to which La Fleur was invited as a guest of honor.

La Fleur was offered a nice sum of money to play her part. And she prinked herself up[4] in style for the party. Heightening the tone of her face and her neck and her arms with rouge, she appeared like a big-mouthed brown orchid. An automobile was sent to convey her from Quayside.

It was a princely banquet with the lady of the house presiding and many pretty girls and La Fleur the only colored one. The personage had a couple of friends with him and the guide was there spruced up like a man about town with another of his fraternity. It was fine eating and drinking.

But the rubicund gentleman did not please La Fleur. He was afflicted with an enormous paunch, which dominated the banquet. When he stood up it ballooned ungracefully against the neighbors in its vicinity. And when he sat down it surmounted the table, a huge bag that any accidental prick it seemed might cause to burst disagreeably. Some of the girls pressed their little elbows mischievously into it and fondled the rubicund's face.[5]

But La Fleur was not so merry contemplating contact. And when after the feasting was finished and a tango unwound slowly out of the pianola[6] and the personage took her dancing, pushing her round and round the room with that panting paunch, she felt that that was as far as she could go with it.

La Fleur could always intoxicate herself up to the point of easy pleasantness in the love trade for any person. But now she felt it was impossible to find any tolerable kind of person in that huge contented bag.

And so a little after she had finished dancing La Fleur excused herself from the attentions of the rubicund and fled to Quayside. Later she telephoned that too good feasting and guzzling had made her ill and unfit to carry through the entertainment.

The rubicund was inconsolable and so Aslima was sent for to substitute for La Fleur. Aslima went and the flagging entertainment went banging over. But the following day La Fleur enticed Aslima into a card game and from her all the money that she had earned.

All the little rats in the holes of Quayside held their tales high, pirouetting in merriment over the practical joke. But from that day Aslima consorted no more with La Fleur and the two wenches became vicious enemies. But La Fleur remained the queen of Quayside.

When Lafala arrived at Marseille, Aslima was absent on a short trip of adventure to a popular summer resort of the region. The first place of recreation that attracted Lafala was the Café Tout-va-Bien.[7] It was the rendezvous of the colored colony and owned by a mulatto.

The freedom of Quayside was practically granted to Lafala on his return. As a onetime habitué it was a big event for him to come back to the old haunt with the status of a personage. There was all sorts of wild talk about him. Some said that he was officially protected and had been granted a large tract of land somewhere in the deep bush of Africa. Others said that he was going to acquire real estate in Marseille.

The faces of his old comrades of the boats had nearly all disappeared, except for an American black who made his nest between the blocks way down the extreme end of the breakwater and was thus called Rock and a Senegalese named Diup.[8] But the girls of Cat Row were still there with new faces among them. They all trooped down to the Tout-va-Bien and chattered about Lafala's unfortunate stowing away and the fortune he had derived from it.

Lafala did not as in his carefree days indulge in any reckless spending yet he was highly esteemed nevertheless, representing as he did to the Quaysiders almost one of themselves who had legitimately succeeded in getting his hands deep into the pockets of the high-and-mighty.

La Fleur attached herself to Lafala and was making just a regular little affair of it until the evening of Aslima's return to the Quayside. That evening Lafala in a honey-sweet and La Fleur in a money-sweet mood were engaged in a corner of the Tout-va-Bien over a bottle of the soft Italian wine, spumante,[9] when Aslima appeared. She was wearing a red frock. Lafala looked up at her and was surprised to find himself feeling that she looked better than ever. But he surveyed her coldly, proudly with a sarcastic set of the mouth and his manner said "Look at me! Here I am come back a bigger man than you ever dreamed of when you robbed me and went away."

Aslima had already been informed of Lafala's triumphant comeback and she had fully made up her mind to challenge La Fleur and stage a comeback of her own. She sized up the situation immediately and rushed it putting herself between La Fleur and Lafala. She patted his cheeks, hugged him, felt his feet, had him pull up his trousers to show the corks—all in a flutter of sympathetic enthusiasm. She was really sorry for his accident, yet really glad about the fine result, glad and sad for him in the same feeling. For the moment Lafala's rancor was fairly swept away by Aslima's warmth. It seemed so natural. He invited her to sit down and drink and she appropriated the seat on the other side of him and clapped her hands for the waiter. The proprietor came and Lafala ordered another bottle of the same wine.

But La Fleur stood up full of anger, yet trying to hold herself calmly and get Lafala to go, saying it was time for them to eat; for it was the dinner hour they had been spending unconventionally drinking sweet wine before eating because they were feeling sweet. La Fleur had been suddenly put to confusion and was rather helpless. Aslima had never crossed her ways since the day of the famous card game.

"Let's go," La Fleur said, "I want to eat."

"Have some more wine first," said Lafala.

"Don't want any more wine," said La Fleur.

But the cork had already popped and the sweet yellow stuff was foaming in the glasses.

"Oh sit down and drink with us," said Lafala.

But La Fleur was already making for the door.

"Fleur! Fleur! La Reine Fleur!"[10] cried Aslima on a mocking note.

La Fleur had to look back. Since the party of the Paunch, Aslima had never met her full in the eyes much less spoken to her. She looked haughtily at Aslima, but Aslima merely said, "Adieu, Fleur," and making a low-down naughty sign at her with her finger and shrilling laughter she jazzed a few steps.

The café was filling with habitués straggling in from feeding and as La Fleur pushed her way out without a retort to Aslima a salvo of mocking laughter came from her old admirers, who were quite ready to bait La Fleur in her discomfiture as they had once flattered her in her triumphs. . . .

Lafala and Aslima had finished eating in a little food shop on Number One Quay.

"And now what's the next thing?" he asked.

"That's up to you."

"Want to see where I live?"

"That's alright."

"Come on, then."

"Get a taxi."

Lafala acquiesced and they went off in a taxicab. . . .

Aslima remembered what a dancing dog Lafala used to be, how infectious and tantalizing the jigging of his feet. His long legs then, uniquely handsome though they were, had been just like any other pair of legs to her. But as she looked at Lafala on the bed, the shrunken stumps tapering to the knobs where once were lovely feet, she was moved to a great pity and a great shame.

And she knelt down caressing and kissing his knobs: "Poor man, poor man, and so young, so young. What a pity!"

"That's a present from you," said Lafala maliciously.

"But I didn't send you to stow away!"

"Yes, you did too. You think I was going to hang around here and go to rags like those no-count fellows on the beach? No sir! After you gypped me and skipped I made up my mind to stow away and this was what I got for stowing away: my feet sawed off. Yet here I am with you again. Don't you think I'm crazy?"

Aslima put her hand over Lafala's mouth. "Don't talk about it, darling. You know all we girls treat a stranger like that when we can get away with it. It's the law of Quayside. But I didn't mean to hurt you. I'm sorry, oh my God! Poor half of legs." She began to sob.

"Don't cry," Lafala laughed. "I can't stand tears. I got something that must be better than sound feet, alright, for now all the chippies at Quayside are making eyes at me."

"But how you could dance, darling, all sorts of movements. Oh là-là! Tonight I'm going to be better than I ever was to you the first time you were here. I'm going to be a sweet pig to you. Tonight I'll show you. I'm going to be a darling pig."

That night Lafala was very happy. For Aslima revealed herself to him as she had never done before nor to anybody in Marseille. Lafala was so happy that he became afraid of his happiness, for it was the kind of sensation that always started him off like a fever gripping madly and sweating him dry for a crazy season. He never could take love casually as most of his pals. That was his weakness. It had a way of getting him. Some strangely different body captivating and clinging, haunting and tormenting. But this time he wasn't going to fall that way like an overripe fruit. No, not for Aslima. I never will again for I have never fallen the same way twice.

However, in the morning when he handed her money, she obstinately refused it.[11]

"No, I don't want anything. Last night I paid you back what I owed you. Now we are quits."

"But I don't want to be quits. I never said you owed me anything and I want to see you again. Here!" He pressed the money upon her.

But she wouldn't accept it. "I don't want your money. That was why I made you take the taxi, so nobody should see us go off together and Titin[12] wouldn't know I was with you."

Titin was Aslima's pimp and reputed to be one of the meanest from Quayside.

"But we must see each other again," said Lafala.

"We can every day down there."

"But I mean for another party."

"We'll see."

CHAPTER EIGHT

On his next visit to the Tout-va-Bien Lafala flaunted a large, important-looking envelope, conspicuously displaying the foreign stamps. Although the contents were of no actual value, the letter was highly prized by Lafala. For he had received it through his official representative and it gave him a luxurious feeling of importance.

It was a letter from a solid established banking house which was handling the transference of Lafala's funds. And it contained slips of accounts paid, balances and transferable bonds. Lafala felt fine to be a little on the inside of great big firm things and being addressed as "Mister" and "Esquire." That was so different from the vagabond black troubadour days.

Sometimes he tried to get out of his skin to measure himself as he once was against his present state. Marseille was a vastly changed place for him now that he had money. In the air of Quayside there was something romantic, quite different from the realistic atmosphere of the nights he used to jazz through there like any other stoker.[1] Sometimes a wave of regret swept over him dampening his heart when the music tickled his upper half and the lower could not respond to it. But that sadness soon vanished under the sensation of the new power that having money gave him.

With their arms over each other's shoulders, Rock and Diup, the funny fixtures of Quayside, barged into the café. They had been drinking plenty of new red wine down the docks and were in a mischievous mood.

"Heah's the jungle kid looking as good as a million," cried Rock. "And carrying a cane too like them Englishmens."

"I got a jungle magic here to gag your mouth," said Lafala. "Takes a Jungle kid alright to put something over."

"I know youse one ace pardner," said Rock, "and no hahm meant to you. Ise always a kidding kind a fellah."

"Didn't think there was any harm," said Lafala. "After all I come from the jungle. I was born there and am going right back with a little civilization in my pocket."

Heavy laughter rolled up from Rock and Diup who remarked "Look out the white ones don't take it back out your pocket when you get there. Take my advice and stay here where Civilization can protect you and leave jungle Africa to white men. What you want to go back there for? White man don't like black man with brains nor money near him in jungleland."

"Going back all the same, Diup," said Lafala. "And you, Rock, I tell you there are many jungle places better than all your Lynchburgs in the States.² I'm going back to make good. Put lazy no-count fellows like you two to work."

"Oh Gawd-an-his-chilluns!" cried Rock. "Jest listen at this swell kid. Ain't no time gone you was a no-count like us all."

"Never was a fixture like you," said Lafala. "I dropped in and fooled around for a little while and then beat it. That was my style when I was a wandering fool. My way of making it before I had this accident."

"Which just landed you slam bang in a mess a good luck," said Rock.

"Was as much having a good head to handle my stuff as good luck that got me where I am," said Lafala. "Every man's got a chance once if he knows how to use it."

"Now jest listen to this wise Jungle kid!" Rock said, his eyes popping. "Why, kid, if a chance had evah brushed anywhar near me in all mah lifetime I'd a grabbed it by the tail and nevah turned loose if it carried me way into hell. The chances in life ain't moh'n a lottery with a million trying and jest ten winning." Rock held up his hands, his fingers apart.

"What about some wine, Lafala?" asked Diup.

"I think you fellows got enough. However, one bottle of ordinary and no more. I'm not going to spoil you for you ought to pull out of this sort of life." Lafala smiled. "And I don't mean to be foolish, even with the small allowance they're giving me. Negroes spend too much. Always showing off and spreading themselves big on nothing."

"What you say is alright, Mr. Lafala," said Rock. "Youse the big boss. Come on," he called to the barmaid, "bring us that bottle a wine on the boss. Bring it heah and le's drink to the health of the United States of America, Gawd blastem with long life and prosperity."

"Let's drink to Marseille and forget America," said Diup.

"Fohget the biggest piece a business in this white man's Civilization!" cried Rock. "Ah couldn't no moh fohget it than mah piece a black person. Why is only in that country theah's miracles still working? Now tell me whar in any other part a Gawd's own wurl a jungle kid like Lafala nor any other poah kid without backing and a pull coulda gotten such a mess a money? Jest look at him setting pretty there with two feets to him as good as any flesh-and-blood ones and the slappiest pair a shoes on them. Why anywheres else perhaps they wouldn't a gived him a pair a pegs. He woulda been lucky to get away with a long shirt like our fourth cousins in Africa wear and a pair of crutches to lean on."

The café resounded with a bellyful of laughter, ebony-smooth-and-shining laughter, bronze-sounding laughter, tawny-throated laughter, sweet-money laughter over Lafala and his luck.

Lafala laughed himself weak. The face of the boss of the bistro[3] caught color, the muscles relaxing in amusement. The boss was a tall and stout mulatto, a silent sort of fellow, casual-looking, but his sharp eyes and ears received every note of significance. One was never sure to what side his sympathies leaned, but suspected they leaned to the strong and cruel. He was a good man for a bar at Quayside.

A guitar and a mandolin were hanging up behind the bar. A white youngster walked in and, asking the proprietor for the mandolin, he tried his hand at a popular tune.

Lafala was an amateur flutist. He extracted a little black flute from his pocket and joined the mandolinist.

"Come on now," said Rock to Diup. "Let's do that split[4] that we were betting on the other day."

Rock shuffled around and flopped to the floor with his right foot out and his left half doubled up. Diup followed suit imitating Rock. They were like two mischievous monkeys. None of them could make the split.

"This heah one got me beat," said Rock. "I done made all the new stunts in mah lifetime, but I kain't make this."

"It ain't natural to us," said Diup. "The split is women's business. God made them natural to split."

"A woman's business is anybody's business," said Rock. "Ain't nothing a woman do you can't find a man to do. If you haven't a way, make one they say. Every white, black and brown man at Quayside knows that. And the womens know that too."

"But it ain't right," said a little white unprosperous-looking protector. "That's just what's wrong with the whole world today. Women trying so hard to do men's stuff and men doing women's stuff. God made man and woman different to do different stuff. That's all."

"Well, we'se all jest imitating Gawd," said Rock. "Gawd done make everything and finish. And since he was so crazy in the head as to make man in his own image we jest nacherally want to make everything that God makes. Get me, pink? I don't believe in laying down no laws for nobody, for the biggest law-makers are the biggest law-breakers undercover. Come on, split, let us ride."

And Rock and Diup started splitting again urged on by the cheering laughter of the clients. It was the *apéritif* hour[5] and the habitués[6] of the bar began dropping in. The men with girls took tables, but some of the stags, especially the Negroes, stood round the counter.

"Just that way, that's a good split," said Rock to the mandolin player. And round and round he went flopping down and up and followed by Diup. And once Diup went down and could not get up.

"Whasmat, pardner? You done split you bone?" cried Rock.

"Wonder where that split stunt comes from?" said Diup still sprawling and looking comically around him. "It's a bone-breaker and a piece-cutter."

"I guess it's American," said Rock. "All the mahvlous-crazy things them come from America. Theah's a sweet-eating stuff ovah there they call banana-split full a rich cream. It's one A-number-one American dessert that everybody is foolish about."

"Well this stunt must be a banana-splitter," said Diup.

Aslima entered swinging herself as always from side to side most tantalizingly and seeing Diup in his funny squatting position on the floor she went and playfully kicked his behind.

"Always monkeying, you and that Rock," she said.

She bounced over to Lafala and ostentatiously began to vamp him. "Play 'Toujours,'"[7] she said, "and I'll dance the jolly pig."[8]

The white lad tuned the mandolin for the piece and began, Lafala joining him, and Aslima started a dance. If you have ever seen a pig dancing before rain, Aslima's movement was an exact imitation. She struck an attitude as if she were on all fours and tossing her head from side to side and shaking her hips, like an excited pig flicking and trying to bite its own tail, she danced round and round the little circle of the café.

The habitués let loose a salvo of applause. "Bravo! Bravo, Aslima! Carry on! Don't stop! Don't stop!"

When she passed Lafala she clutched his hair savagely and said "Going to rain tonight."

"And soak the earth," he laughed.

As the music finished she pulled herself up with a jerk.

"Halouf!"[9] cried a little Arab at her.

"I dance it and you eat it," responded Aslima.

The Arab rushed at her crying "Me eat pig? You dirty slut."

But the Negroes at the bar barred his way. Aslima shrugged, dabbing her face with a handkerchief. The Arab didn't mean to do any harm anyway, but as a good Quaysider he had to show his mettle.

A little after Lafala left the café, his blood warm with carnal sweetness. Aslima had secretly seized an opportunity and made a rendezvous to join him at midnight. And all of Lafala's thoughts were concentrated upon that hour. In spite of himself, Aslima had stirred him deeply again.

He remembered that he had almost been stirred like that once by a mulatto girl in Cardiff.[10] Her color was rich and sweet like a tropical plum. And all the seamen worshipped her. She was a lovely-bodied girl but with a heart-breaking heart. And she used to play with Lafala, teasingly, mockingly, for he was just an adolescent almost innocent among the more experienced seamen. And he did not worship her the way they did, but differently in an adolescent way as if she were an angel. She was the first mulatto girl he ever loved.

Lafala dawdled through his dinner thinking of midnight. He tried to deceive himself to think that it was the assignation only and not the object of it that filled his thoughts. But his eyes without and within could see nothing but Aslima as the "jolly pig," while his ears were humming with the music of her honey-dripping words: "I'll be a sweet pig to you."

A sweet shiver shocked his whole body.

"Oh you're one black liar!" he cried at himself. "You know you're just crazy about her."

At a late hour when he returned to the hotel, he tipped the night porter and asked him to let Aslima right up when she came. He sat down in a comfortable old easy chair and removed his corks. Then with his crutches he swung himself over to the bed and pushed between the sheets.

Aslima arrived with the hour. She went to the bed and kissed Lafala, asking him if he liked her new frock. It was a purple thing bordered with that peculiar cerise[11] that is so popular among the North African women. The dress harmonized charmingly with her chocolate-brown complexion. Lafala said he liked it and Aslima turned and admired herself in the full-sized mirror of the old wardrobe.

He watched her gestures as she undressed and the thought of Titin, Aslima's lover, studying her in his place tormented him. So when she came to him he said, "Suppose Titin should see us now!"

"Why think of him now?" she asked. "He doesn't care what I do so long as he knows that I am doing it for money and not for love."

"He's jealous of your betraying his love, eh?"

Aslima shrugged: "I am doing it now with you."

"Oh no! It's pity and pride bring you here to me. You know I can't love you like Titin. I'm just half a stick that you take pity on, but Titin is your whole loving man."

"Maybe he loves me more than I love him."

"With a lousy love. Well, I've done lots of hoggish stuff in my life, but I'd sooner clean the rusty pipes than be a pea-eye."[12]

"That is a *métier*,"[13] said Aslima. "There are many who prefer a pimp."

"The girls are all crazy about their protectors."

"Not all. Some of us fight with them all the time. But we put up with them for the life is too tough down here without them. You can hardly do any business. In my country it wasn't necessary to have protectors."

"But how is it La Fleur hasn't a Titin?"

"Because she's different from most of us. She doesn't go crazy over men. She hates men and goes with them only to make money. Her Titin is that Greek girl."

"Oh, that's why she's so haughty cold."

"She attracts lots of men," said Aslima. "Because they think she's got something hidden in her to give up, when she really has nothing at all. Nothing for men."

"While you have everything—but for Titin only," Lafala laughed.

"Let's finish chatting and be loving pigs," said Aslima.

"I can't be as piggish as in my able-bodied days," said Lafala.

"Pigskin!" Aslima exclaimed. "Forget about your feet now and thank God it wasn't something worse that was cut off."

"Alright, piggy."

"I've been a pig all my life," said Aslima. "But with you I don't feel that it's just a mud bath. I feel like we're clean pigs."

In the morning Lafala again offered Aslima money, but she refused it.

"Think what you want and do what you will but I don't want your money."

"Look here, don't hand me that stuff. I have money and I know you've got to love to make money. That's your living. I want to be with you as long as I remain in Marseille so take the dough and don't hand me a lot of crap."

"Listen," said Aslima, "we'll be happy pigs together as often as I am free. I want to convince you that I am human at bottom. That I really think more about your accident than about your money. And when you go away from here this time you will think differently of me from what you did the last time."

Now at last Lafala thought his revenge was perfect and complete. Such words coming out of the mouth of Aslima, the Tigress. When she robbed him and escaped that time of their first liaison he had had his thoughts of revenge. But after his illness and the amputation of his legs, lying there in the hospital, the idea of a little revenge had faded away before the contemplation of the enormous tragic joke of himself. Then when he received the compensation for damages all that remained in his mind of Aslima's little joke was the desire to see her again and show himself, even though physically half a man, in spirit a stronger, new man.

"Are you satisfied now, pig?" Aslima asked after a silence.

"Well, it's nice to meet with one person who is not out and out right after my money," said Lafala in a suspicious accent.

"I'm not better than the rest," said Aslima quickly. "But I did play you a rotten trick once. And now I want to show you I have a heart."

"Look out! Titin will carve it up if you start fooling with it that way."

Aslima shrugged. . . . And then an idea entered Lafala's brain. A mixture of mischief and humor and a desire to test Aslima. And he said, "Why don't you quit Titin and come with me?"

"Me!" exclaimed Aslima. "Where? Quit Titin to go where?"

"Back to Africa with me for a change. Wouldn't you like to go back? Think you could stand the life there again?"

"Sure! See me quitting Quayside to go and be your Lalla[14] in Africa. That's very fine! What a chance! What happiness!"

"I mean it."

"Now you're trying to make a fool of me. Getting even, eh? Go on!"

"No, I really mean it. I think it would be a good thing if you went back with me. I don't like the idea of going alone."

Aslima spat a common love word: "Big pig! Now it's your turn to take your revenge on me. See me quitting Quayside to go back with you to the bush to live on palm wine and cane juice, bananas and nuts."

"All of that," Lafala laughed. "We'll be happy wild pigs over there."

"The pork-eaters rooting in the bush might get us," said Aslima.

"No. We'll hide deep down in the bushes and only come out when we're dirty to swim every day in a warm, blue river."

"And what about the crocodiles?" asked Aslima with a pretty singing shriek.

"We'll climb high up on the banks when they open their traps. And we'll go to sleep and dream that Quayside is Paradise."

"Well, I'm willing to take a chance if you don't change your mind, big-money pig."

"And suppose I change my mind?"

"I should worry. We'll just treat it like a joke. One can go far on a joke and with money. Money will lead a woman to the devil and a man to hell."

"We'll take it as a serious joke," said Lafala.

"I'm all excited now," said Aslima, sitting down on the bed again with a tantalizing air.

"Want to make a day of it too?" said Lafala.

"Why not, big pig? It's the life."

"Especially when one has money," agreed Lafala, sitting down against her.

"Oh, pig-pig-pig, piggy-pig," Aslima chanted in an ecstatic fit. . . . "We are all pigs."

CHAPTER NINE

Aslima was a child of North Africa out of Marrakesh,[1] that city of the plain where savagery emerging from the jungle meets civilization. Marrakesh, that amazing city that excites to wonder—a city like jewels of wild tropical extravagance set at the feet of majestic encircling snow-capped peaks.

Aslima's mother was a robust Sudanese who had been sold a slave to the Moors. Aslima was born a slave. She retained a shadowy remembrance of her mother, recalled running by her side clutching her voluminous skirt when she went upon errands. She held in the child's chamber of her mind a picture of the Djemaa el-Fna,[2] the great wild square of Marrakesh: the elegant white-robed-and-veiled women exhibiting the margin of their rich colored dresses, the dainty shuffle of their painted feet in bright embroidered slippers; the merchants and peddlers and purchasers haggling over a thousand odds and ends; the storytellers, the snake charmers and boy dancers clapping hands and chanting to the unceasing monotonous beat of the drum; the muezzin[3] calling, the marabouts[4] praying and the weird noisy rituals of religion-frenzied groups. . . .

And one day she was separated from her mother, confused with many things in that strange place where child stealing is practiced and secret hawk-eyed slave dealers are ever looking out for little victims. . . .

Next we find Aslima among the hetairai[5] of Fez[6] growing up a pretty little girl, a decorative thing in the house of a wise old courtesan.

Aslima grew to girlhood in Moulay Abdallah,[7] that alluring quarter of Fez full of strange antique interest where affairs of love are conducted in an atmosphere of almost otherworldliness.

Aslima's mistress had a nice house bright with Moorish rugs[8] and curtained walls and gleaming bronze trays and candlesticks. And Aslima performed little tasks such as making a fire in an earthenware bowl, serving tea and running errands to the grocer's. And she wore pretty clothes.

Her mistress brought her up in a fine spirit of materialistic interest. The girl was worth a little prize and someday a nice little sum could be realized on her virgin beauty. Aslima's first personal adventure was with a colored sub-officer from one of the French West Indies who, taking a liking to the girl, made a bargain with her mistress and paid a few hundred francs to take her away and live with him.

The soldier took Aslima to Casablanca.[9] And when after some months he went to Algeria, Aslima accompanied him. At the end of two years the soldier was transferred to a Far Eastern regiment. And he was obliged to leave Aslima. He gave her a sum of money.

After the soldier's departure Aslima carried on transient love affairs with native and white. And one day she was approached by a young Corsican.[10] He was a tout who went to sea sometimes when business was slack. He obtained a passage to Marseille for Aslima. There he got her into a house of love and received money for her.

It was Aslima's first experience with a protector. From one house of love she passed to others. She never remained very long in a loving house. For she was always having trouble with the management and with clients. They said she was a savage girl. She was vigorous, rough-tongued and reckless. And being quick-tempered and brown she was outstanding among the white girls in Quayside and soon became notorious as the Tigress.

It was more congenial for her to have an independent lair in Quayside. No one would have recognized in the Tigress the little demure brown child of the house of love in Fez. Indeed there were moments when Aslima wondered herself if she were the same person.

Her lair was a poor little affair but cleverly arranged to suggest the exotic. There was no bedstead. A small mattress in a corner with a gay coverlet. A water pitcher sat on the ground before the mattress and in the center of the lair was a bowl.

The water pitcher was made in Spain and the bowl in France but nevertheless the atmosphere they created was effectively African. And many were the African and Oriental seamen who stopped to look in at the open door at the little savage curled up on the mattress regarding them with mischievous half-closed eyes.

It was that pose and that atmosphere that had magnetized Lafala when he first arrived in Marseille.

And now half-jokingly, half-seriously, Lafala had proposed to Aslima that she should return to his tribal Africa with him. And the idea had grown upon him. After so many years of drifting along European ports he was half-civilized in a Quayside way. And he rather dreaded returning home to his native bush alone.

He had grown accustomed to a vagabond way of life and love. And it was hard for him to wrench himself away from that. But with Aslima companioning him the new life might be tolerable. He might be able to adjust himself to it more easily and happily. . . . And of all the ways of loving he had experienced, none had ever wrought such delicious havoc on his senses as Aslima's.

One evening Lafala treated Aslima to the cinema up in the respectable part of the town. It was a romantic sheik picture.[11] Aslima and Lafala held each other's hands following the quickly developing action. They were excited and looked like happy lovers.

During the intermission Aslima leaned her head upon Lafala's shoulder. When she looked up again she saw La Fleur staring at her from the opposite side. La Fleur's Greek girlfriend was with her.

Aslima became uneasy. She had no money. She was going to spend the night with Lafala and did not intend taking any money from him. She would have nothing to give Titin in the morning. And La Fleur might tell Titin about her being with Lafala and looking so happy.

Aslima decided not to stay with Lafala that night and told him so. But Lafala was displeased: "Why, that's why I took you to the picture, so we should feel sweeter pigs together." Aslima went with him.

Titin was waiting for Aslima when she returned to her lair behind Number One Quay the next morning. La Fleur had seen him at the Tout-va-Bien after the theater and told him mockingly that she had seen Aslima and Lafala at the cinema looking just like two innocent young lovers.

"Where in hell were you last night?" Titin greeted her.

"Try and guess."

"Won't try a damn thing. I'm not kidding."

"But you know who I was with. Didn't that La Fleur tell you?"

"Yes. With Pied-Coupé.[12] Give me that money."

"Ain't got more than twenty francs."

"Twenty francs, you cheapest slut for all night. Show me a hundred francs or I'll cut your throat."

Aslima laughed as Titin advanced on her menacingly.

"What's the matter with you acting the fool!" she exclaimed. "I'll never get away with anything if you keep on interfering and listen to those covetous cats spying on me. That Fleur is just crazy jealous since I made her look anything but a queen that night in the Tout-va-Bien when she was right after Lafala for a hundred francs and I just cut in and took him away. . . . What is a hundred francs when a guy is rich? I am playing a deep game for a big stake."

"Explain yourself!" Titin commanded.

Aslima hesitated. "Promise not to whisper a word to anybody," she said. Titin promised. And Aslima told him that Lafala had asked her to go to Africa with him.

Titin started. "Did he? That damned Pied-Coupé!"

"Keep your shirt on," said Aslima. "And who're you kidding with that open knife, yourself or me?"[13]

She told Titin that she had promised to go with Lafala. And for that reason she was not taking any money from him. In fact Lafala had very little money in his possession. He received money only from the official agent who was looking after his affairs. He was waiting in Marseille for the final settlement and payment. And she was waiting too and working herself into his confidence. She had to be very clever and sincere-like because of the first trick she had turned on Lafala. For this was not a matter of a few hundred francs but thousands . . . and as soon as Lafala got his, she meant to get hers.

Titin was amazed at the plan. "Fine! Fine!" he said. "You're a brick, a born whore. My God, you might get enough out of him for us to buy us a bar in Marseille."

That was the highest ambition of all the Quaysiders. To own a bar over and under which passed a thousand intrigues and upon which flourished the savage anarchy of Quayside.

Titin believed in Aslima with a certain reservation—as much as his type of mind could believe in anybody. He knew all about the slick trick that Aslima had pulled on Lafala before he stowed away. That was before he became her protector. And it seemed like madness to him that Lafala should take up with Aslima again and have confidence in her. But no doubt Lafala was just like all the rest of the Quayside Negroes. They were just a band of savage children, flaring up like fire when they were badgered and angered and as quickly subsiding again, forgetting their injuries and those who inflicted them, thoughtless and changeable. They did not know how to organize revenge like the white Quaysiders.

Titin discussed with Aslima the different plans they might use in mulcting[14] Lafala. As they talked together and he warmed up to the idea of raiding Lafala and buying a bar he felt finer towards Aslima than he ever did. She became more important and desirable to him than ever. His blood mounted and he embraced her feeling like loving her. But Aslima said she was tired and found a way out of it.

When Aslima saw Lafala again, she did not tell him what had passed between her and Titin. She had reasoned that Lafala who had grown as suspicious as a fox under the responsibility of money might become more so. Things were complicated enough already and among men as well as women the law of Quayside was "Never trust a woman."

And as for Titin, walking into the Tout-va-Bien one afternoon when it was full of clients, he bawled loudly at La Fleur, asking her if it were because business was so dull that she should spend her time spying on his woman. Ashamed and unable to stand the jeering faces of the habitués, La Fleur left the café without a retort.

CHAPTER TEN

Since the battle with Aslima over Lafala and her defeat and the public rebuke administered by Titin, La Fleur's popularity was on the wane in Quayside. The Quaysiders were turning their interest to Aslima who had Lafala, the money man, in hand. And La Fleur felt very spiteful towards Lafala, considering him the cause of her setback.

One week Marseille was all beflagged and gay with colors and music for its yearly festivities.¹ Quayside had cleaned and polished its front for the event and the Quaysiders were all in contagious holiday mood. The square was fenced in and an orchestra installed on a stand. And the fishermen and dockers came with their sweethearts to dance and mingle with the girls let out of the houses of love with their lovers for the occasion.

The sailors from the boats along Quayside turned out in full force and many of them were attracted to the sweethearts of the dockers and fishermen charming in their homely dress, some wearing aprons. But those girls would not dance with them. And so they had to be contented with the girls out of the houses of love dolled up in the latest fashion.

The Tout-va-Bien had its little flags out and the proprietor and his paramour were as busy as could be. Midweek of the festivities one evening during an intermission in the program on the square, many of the habitués crowded into the bar on the quay to drink.

There were some Quayside girls in the bar who had not been dancing in the square. And they were not so very happy over the festivities, for it interfered with the routine of their lives. They were the café girls and the bars during the festive week were monopolized by honest working folk: docile dockers and fine fishermen with their sweethearts. The girls were elbowed aside and out. There was no room and no chance for them to pose and vamp. The men who wanted a little loving in a hurry went to the shuttered houses.

Lafala had been wistfully watching the fun in the square remembering how he had danced himself sweating tired during the festive week that was held in Marseille before he stowed away. He had stood around so long that his corks began to hurt him and so he went around to the Tout-va-Bien to rest himself.

The discontented girls were playing the pianola and dancing listlessly with their lovers. La Fleur was there with her Greek friend and another white girl. Lafala entered, greeted them cordially and hobbled to the WC. But he was followed by loud derisive laughter, started by La Fleur, in which the other girls joined.

Lafala was nonplussed by the laughter which he felt was directed against him. Then he heard La Fleur's high mocking voice shrieking "Pied-Coupé! Pied-Coupé! Watch him strutting!" He cracked the door of the WC a little ajar and saw La Fleur giving an exaggerated imitation of his walking. And the entire café was amused and laughing.

Rock was there and did not appreciate La Fleur's joke. And he said to her, "Him's got a fortune foh them feet all the same. Theah's other gals don't mind them pieces a feet. Aslima likem."

The mention of Aslima was like a prick in La Fleur's flesh. She was tortured by the memory of Lafala allowing Aslima to wrest him right out of her arms. "It's because she's a cheap slut," cried La Fleur. "Everybody knows she'll love for five francs. She's acting up to Lafala as if she was loving him. I saw them at the picture the other night. They were a scream."

"Maybe Aslima's really got the beguine² for Lafala," said the white girl, "for he's one handsome black man."

"It's because you don't know Aslima," said La Fleur. "When he was here the first time with his two sound feet, she didn't love anything in him but the purse she snatched. And you think it's any different now? He's waiting for his money and she's waiting too. Aslima is one wonderful actor."

"He looks better now than before," said the white girl.

"Then he was nobody, but now he's somebody with good clothes and good money."

"Why don't you try your luck?" asked La Fleur.

"I'd like to stick an iron pole into that thing," Lafala said to himself, "and set her up in the square for everybody to mock at her."

He went from the WC to the bar where Rock and Diup were standing with a group and he stood them drinks, telling them to have whatever they wanted with a swaggering gesture.

"You're the prince of Africa," said Rock, caressing Lafala's shoulder.

"And you're the clown of the Congo," replied Lafala.

"No pardner, Ise original American."

"What? You think you're a redskin?" asked Lafala.

"No, but Ise as good as them with some real red in mah skin. Don't you know, pardner, when them redskins wouldn't stand being good an' native them ofays had to import us to implace them?"[3]

The African boys laughed spaciously to the echo as if they were camping in the Sahara.

"We all sold you to the Yankees so we could have more room in the jungles," said Diup.

"Monkey nuts!" replied Rock.

The girl that had been defending Lafala spoke up: "Can't you pay me a drink too?"

"Have one," said Lafala with a princely gesture.

Lafala drew his chair towards her. He had taken the café by surprise. He had never been in such a spending mood before. Others clamored for a treat and soon all the old habitués were drinking at his expense.

La Fleur looked quite discomfited and her girlfriend said loudly "Why, it seems we're out of it!"

"You can have a drink too, if you want," said Lafala.

"Oh, what we want you can't afford!" said La Fleur quickly.

"I can afford anything in this place," said Lafala. "Money is no object to me."

"My faith! What style!" exclaimed La Fleur. "Well, give us champagne."

Lafala ordered champagne. All the proprietor had was Vin Mousseux⁴ which he always served as champagne.

La Fleur looked proudly over the crowd, threw her head back and drained her glass at a draught.

"I thought you'd treat Aslima only to champagne," she said mockingly.

"I am one independent cuss," said Lafala. "I treat who I want to when I want to. Tonight I feel like treating you."

La Fleur laughed and shook her head vigorously. She extracted a tube and pad from her vanity bag and began fooling with her face. Her big bright eyes seemed more spiteful than ever as she stroked the lids. As soon as the champagne was finished she said she would like some more. Lafala ordered another bottle.

La Fleur called to the little boy who always operated the pianola. "Here, pigling, put this coin in the piano and start it going."

La Fleur stood up castaneting her fingers⁵ and went to dance the beguine with her girlfriend. When she returned to her seat Lafala said, "No more dancing for me. Poor Pied-Coupé."

La Fleur felt a little embarrassed. "Don't pity yourself. You're alright. If you can't dance you can do something else."

"Sure. Like paying for champagne. . . . Or—invite you to my hotel tonight."

La Fleur giggled happily. "The last time you were going to, you changed your mind for a cheaper party. I'm not changed any. Indeed I feel a little dearer after champagne."

"That's all right. Don't think about the price. Money is nothing to me."

La Fleur whispered to her girlfriend: "I think it's going to be black tea tonight."

"Save the sugar for us," her friend whispered back.

"That goes without saying," said La Fleur.

Lafala was preparing to leave with La Fleur when the proprietor brought him the bill.

"Chalk that up to my account," Lafala said without looking at it.

"It's a big one," said the proprietor.

"You worried?" asked Lafala.

"Never in my life, Grand Duke of Dakar."

"I'm not a Senegambian," said Lafala.[6]

"No difference. You're just like one of them."

"One of us, you mean, Yaller."

And with a swagger as much as his feet would allow him Lafala departed followed by La Fleur who imitated his walking a little as she went, winking at her friends.

They taxied to the hotel. Arriving, La Fleur threw her gaudy Spanish shawl on the back of a chair and went to the lavatory. When she went out Lafala quickly removed his corks and got into bed covering himself. He was sensitive about being seen without the artificial feet.

La Fleur returned and looked around the comfortable room. She glided to the window, drew aside the curtain and looked out. Many cats were amusing themselves noisily on the roofs.

"The cats are carrying on terribly on the roofs," she said.

"And the two-footed ones are just as bad under the roofs," said Lafala.

"It's the same life everywhere," La Fleur giggled.

Lafala's black head stood out conspicuously among the white bed things, his bright eyes following La Fleur's movements. She was like a lizard, a tropical green lizard that is beautiful but cold among the hot colors and sensations of the tropics.

She sat down in the easy chair and examined the artificial legs, thrusting her hands into them. And after a while she glanced speculatively at Lafala and smiled faintly.

"Well, here we are, all set," he said.

"All set," La Fleur repeated. But she showed no eagerness about undressing. She went over instead to the wardrobe mirror with her beauty pad and began dabbing her face.

"Your color is alright," said Lafala. "Undress and get into bed."

"I know *my* color is all right," replied La Fleur, "but I don't know if the color of your money is. I'd like to see it first right there on the night table."

"The money is alright," Lafala said in an evasive tone.

"Then where is it? I'll feel better with it in my stocking than in your pocket."

"Well, I have no more than five francs on me now. You'll get it Saturday when I draw money."

"Me wait three days! I'm not on the credit system. What the devil did you mean by bringing me here tonight?"

"The barkeeper waits, you saw it yourself. And the hotel manager. Aslima—."

"Don't mention the name of that no-count slut to me. You had your nerve bringing me here when you didn't have enough money to pay."

"What's the difference?" Lafala said indifferently. "My credit is good and everybody in Marseille is glad to give me credit."

"Except me. I am not everybody, you dirty black block of a swine," said La Fleur viciously.

"You don't mean what you say, do you?"

"I mean more and I'll say more. Why did you bring me here when you hadn't the money? Do you think I'd trust any man? If you don't pay me after you've satisfied yourself, can I force you? Can I go to the police and say 'This man loved me all night and refused to pay?' You think I'm a fool, don't you? Or perhaps you brought me here to play a trick on me."

Lafala grinned a little.

"Don't laugh at me, you miserable Pied-Coupé. You think I'm Aslima pretending to be in love with your withered stumps of legs, because you've got money? You look like a mess to me. You're strutting like a monkey and crowing over everybody because you got money. But you can't crow over me, Pied-Coupé, though you think you're such a nice cock."

"You can't talk to me like that in my own place. If I could stand on my feet I'd slap your messy mouth shut."

"Go love yourself or get somebody to. You got a block as good as mine."

And La Fleur continued to abuse Lafala. Loads and loads of filth falling from her orchid-like mouth and piling up a pyramid until Lafala felt as if he were buried under the stinking heap and could not crawl from under it, until he was sorry he had brought her there to revenge himself upon her.

"Now I know what you really are," he said. "Nothing but filth. A sewer full of filth. I wouldn't want to touch you at any price. Get out of here, you dirty piece of tail."

"You give me the money to pay the taxi back home," she said.

"Not a damned cent. You can walk on all fours, bitch that you are."

"The idea of bringing me here to mess with me. I am not Aslima."

"Aslima is a thousand times better than you. I'd give any money for Aslima, but I wouldn't give a cent for you. Aslima is rough but she isn't WC. You're nothing else."

"Don't, don't compare me with that Aslima," cried La Fleur. "I don't want to hear any more. You pay the taxi to take me back and I'll go."

"Pay nothing, you rotten stinker. Get out! You're nothing but a load of filth. I can't stand the awful smell of you. Get out, I say!"

"I won't go unless you pay the taxi," said La Fleur.

She sat down, and began thinking. It was late. She did not want to walk all the way down to Quayside. And she had no money. She hated to go back to her Greek friend like that. Soured and empty-handed after she had left the Tout-va-Bien so triumphantly with Lafala. The champagne was having its effect and she felt a little drowsy. She was also piqued because Lafala had said he would not love her even for nothing and called her a load of filth. It would relieve her to make him eat his words.

I'll sleep with him for the night, she thought.

She began undressing. "You shouldn't have brought me here to play such a trick on me," she said. "But I'll sleep with you since I'm here and you can do anything you want with me."

Lafala did not reply. But La Fleur continued to undress until she had nothing left but her stockings and shoes. She minced to the bed and bent to caress Lafala but before she could achieve the gesture he shot his stump into her belly. Quickly he pressed the button by the bed and before La Fleur could gather her senses together the night man entered the room. Hastily La Fleur grabbed her shawl to cover herself.

"Put that slut out!" Lafala said.

The man hesitated. He knew La Fleur. He himself once had a girl at Quayside.

"It's alright. It's nothing. I am going," said La Fleur.

She dressed hastily, the man standing by. As she was making for the door he saw her vanity bag on the window sill and
arresting her with a gesture, he picked up the bag and handed
it to her. La Fleur took it without meeting his eyes and ran
down the stairs.

Left alone, Lafala felt that he did not want to see another
woman in his life. He felt sticky, slimy, sorry that he had
invited La Fleur to his room for the sake of revenge.

He had gone through some nasty things, but in all his experience he had never had such a filthy feeling. He made a resolve
to keep away from Quayside. He turned out the light and tried
to sleep, but sleep refused to be wooed. And very soon something stronger than his resolve began to assert itself. His body
was aching for love. He thought of Aslima. There was a time
when she was the only person in Marseille who stirred in him
a feeling of hatred and revenge. Yet now he felt closer to her
than anybody. How changing were the emotions!

He got up and dressed, put his feet on and hobbled out of
the hotel. He took a taxicab down to Quayside. The Tout-va-
Bien, now closed, looked like a comfort station with an "Out
of Order" sign up. Lafala went past it navigating the intricate
arteries towards Aslima's lair.

Titin was there and, annoyed at being awakened at that
hour, he opened the door in an unfriendly fashion to Lafala's
knock. But when he recognized Lafala he greeted him with a
smile. Then he half-closed the door and turned to tell Aslima
that Lafala was there.

Aslima dressed quickly and joined Lafala outside. They
strolled along to Number One Quay where there was a little
open-all-night bar. There were not many clients. They sat off
in a corner by themselves. Aslima asked Lafala why he had
come to see her at that hour. He told her what had happened
between him and La Fleur.

"She's finished down here now," she said.

"I don't care about that. I feel rotten."

"Don't feel rotten because of that La Fleur. It would have

been fine if you had been in a fit state to throw her out naked into the street."

"Tigress!"

"No. I'm just a chummy pig. Scratch me and see how I'll lie down at your feet."

Lafala laughed. "I won't do any such thing. Not here."

"Alright then. Pay up and let's go where we can be scratching pigs."

CHAPTER ELEVEN

Titin turned out of bed on the wrong side of life with a sore soul. Money had been getting scarcer and scarcer with him for too uncomfortably long a time. It appeared as if Aslima's liaison with Lafala was incapacitating her as the hardiest hustler of Quayside. There was something gone wrong there. It was alright to work-and-wait on Lafala. He was entirely in agreement with that and always ready to give Aslima good advice. But there was no reason why that should change the good old way of Aslima's life and deprive him of his regular daily bread and pocket money for *apéritifs* and the indispensable after-dinner cigar which was the protectors' trademark at Quayside. And it was about time he should be getting a new suit. He had been feeling a little seedy of late among his comrades in arms. And now he was wondering—there was a possibility that Aslima might be betraying him with Lafala.

Things had come to such a pass that he had not even money to pay for his meals and was eating on credit at the Pig's Tail—a little clan restaurant on Number One Quay. Formerly he used to be accompanied by Aslima, but now she was taking most of her meals with Lafala.

There was a subtle change in Aslima which did not escape him. However much she tried to be the same girl externally, she was a different person in their intimate relations. He did not feel in her body that desire and dependence upon him as a protector that had formerly been psychically communicated to him.

Today he was having lunch with Aslima. They went together to the Pig's Tail and removed from a nail their serviettes[1] knotted together and covered with flies and flyshit. They ate in silence. They had had an ugly dispute and for a couple of days there was acute nervous tension between them.

After lunch Titin went to a café where a group of his colleagues usually met to gamble. All he possessed was ten francs which he lost playing French poker. It was much the worse for his temper to sit there impotently hearing the clink and rustle of money and watching coins and notes piling up under the palms of his colleagues.

Late in the afternoon when he looked in on their lair Aslima was getting ready for a rendezvous with Lafala. From outside he had heard her humming an African melody, reiterating the monotonously wistful notes, and that increased his irritation.

"Where are you going?" he said.

"Why, you know I'm going to see Lafala," Aslima replied shortly.

"It would be better you go and hustle some money elsewhere," said Titin. "You're wasting too much time with that guy."

"I've got to jolly him along. It's the only way to do. I promised him I'd come tonight."

"But listen to me! I don't think you're playing the game right. You're too easy. You ought to keep him guessing and worrying over you."

"If you think you know this game better than me," said Aslima, "you'd better put on a skirt."

"Don't you try to crap on me because of that Pied-Coupé, you snotty slut. You spend every evening with him and eat a swell meal and drink good liquor. And you don't care a screw if I starve—if I can't buy a drink."

"I'll stop going then if you don't want me to," Aslima said in a cold metallic tone.

"I didn't say you should stop. But I don't think you should be with him so often and not hustle on the side at all."

Aslima shrugged and again began humming the African melody.

"You're acting in such a way as to make me think you are in love with that damned stump," said Titin.

"Suppose I am," Aslima laughed mockingly. "It isn't impossible."

"Oh, it isn't, eh? What would you do with it? Go and nurse

him in the jungle? Guess it would be nice to go naked again. Just get rid of all your silk shifts and stockings and wear a banana leaf. Say goodbye to Quayside and all of us and be a good and naked squaw to Pied-Coupé in a hut in the bush!"

"You dirty rat!" Aslima cried, "Lafala is a better man than you although he has no feet. Do you think I am afraid of the jungle? I'd rather go back there than live like a dog here."

"You would, eh?"

"Yes I would and I'm going." And Aslima flung herself out of the room.

But instead of taking the way along the quay that led towards Lafala's hotel, Aslima turned up an alley. The alley sloped up to a terrace which overlooked the beautiful bay. The terrace was shored up by a fine wall from which the main road dropped sheer down from a height of some fifty feet and ran for miles and miles along the waterfront.

The families of the houses around the terrace were taking the evening air before supper. Children played in the sand. Loving couples sat spaced apart with their backs to the sea.

Aslima sat on a bench and gazed out over the big bay. From up there Quayside was so charming a dream with the soft-gray buildings forming a fence along the water and the little fishing boats huddled together coloring the slightly moving waves. Farther off the big ships loomed upon the horizon in shadow and gloom.

The night came quickly down throwing a heavy cloak over the city and the sea. And Aslima was lost in it. The lights glimmered along Quayside and in rows and clusters in the town but the margin of the bay was in heavy obscurity.

The darkness became thicker and damp with dews and Aslima remained alone with it, inert as if her spirit had fled her body. And after a long strange interval a red light appeared in the horizon revealing to her a different scene. She was in the heart of an antique white-washed city. And there was loud mounting music of voices as if a thousand golden-throated muezzins were calling in one mighty chorus.

And there was a rushing movement of hurrying feet as if all the houses had brusquely emptied their inhabitants into the street. And started a great procession of loose-robed men and women and children marching as to a midnight ritual, stamping and dancing to barbaric music, the men brandishing swords and women chanting and keening and children capering and Aslima foremost among the hysterical women.

And the procession went winding into a vast marble and malachite court of beautiful balconies filled with kindred people and all the people marched around a gushing fountain dipping their hands in limpid water. And perfume was shed down upon them from on high.

There followed a loving feast.[2] The people gathering unceremoniously together, old and young, men, women and children, kneeling and squatting upon magic-like carpets and piles of rainbow cushions under lights like variegated flowers and shrouded in clouds of rarest incense, there was a gorgeous gorging. . . .

When the feasting was finished the belly-moving beat of the drum roused the people again after an interval of rest to dancing and chanting over and over again repeating and reiterating from pattern to pattern unraveling the threads of life from the most intricate to the simplest to the naked bottom as if in evocation of the first gods who emerged out of the ancient unfathomed womb of Africa to procreate and spread over the vast surface of the land.

Dancing and dancing down into a deep darkness. . . . And when they came up into light again the court was transformed into a place of worship. And all bowed down together submissive in a warm circle. And timidly raising her head Aslima saw a beauty that dazzled her. Overshadowing all an immense dome studded with all the jewels of earth and reflecting all the colors of life.

And as she gazed she was repelled, fascinated and awed by a flaming sword suspended from the center of the dome. And a golden voice was chanting its praise: "The Sword of Life! The Sword of Life!"

All the people of the earth were assembled under that dome and worshipping that sword. Some were slaves and some were free; some were wanton and some were happy. Some were strange and some were sad; some were lighthearted and some were heavy-burdened.

But all were worshippers, subject creatures, making sacri-
fices to it: budding flower of childhood, fruit of adolescence,
honey of maturity, wine of experience, vinegar of disillusion,
bitter broth of cynicism, lamentation of blasted hopes.

And among the multitude was one group apart that was
offering up body and soul as a sacrifice. And in the midst of
that group was Aslima divided and struggling against herself.
She did not want to surrender all of her, but she could not
detach herself. Fighting for release, she saw Lafala among the
free and cried out fearfully to him. But he could not go to her.

Lafala! Lafala! Lafala! But a high wall arose shutting her off
and all was darkness.

"Oh, God, I'm free!" Aslima cried, springing up. The terrace was deserted and silent. "God! How long I've been here.
What a vision! Awful and sweet! Oh, I wonder if it meant
good or bad? I must go and tell Lafala about it right now."

CHAPTER TWELVE

Titin was a son of country laborers, born and raised in a small village. It was while he was doing his service in the army that he got onto the tricks that eventually determined his career. His parents were too poor to send him even the smallest of remittances to help eke out his miserable army pay. Titin belonged to a group that had no cigarette money, no beer money, no money for loving while their comrades had.

Titin soon learned the ways of earning a percentage from the loving houses by procuring clients. By that means he obtained a little pocket money.

With his face prematurely caved in he was not at all a handsome type, but there was a fascination in his glassy beady eyes and spoonlike mouth. He possessed a tough little body and his manner was brusque. And so he was a good type to do business for a loving house. He picked up a store of knowledge about the secret desires of men and understood the mawkish weaknesses of the hetairai. And so when his military service was finished he just slipped from amateur to professional.

However, he was among the lesser fry in the loving business. The loving houses he frequented when he was a soldier were all small establishments in small towns. Titin did not possess the quality and the presence for the luxurious places. And so he had never reached above Quayside. Even in Marseille he was not associated with any of the big fellows who played his line.

But Aslima losing control of herself and getting madly angry because of Lafala convinced him that she might really be playing a double game and against such an eventuality he decided to enlist the help of the bigger fellows.

There was a fellowship in Quayside known as the Domino Association that usually met at a café called the Domino.[1] It was an international association, a kind of loose federation of men of common mind and ideals who kept in touch with one another by secret correspondence, keeping tabs on their protégées, boycotting or hounding into submission or out of existence those who were refractory.

The president of the organization at Quayside was a Levantine sort of person,[2] a thick-set, well-fed man with enormous jowls reminding one of the types of men pictured as guardians of harems, excepting that this man was not black, but had a complexion something like old yellow paint dirty with soot. He was a highly-honored personage in all the loving houses of Marseille. Formally he was known as a guide and commercial traveler. He was a great crony of the cavalier seamen who went to sea sometimes to prove that they were not sans profession, and through them he kept up a regular correspondence with those Near East ports that are as fascinating to the mind as Marseille.

Titin did not find this man at the Domino Café (so-called because the clients always gambled at dominoes, preferring it to any other game). He left the Domino thinking of Aslima and Lafala and the thought of what they might be doing together excited him so that he was irresistibly compelled to visit Lafala's hotel.

The night man unsuspiciously gave him the number of Lafala's room on the first floor back. He went up and listened outside the door to catch what was going on. Hearing nothing, he knocked. Lafala said, "Come in."

Titin's entrance startled Lafala. He had thought it was Aslima.

"What is it? What do you want?" Lafala asked.

"Where's Aslima?"

"I don't know."

"You're a damn liar. You must know when she left me to come here."

"I can't understand why a rat like you should come here to insult me."

"Don't dare call me a rat, Pied-Coupé. I came here to look

for my woman." Titin looked behind the screen where the wash bowl was under the bed.

"I tell you she isn't here. What sort of game are you up to? Why should she be hiding if she were here?"

"Because she knows I'm going to get her."

"Well, go and get her where she is," Lafala's voice rose in contemptuous anger. "You'll never find her here now or any time. I don't want to have anything to do with a woman whose pimp comes butting into my hotel. You get out!"

"I will when you pay me the money you owe Aslima."

"The money I owe her! Did she send you here for that?" Lafala was very suspicious. He had never really reposed any confidence in Aslima.

"Yes! The money you owe her. You've never paid her anything, but you'll pay me."

"I offered money to Aslima many times and she wouldn't take it. I suppose you're both up to some hellishness. But I don't care a damn. I have no money for you."

"You lie! You have plenty of money, you black Pied-Coupé."

"I'm a Pied-Coupé, alright, but I'm a man!" said Lafala. "You're nothing but a white dung-eater. Money is your only passion, yet you never think of working for it. All you're good for is riding some goose like Aslima until she plumps money out for you."

"Sure, I ride easy and make the pigs like you pay. How did you get your money? You didn't work for it any more than all the other hogs who're rich. You just got it by chance."

"Chance here." Lafala tapped his head with a contemptuous smile. "Yes, I got plenty of money. All of you down Quayside know that. But it isn't for any of you and you won't find five francs here. You're in hard luck with me, my friend, but the life of a pimp is not as easy as you say. It's just like the life of a rat."

Titin was enraged. Lafala was actually laughing, mocking at him. "You dirty blackamoor," he cried, and his hand sought his hip pocket, but he had forgotten his revolver. He approached the bed. Lafala felt afraid and turned to press the button of the bell, but before he could touch it Titin was upon him.

"Give me that money or I'll kill you," he said. And suddenly he threw the heavy blanket over Lafala and began choking him.

"I'll kill you and finish with the damned business!" Titin cried, tightening his hold on the twitching stump.

CHAPTER THIRTEEN

Arriving at Lafala's hotel in an exalted condition after her vision Aslima was rather distressed when the night man informed her that Lafala had a visitor.

"Well, I can't go up then." But the man assured her that she could for it was a he-male and not a female.

Aslima ascended the staircase. Approaching Lafala's door she heard Titin's voice: "I'll kill you! I'll kill you!"

She rushed in and saw him in the act: Lafala was being murdered. With a sure and quick presence of mind she seized a chair and brought it down upon Titin's head, knocking him flat against the bed. She snatched the blanket off Lafala and, seizing a jug of water on the night table, dashed it in his face.

"Are you hurt, my God! Are you hurt?"

"Almost," said Lafala, shaking himself like a dog come up out of water.

"Thank God, you're alive," she said.

"You saved my life!" he said.

"Sh-h-h-h! I got to look out now," she replied.

Titin stirred, coming back to his senses. Aslima pulled him up and pushed him through the door into the corridor.

"Who hit me? Who hit me?" he demanded.

"Better let's beat it before the police gets on to this," said Aslima.

Outside in the street Titin started to quarrel with her for hitting him so hard.

"Guess you'd have preferred to finish him and get ready for the guillotine,"[1] said Aslima.

"What guillotine?" said Titin contemptuously. "I wouldn't catch more than six months if any for that stump."

Aslima turned upon him tigerishly: "But what profit is there in such a fool act? We had a perfect plan to carry out and now you've wrecked it."

She burst into tears. She declared that Lafala would never want to see her again now that Titin had frightened him with an attempt on his life. Lafala was suspicious. He would think that Titin's attack and her coming to the rescue at the opportune moment was a planned affair. She was sure Titin did not want Lafala's life. What was he going to do with it? Take it and then fly a fugitive from his beloved dream port? All the days and nights she had devoted to the scheme were lost through Titin's folly. Women were always suffering for men. She had sacrificed herself perfecting her plan and Titin like a madman had destroyed it in a moment. Aslima wept copiously.

Titin was confounded. He could not answer Aslima. The force of her argument sunk into him. He had made a fool of himself and perhaps wrecked the bar of his dreams. He suggested that he might beg Lafala's pardon. But Aslima said that that would be worse and that Titin had better think of getting into hiding, for Lafala might put in a charge of assault against him. But Titin stood out against that suggestion. He was not afraid of an affair like that. And Aslima continued to mourn the wreck of their plan.

They drifted along without direction until they found themselves before the cathedral high on the hill above Quayside. There Titin broke down completely and confessed that he was altogether wrong. He had gone crazy when Aslima left the house in a fit and at the hotel the craziness turned to madness before Lafala's taunts. He shouldn't have gone to the hotel, but some power stronger than himself had just taken him along.

"But swear to me before God and this cathedral, Aslima," concluded Titin, "that you won't double-cross me in this business!"

"What business?" demanded Aslima. "It's finished."

"It isn't finished! That Negro likes you more than anything except his money. We can fix him yet. But you swear now that you're on the level."

How abject and detestable he was, asking her to swear before the church, Aslima thought. She swore with her mouth, but her heart went out to her own God. "Help me oh God and forgive me," she said. An oath before the God of Titin could not bind her to anything. She had heard the story of the warriors of the golden age of her people conquering all that romantic stretch of earth between the Pillars of Hercules and Marseille.[2] And there was a legend that the cathedral was built on the site of a mosque, over the bones, maybe, of a marabout. And she uttered a silent prayer that the lost dominions of her people might be restored.[3]

Arriving at their room Aslima threw herself on the couch continuing her sad state of lamentation. Titin went down on his knees to her to plead for forgiveness. Pretending to shift herself on the couch Aslima purposely kicked him in the face and asked him to excuse her. And she felt that laughter was taking possession of her, an uncontrollable overcoming laughter that would sweep her away and betray her and with a strong effort she channeled it into another outburst of hysterical weeping. It was too much for Titin. He cursed himself a damned blunderer and fled from the room, slamming her door.

Meanwhile, Lafala was anxious about Aslima. She had saved his life. That was the big thing. However much he had doubted her before, he was compelled to change his mind before that big fact. Even though he had been loving her all the time, he had never permitted the exigencies of the flesh to befuddle his head. But it was different now. Suppose Titin should find out at last that she was playing a double game!

In his agitation he made up his mind to go down to Quayside and find Aslima, although he felt that it was dangerous. He was sorry now he hadn't bought a revolver since his return to Marseille. He asked the night man if he had one to spare, but the night man had one only with which he could not part.

Nevertheless, Lafala decided to go and took a taxicab to the square at Quayside. He went a roundabout way through a rusty and moldy row of buildings to Aslima's lair. When he approached the door he heard Titin and Aslima arguing excitedly. He stepped into the shadow of a hallway foul with piled-up garbage to listen. He was happy to hear Aslima's voice.

But now she was crying. Suddenly the door flew open and Titin dashed out brushing against Lafala in the shadows.

Lafala stepped into the room and to his greater amazement found Aslima flat on her back laughing hysterically.

"What's all the noise about?" he asked.

"Did he see you?" she asked eagerly, turning over on her side.

"No."

"Good. Then I can keep him up in the air a little longer."

"What's the game now?" Lafala asked. "Tell me everything."

Aslima related how she had contrived to turn Titin's attack upon Lafala against Titin and to their account.

"Suppose he's come back and should be out there listening now," said Lafala when she was finished.

"He won't come back tonight," said Aslima. "But all the same let's go up on the terrace where we can talk freely."

Lafala said his artificial feet were not any good climbing.

"I can carry you," she said, and did most of the way. She wanted to return to the terrace of her vision with him. Arriving there she told Lafala everything about the plan that Titin and she had in mind to ruin him. She explained however that she had invented the plan herself, considering it was the best means of allaying the suspicion of Titin against her.

"Oh, that was why he was so nice to me when I came to see you that night I threw La Fleur out. But how can I trust you? How can I know for sure you're straight?"

"I can't tell you. You got to find that out yourself."

"And I have. You saved my life. That's proof enough."

"I didn't do much. It was the vision."

"What vision?"

Aslima told Lafala the story of what had happened up there on the terrace a little earlier in the evening.

"Do you believe in visions?" she asked him.

"Oh, you just fell asleep and dreamed a lot."

"Maybe it was a sign that Titin was going to do that and you and I go away together," she said.

"Whatever it is, I think we better get away from Marseille as soon as possible," said Lafala. "Tomorrow I'm going to tell the official about it and ask him to arrange the passage for us. I was never sure in my mind about taking you, but I am now."

"There's one thing we must look out for in the meantime,"

said Aslima. "I don't want Titin to know that you've made up with me. And if I'm at the Tout-va-Bien when you come there, don't speak to me."

"But we've got to see each other."

"Sure, but Titin mustn't know. I want to have him so that he'll keep his tail down and eat out of my hand like a dog."

The dawn surprised them on the terrace. They arranged a rendezvous for the following evening in another part of the town. Aslima returned to her room. Lafala went in the direction of the cathedral.

The incidents of the night had stirred him with a new victorious feeling and he felt that he could walk a long way on his artificial legs. He continued past the cathedral towards the docks. The dockers going to work brought to him thoughts of the near yesterdays when he himself often went with the early rising stream to take his place in the waiting line for a day's work.

Even minus his legs he felt fortunate with the fresh buoyant dawn in his face that he was free now to think about love instead of the depressing possibility of whether or not he would have today's daily bread. How good it was to be able to live comfortably. And how ugly the thought of the thousands who lacked the barest civilized necessities.

In the primitive life such as he had lived as a boy, civilized necessities were superfluous. But how depressing it had been to exist in the heart of civilization and be too poverty-stricken to afford them.

He entered a little café. The bar was crowded with workers hurrying through coffee and rolls. He sat down to a little table in the corner and ordered a bowl of steaming coffee and milk. He had a little talent for drawing, and fishing out a scrap of paper and pencil, he made a sketch of his native village as he remembered it with a road cutting through the bush and a European house dominating the huts.

He returned to his hotel at sunup. At ten o'clock he presented himself at the office of his official agent. The official's sentiment towards Negroes was based upon *Uncle Tom's Cabin* and David Livingstone.[4] And he took a sort of patriarchal interest in the black boys drifting into Marseille—those who broke through the petty-clerking cordon and came under his notice—so long as they were good children.

Lafala told the official that he was anxious to know when his affairs would be settled so that he could leave Marseille and also that he wanted passage to be reserved for two. The official looked bewildered. Passage for two! Perhaps it could be arranged, but would Lafala mind telling him who was the second person? Lafala said it was a girl. The official frowned, scenting a black-and-white romance. Lafala had perhaps become entangled with one of those lost white creatures of Quayside.

He wasn't to be encouraged. It would never do for a black man to take a white woman back to an African colony, especially a woman of Quayside who would certainly be a disgrace to the European colony and make it look morally small in the eyes of the natives. But—.

"I suppose it can be arranged, Lafala. But we'll have to make special arrangements. H'm, er—of course you know it isn't as easy for Negroes to travel in and to Africa as it is here in Europe. But let me see. Do you have any objection to bringing the girl here so that I can talk to her? Who is she? Is she a—a—a European?"

"No," said Lafala. "She's a colored girl, an old sweetheart." The official relaxed, relieved from his embarrassing attitude, to all-smiling sentimentality, his imagination taken by a romance in color. "I think the best and easiest way is for you two to get married," he advised Lafala. "Then your lady will have the status of a wife and so be protected against any untoward incidents on board."

Lafala said he had not thought of marriage, but it was a good idea. "Why, yes, my boy," said the official. "Just the thing for a lad of your age to do . . . now you're crippled . . . with your money . . . a nice colored girl to help you start life in your own home. . . . Just the thing."

The official said he had received good tidings about Lafala's affairs and that perhaps he could leave in a short time.

Lafala left the bureau with the intention of getting married quietly and as soon as possible to Aslima.

CHAPTER FOURTEEN

Besides its gorgeous breakwater and Quayside where all the
drifters and bums, the outcasts and outlaws of civilizations,
congregated like wasps together in hate and love feeding and
buzzing over the scum of the Vieux Port, Marseille possessed
also a Seamen's and Workers' Club.[1]

This club was a very different affair from the sanctimonious
British-bossed Seamen's Mission down the breakwater way.
Late in the decade following the era of the Russian Revolution,[2] there began springing up in the principal European ports
seamen's clubs that were very different in spirit from the old-
style missions and rests.

The Seamen's and Workers' Club was situated—God knows
why—in the drabbest and least interesting proletarian and
factory quarter of Marseille. It was a fine large place with bar-
room, recreation rooms, reading room and theatre. The atmosphere was right. No sermonizing nor psalm-singing, neither
of the old religious or the new radical brand. But not many
seamen could be persuaded to go up there. At least those that
frequented it did not seem to be anything like the healthy-
rough body of seamen and dockers.

The club was so far removed from the seamen's haunts.
Quayside was more attractive. Even though the sordidness of
Quayside was stinking, there were broken bits of color in the
dirt. The gnashing dogs and cats devoured the offal and inces-
santly by day and night the Mediterranean sprayed the pave-
ments, the mistral wind[3] blew through the gloomy houses and
the meridian sun quickly burned away the stench.

One of the active workers of the new Seamen's Club was a
mulatto from Martinique, Etienne St. Dominique.[4] He spent

much of his time in Quayside trying to induce the seamen, especially the colored ones, to go to the club for recreation and reading and lectures.

St. Dominique had formerly been a student. He had obtained a scholarship to study in France. He was very clever but not a good student. He was something of a philanderer and through an unfortunate incident he was compelled to leave college and forfeit his scholarship. His time for compulsory military service was overdue when he left college and he entered the army. There he met comrades of radical ideas which he assimilated. And upon the completion of his service his curiosity carried him into association with the proletarian intellectuals.

St. Dominique had heard about Lafala, his misfortune and his return. But he had not had an opportunity of meeting him.

Lafala had drawn some money from his agent. On his way from the office, which was situated in one of the fine tree-shaded avenues of Marseille, Lafala stopped under a chestnut tree, spreading out over the sidewalk, and began counting and dividing up his money. He put some bills for debts and immediate use in his pocket book. The rest he thrust into a thick envelope. He was buttoning this envelope in his inside vest pocket when he was touched upon the shoulder. Lafala wheeled around, startled, knowing that Marseille was notorious for its daring hold-ups.

He faced a tall and striking mulatto who introduced himself as St. Dominique. St. Dominique told Lafala that he had guessed his identity by his figure and his walk and had followed him down the street. He asked Lafala about his affairs, how long he intended to remain in Marseille. And invited him to visit the Seamen's Club. He asked Lafala if he could go in the afternoon. Lafala said that he was free and St. Dominique said he would meet him after lunch at the Tout-va-Bien down in Quayside.

"You don't want to go to that hole down there, do you?" Lafala said. He was very much impressed by St. Dominique's cultivated accent and his refined manners. Even though Quayside was his rendezvous of pleasures the most delicious, the place and kind of life in which he was most at ease, he felt a little ashamed of it before St. Dominique.

St. Dominique smiled and assured Lafala that he liked Quay-side and the Tout-va-Bien. Lafala was just another of the many working folk he had known who were a little ashamed of prole-tarian places of amusement before respectable people. And it had always amused him that while bohemian radicals of the better classes were romantic or sentimental about common pro-letarian pleasures, the proletarians themselves were contemptu-ous of such and hankering after the better-class patterns.

"I always go to the Tout-va-Bien especially to see the fellows when the boats arrive," said St. Dominique. "I like it but I don't think the proprietor likes me."

"He doesn't like anything but brisk business," said Lafala. "Awful yaller nigger." Lafala said he was on his way to the Tout-va-Bien to pay the proprietor some money.

They agreed to meet in a brasserie[5] in the center of the town, as it was nearer to Lafala's hotel and he was not going down to Quayside that morning.

Lafala arrived at the brasserie before St. Dominique. And while he was waiting he noticed two men looking at him sus-piciously through the fine mirrored front. Presently they entered the café taking seats at an oblique angle from Lafala. And he was uncomfortably aware of being the object of obser-vation and comment, the men averting their eyes whenever they caught him. However, he betrayed no signs of uneasiness although he was very perturbed.

He was relieved when St. Dominique appeared with another Negro, a shining ebony also from West Africa who was intro-duced as Falope Sbaye.[6] Falope was St. Dominique's dearest friend in Marseille, although intellectually they did not agree upon anything. Falope held some kind of minor clerical post in the town with a company that had extensive trade relations on the West African coast. Although of the same ebony as Lafala, he was a different type. His features, especially the nose, had more in common with the European than the Afri-can. He claimed Arab and Portuguese blood in his family.

Because of Lafala's impairment they took a taxicab instead of walking to the Seamen's Club. The hall was a vast affair: lecture and reading room, billiard room, theatre, bar and restaurant, office, phonograph and piano. As one entered the reading room one faced an impressive magnified photograph of Lenin on the right of which there was a smaller one of Karl Marx.[7] Under them was a drawing of two terrible giants, one white, the other black, both bracing themselves to break the chains that bound them. And under the drawing was an exhortation: "Workers of the World, Unite to Break Your Chains!"[8] All over the walls there were drawings and photographs of workers and workers' leaders from many countries, Soviet Russia taking first place. There were piles of pamphlets and newspapers in several languages, European and Asiatic.

St. Dominique introduced Lafala to the president of the club. The president was a very polite person from the middle class. Before he came to preside over the Seamen's Club he had been a professor. He was in no way ambitious. All he cared for was the devoting of his life to service—given a place where he could help serve the cause of the ignorant workers as conscientiously as he had once instructed young students.

Shaking Lafala's hand he told him that he was happy to see a black from Quayside interested in the new social truth.

"We are trying to help your people here in Marseille," he said. "And we want you all to help us help yourselves." He showed Lafala all over the building talking to him as a teacher. . . . Lafala's being there with his yellow and white comrades was a symbol of the all-embracing purpose of the new social ideal. Lafala's race represented the very lowest level of humanity, biologically and spiritually speaking. But that was no hindrance to its full participation in the coming social order. For it would be a universal order including all peoples without difference of race and religion. Marx was a Jew but his vision transcended his race to become an ideal for all humanity.

All this was like an unknown tongue to Lafala, but interesting to hear. His civilized contacts had been limited to the flotsam and jetsam of port life, people who went with the drift like the scum and froth of the tides breaking on the shore, their thinking confined to the immediate needs of a day's work down the docks or a trip on a boat or any other means of procuring money for flopping, feeding, loving.

Existing thus he had often thought of more comfort, more spaciousness and cleanliness as he was accustomed to in the bush, but never of such toilers achieving anything different or changing that way of life that seemed as eternal as the rhythm of the waves along Quayside which they so much resembled.

"And so you're going back to Africa," the manager said.

Lafala said yes, adding that he was really being sent back.

"You must help us over there as much as you can. We need the cooperation of your people. For the white workers alone cannot create a new society if the capitalists have vast reserves of ignorant black and brown workers against them."

"What about the vast reserves of ignorant whites?" asked Falope. "They may be even more dangerous than the backward colored. Why not try to convert them first?"

"There is no first and last in the class struggle," said St. Dominique. "We need advanced groups of workers everywhere regardless of race to be the vanguard of the class struggle."

While talking the president had been gathering from the piles of literature a little bundle of pamphlets and papers bearing on the subject of the Colored Races and the Class Struggle. These he handed to Lafala (as was his custom with all new visitors) asking him to distribute them among his friends.

"Is it the same as the Back-to-Africa organization?" Lafala asked. That was the only movement that had penetrated his ears in the portholes.[9]

"Oh, no," said St. Dominique. "The Back-to-Africa movement is different. It began like a religious revival and is dying out the same way. Because it wasn't founded on the facts and needs of our time. It was a race movement. But we can't go back to Africa. *You* can as an individual. But we can't as a people. Our movement is a bigger thing. Each group of workers must stay where it is but all fight the battle of the class struggle for a new society."

"I don't believe in any working class having the absolute power," said Falope. "I can't see where they have more intelligence to rule than the present ruling classes."

"They have the intelligence in Russia," said St. Dominique.

"Oh, the leaders are all well-educated men," said Falope. "Like our president here." The president smiled.

"It's a government in the sole interest of the workers," said St. Dominique. "That's all I can say."

"I don't care a damn for the workers," said Falope, "and don't want to see any working class ruling the world. I get on better with the bosses than the workers every time."

"You're reactionary as always," said St. Dominique. "You know we did promise not to argue about politics."

"All right, I'll shut up," said Falope. "I'll leave you to convert Lafala. I've got to go now and work like a good bourgeois. You're a proletarian and so you can take it easy with Lafala."

"We're going too," said St. Dominique.

They said goodbye to the president of the Seamen's Club and left. Outside they hailed a taxicab on the corner. As Lafala was entering he saw the two men of the brasserie sitting in a café opposite. He felt panicky.

"They're after me," he whispered agitatedly to St. Dominique.

"Who? Where? Why?" asked St. Dominique.

"Two men in the café. They followed me from the brasserie." Lafala explained about the suspicious-looking men in the brasserie.

"Oh, it's nothing! I know what it is," said St. Dominique. "It's your being with me and going to the Seamen's Club. I am followed you know and they follow you because you are with me to find out who you are. It's nothing."

But Lafala was not at all convinced by St. Dominique's plausible explanation. He remembered he had been kidnapped in New York and the misunderstanding with his lawyer. He had an idea the two men had something to do with his case. He did not feel safe.

Falope thought that as the shipping company had paid Lafala a handsome compensation and brought him safely back to Marseille on its own boat, there was nothing to fear from that source. St. Dominique agreed with him.

"I'm sure it's the political police," he said. "They haunt all the left radical places and try to know about everybody and everything."

"Political or criminal, the police is all the same to me," said Lafala. He didn't like to be followed. And when the taxicab reached the crowded square in the center of Marseille, he stopped it and hastily hustled out and mingled with the crowd.

But that evening he did not appear at his hotel, the Tout-va-Bien or any place down Quayside. He had vanished like a spark in the air.

THIRD PART

CHAPTER FIFTEEN

Lafala had had a partner in stowing away. He was a huge West Indian from a British island who went by the name of Babel.[1] He was routed out of his hiding place a day after Lafala had been discovered. He was also locked up but came all right out of his confinement skin-clean and foot-whole.

Babel caught a glimpse of Lafala on a stretcher being taken to the hospital, but did not know what had happened. He was held as a prisoner to be taken back to Marseille on the same boat. Babel did not relish going back there to stand trial for the misdemeanor of stowing away. So when the boat appeared in full view of Marseille and the officers were busy preparing for the visit of port officials, he leaped overboard and dived to safety. Getting clear of the ship, he swam to the far out-of-the-way end of the breakwater. And he hid himself for nearly two weeks before he struck a job on an outgoing freighter. . . .

It was in a North African port, after many months of unworried silence, that Babel heard the good news about Lafala. He went up in the air all agog to see his former pal in his new role as a money man.

The whole crew of Babel's boat was anticipating leaving the charming blue-white North African port for the fascinating nocturnal revels at Quayside. But the boat went instead to a little antique port near Genoa.[2] And from the little port they were due to go back to a Greek island.

That was more than Babel could stand. He made the freighter leave him in the little port. When it had disappeared, Babel went and planted himself in the town square like a big banana tree and stretched his limbs. He had no money. He would have to depend on his wits to carry him over the frontier to Marseille. A group soon formed pressing around Babel and yelling "Negro!" in rough friendliness. Men, women, girls, children, Babel took it all grinning. The men invited and escorted him into a bar. And while he was being treated to a rich black-red wine, a man pushed his way in and addressed Babel in Americanese.

The man was chance itself. He knew an agent in Genoa who put up stranded seamen until he could place them. He proposed sending Babel up to Genoa, and Babel accepted. That night Babel had a good plain board and bed and the next day he entrained for Genoa.

Nothing could pleasure Babel more except going directly to Marseille. Genoa was a pretty good start. It should be easy for him to pick up some old kind of craft going across to Marseille. Babel was duly met at the station by a runner of the agent and taken to the bureau. The agent greeted him warmly, took his name and promised to keep him until he could place him.

For the first time in his life Babel started in living the life of an honored guest. He was given a room and tickets for regular meals in a seamen's eating place. On top of all this came Maria the housemaid who took a great liking to him.

But after nine days (during which Babel discovered nothing available sailing between Marseille and Genoa) the tenor of that lovely existence was endangered by an incoming freighter that needed a fireman. The agent secured the job for Babel. There wasn't much shakes to the freighter—a rusty-looking affair engaged in toting lumber and copra up the West African coast. Babel took a look at it and walked away. He reported to the agent that the galley was in a mangy condition and didn't appeal to him for the hard job of a fireman.

The agent had a sharp sense of humor. There was a comical sharp-featuredness about him. His flesh was a sharp growth over his frame. His forehead was sharp. His ears pointed sharply, likewise his nose, his mouth, his moustache, his hands, his clothes; and the long peculiarly Italian cigar he smoked was an indispensable spot of color in the whole sharp composition.

He smiled at Babel sharply and said, "Alright, me get you

one other ship." And he gave Babel a couple of long cigars. "Have a smoky, you," he said.

The second opportunity was a boat going out to the far east "on the fly"—to stay out there.

Babel grew indignant in the bureau of the seamen's broker and made a big noise. The crew was East Indian and Babel voiced the fear that if he signed on, they might want to reduce his pay to the East-of-Suez rate.[3] The agent said he could guarantee there would be no reduction.

"But I wouldn't know going out theah with a coolie crew,"[4] said Babel. "I wouldn't know foh sure. And when I goes out yonder in that country they might want do anything with me. I won't go with no coolie crew. I want white man wages."

Meanwhile, Babel was full up with exasperation not finding a chance to run away to Marseille and Quayside. He was crazy to see his old pal Lafala and determined to get to Marseille by any means. Quayside was big in his body, singing in his head and calling, insistently calling him as if something important was happening there in which he should be meddling.

"Got to make it! Coming back to you, Marseille. Got to go back right there."

The third boat was going to the same Greek island that Babel had from the first funking decided to miss. This time he pulled off a heavy drunk. Two days after he appeared in the bureau. The seamen's broker was jaundiced from anger.

"I did hopes never see you no more," he cried. "I see you wanta ruina me. I treaty you better than any other seamen. Feed you and bed you and you living a fine. Me losea lotta money on you. But you gotta no conscience. Finish, me finish, no lose a no more money. No more job, no more sleeping, no more feeding. I never before had no seaman likea you to handle and I hopes I never see another like you. You don't wanta leave this port so you can go live on the beach."

Babel had no words left to defend himself this time, but he hesitated there like a shamed boy, a comic picture from being so big, tricky and simple.

"I mean what I said," continued the agent. "Me finish. Get outa here."

Babel realized that the game was at last played out and left
the bureau. He climbed up a narrow stone way and went into
the public gardens along the waterfront and sat down. It was
after the lunch hour.

There Maria came to him with a way out and of her own
planning. Maria had found Babel all right whatever he did.
And she had consulted the police on his behalf. The police had
told her that the agent could not turn Babel out of doors
because it was he who had brought him to Genoa. The agent
was bound to place Babel on a boat or be responsible for him
so long as he remained in Genoa. Babel could go back to the
lodging house and if the agent tried to put him out he should
report to the police.

"I don't want no police messing with that man because a
me," said Babel. "That man know his business and I knows
mine. The picnic is over and me—I is through."

"And what you going to do?" asked Maria.

"Something in some ways."

"Come back to the house just for tonight."

"No, man. I ain't never going back on meself."

Unable to persuade Babel, Maria went back to her work.
And Babel philosophized: "She's a darter of a dawg."[5]

In a barrelhouse on the quay that night Babel struck up conversation with a slim sailor boy—a reddish Negroid who was
a native of one of those miniature republics strung together in
the Spanish Main.[6] The lad too was waiting for a ship. And he
had been waiting long. He complained that he was fed up with
Genoa and wanted just to get away from it. Babel asked him if
he had ever been to Marseille which was just across the frontier. The lad had not. Babel painted in thick splashing colors
the pleasures of Quayside until the boy's imagination was lit.
There were many ships in Marseille. It would be easy to get a
place. The boy thought it would be fine fun to go to Marseille
with Babel.

Why not leave for Marseille right away? Babel urged. Both
of them. Babel explained that it was easy for the lad to go. All
he needed to do was ask the representative of his country in
Genoa to send him to Marseille by telling him that there was a

better chance for him there. The lad was representatively better off than Babel who had been turned down and away from all official consideration.

But the boy wanted a pal along with him and felt that Big Babel was about the best person with whom he would like to be in Marseille. And so they concocted a plan. Babel could make his way with a little Spanish, for he had lived in Panama. He should pretend that he had lost his seaman's papers. And then he could go to the representative of his pal's country and ask his pal to say that he was a citizen of the republic and that once they had both been on the same ship.

The plan worked splendidly and two days later Babel and the boy were speeding by train over the frontier toward Marseille.

CHAPTER SIXTEEN

The disappearance of Lafala had created a fever of suspicion at Quayside. All his things were intact at his hotel. The worried owner went to inform the official, who was taking care of Lafala's money, of his absence. Recalling Lafala's last visit to him about a sweetheart and the probability of his marrying, the official jokingly suggested that Lafala might be off on his honeymoon. But he became uneasy when the days slipped by without any news. Quayside under the surface was a vicious place. Lafala might be the victim of mischief, gangsters framing him to get at his money.

But Quayside felt itself very clean of the affair. To the Quaysiders Lafala's disappearance came as a shock, but not a mystery. They considered that if any harm had come to Lafala it had come from above and not from below. They had never ceased marveling that Lafala had received such a large amount of money. And as it had been rumored that he was waiting in Marseille for a final settlement, many of them thought now that his disappearance was that final settlement. The people who had been hit in the pocket had hit back.

But the proprietor of the Tout-va-Bien had a different theory. And to air it he relaxed from his habitual taciturnity. On the last day Lafala visited the Tout-va-Bien he had casually mentioned to the proprietor of his intended visit to the Seamen's Club with St. Dominique. And he had remarked, "You better keep away from those anti-government people." He believed that Lafala had got into trouble there. The proprietor did not like St. Dominique visiting the café and distributing leftward tracts among the seamen. The café was sometimes used as a meeting place by politicians in good standing to harangue the voters of Quayside. And on such occasions the proprietor made plenty of money selling plenty of liquor.

Titin and Aslima were in a state of chronic contention over the same subject. Aslima baited Titin, saying that maybe his attack on Lafala had something to do with his disappearance and if they never got anything out of him Titin would have himself to blame.

Titin grew exasperated and one night he turned savagely upon Aslima and commanded her to find Pied-Coupé wherever he was hiding his stump.

"Maybe you and your gang know where he is," retorted Aslima. "But you're fools if you think you can torture money out of him that way. His money is in official hands. God! I hope they're not torturing the poor man for nothing."

"I don't care what happens to him so long as he shows up with that money. You talk as if you're in love with him."

"I pity him. Seems like it wasn't his feet but his fortune is his real misfortune."

"Hell with pity. Better worry about finding him and putting our business through."

"What business? You know you spoiled everything."

"I haven't and if you don't find him and fix it up your soul will repent in hell."

"I'm not afraid of you. If God wills it you'll murder me yet. But you won't get away free either. I have my countrymen here who will get you yet, by God."

Aslima had no secret relations with the Arabs and only meant to frighten Titin. And he was frightened. He had often encountered her talking to some of them in a tongue he did not understand. If the Negroes boldly encroaching upon their preserves were to Titin and his set the most obnoxious of the foreign settlements of Quayside, the lean tough-bodied Arabs were the most pernicious.

As a group the Arabs were right there among the rattiest of the rats, the snakiest of the snakes in the holes of the quays. But it was a rare thing to find an Arab living on the earnings of a prostitute as her lover and protector. Chinese, Maltese, Negroes, French, Italians, Spaniards, Corsicans, Jews, and many others belonged to the fraternity. But the Arabs as a group did not.

Maybe it was because of some traditional thing in their character as a distinct formation of people. Or the fact that the Arab in his relations to a woman is so possessively personal, making her so much his slave in unconsciously becoming her slave that he cannot tolerate the idea of another man loving his woman. Some of the Arabs had taken Quayside girls away from prostitution to become their mistresses and doing that created a feeling of hostility against them among the protecting class. Indeed, it was quite a joke among that class that the Arabs preferred male prostitutes to female.

"I'm not afraid," he said to Aslima. "I can protect myself and I am well protected besides."

"I know you belong to some gang. Why don't you admit it?" Aslima was curious to know but Titin kept a discreet silence.

"You don't have to tell," she said. And after a brief silence between them she demanded, "How do I know I'll get anything out of all this damned business. Suppose Lafala does turn up and I make up with him? What'll be *my* reward if I put the plan over?"

"Your reward?" exclaimed Titin. "Why you fool, we'll buy a fine bar. We'll be independent and looked up to here in Quayside like all the other business people."

"Yes, a bar, a bar, a bar," mocked Aslima. "But how do I know I would be treated right? I want to be sure about myself. If I promise to get that money will you promise to marry me before I hand it over? That's the only way I'll feel sure about my share. If we are married!"

That sense of the unity of the family that is more deeply rooted in the Latin peoples[1] than any was so strong in Titin that he could not even bring himself to attempt to deceive Aslima in his own interest. Because it was an unthinkable thing—the idea of marrying a whore, a woman whose card of identity was the yellow one of prostitution,[2] a woman without family, without home, without name.

He was proud of his family in his village, poor but intact. No near kinswoman was a prostitute. Aslima could never escape from her record as a prostitute. If she had a son it would be a whoreson.[3] Wherever she went and whatever she did she was in the clutch of the social law, the police record that would trace her down to the third and fourth generation.

There were certain Quaysiders who were married to professional prostitutes but they were creatures of brothels and allied places of the same status as the inmates. Titin referred to such men as degenerates and perverts. He felt sick in the guts from the suggestion at his becoming a member of that class of men.

"Where did you get that stuff about marriage?" said Titin. "Who thinks about marriage down here but idiots? We'll buy a bar and live together. That's enough."

"Not enough for me," said Aslima. "I'm a stranger here and always will be. After you've made use of me God only knows what may happen to me."

"What can happen?" asked Titin, breaking wind with his mouth contemptuously.

"What can happen? You know you despise me for what I am. You know well the first thing you'd try to do after you'd used me. You'd get rid of me. Take everything for yourself and get married to a good girl."

"I'm not a marrying man."

"*You* not a marrying man? All of your kind are. I've been in this life long enough to know the very guts of you all. We're not human beings in your eyes. You're all crazy about marrying a pure girl, *une jeune fille de famille*.[4] I'm not going to go farther with this thing whether Lafala turns up or not. I refuse!"

"If you go back on this thing I'll kill you like a bitch!" said Titin.

"Kill me then and finish with everything. I'm ready," cried Aslima. "I'm tired and disgusted. Once you nearly killed Lafala. Now kill me instead and be done with it."

"You talk as if it's sweet to die, my lady," said Titin. "What's coming over you? You never were like that. Something has surely happened to you since the coming of Pied-Coupé."

"Don't talk to me anymore!" cried Aslima. "You say you'll kill me like a bitch. Here, do it then and be damned with you." Aslima ripped open her blouse baring her breast to Titin in one gesture.

"Woman, you're crazy like a mad cow," said Titin. "You want me to commit murder because of Pied-Coupé." And he ran out of the room.

CHAPTER SEVENTEEN

Babel arrived in Marseille one noon at the height of the confusion at Quayside and his exuberant spirits fell flat when he heard the bad news about Lafala. It was tough luck for him after all the tricks he had set his brains on to arrive at Marseille. He felt cheated and fooled by one trick more.

That very night St. Dominique dropped in at the Tout-va-Bien, visiting Quayside for the first time since the day he had taken Lafala to the Seamen's Club. A boat had arrived from the Near East with colored seamen and St. Dominique wanted to invite them to a meeting at the club which was scheduled for the following evening.

In his dislike of St. Dominique and what he considered his pretentious manners the proprietor of the café had stirred up Quayside opinion against him with hints of treachery. Ever since Lafala's disappearance he kept saying, "They have sold him. They have sold him!" He meant that St. Dominique had betrayed Lafala, which sounded plausible as St. Dominique was the last person that Lafala was known to be with. The habitués of the Tout-va-Bien were worked up into a pretty pitch of hostility against St. Dominique.

As for St. Dominique, he was not aware of what had happened. He had dismissed Lafala's fears from his mind, not imagining they could have any serious consequences.

St. Dominique greeted the proprietor in his usual friendly fashion.

"I don't want to speak to any traitor," said the other mulatto.

"What is this? What do you mean, old man?" asked St. Dominique.

"I mean what I said. I don't want a traitor in my place. I mean you!" He levelled his finger at St. Dominique.

"What damned stupidity. What is all this about?" asked St. Dominique.

With an irritated gesture the proprietor half turned, putting some soiled glasses in the tank of water.

Leaving a group of girls and fellows near the piano where they were sitting, Aslima rushed up to the bar and said to St. Dominique, "You don't know what is it? You don't know that Lafala can't be found since that day he went with you?"

"Oh, it's Lafala!" said St. Dominique. "He *was* scared, I remember. He thought he being followed, but I didn't take it seriously. Perhaps . . . perhaps . . . but I don't know."

St. Dominique told them that Lafala had left him and his friend in the Big Square, and that was the last he had seen or heard of him.

"Nobody here's going to believe that tale. I think you're a liar," said the proprietor. The mulatto felt convinced that St. Dominique was a scoundrel. He had referred to St. Dominique as a poor mischievous blackbird who instead of finding an honest job was an agitator against Government and Society. Such people were not to be trusted. And he had warned the little robbers and cut-throats of the Tout-va-Bien against St. Dominique whom he called a dangerous type.

"You call me a liar?" said St. Dominique.

"Yes, you're lying. You're a liar!" shrieked Aslima. "You just made that up. You were the last person with Lafala and you must know what's happened to him."

Babel pushed his way up to St. Dominique and growled in his face: "Come on you proper-speaking strutter an' jest tell us where Lafala is or I'll whip the trute outa you."

By now the entire café was worked up and shouting against St. Dominique. And although he was not a fighter of any skill he was determined to stand his ground.

"Look here," he said, "I'm not going to stand all this from a set of swine like you all."

"Call us swine again and I'll break you' face, you yaller bastard!" Babel cried. "I dare you open you stinking mouth again, you cat-eater."

St. Dominique felt that he was in for a fight, perhaps a good beating, and that his work would be ruined at Quayside. The seamen had always been respectful to him despite the hostility of the proprietor. But at that moment a white Quaysider known as Big Blonde barged in.

"What you all have against this man. It's not fair. He's a good friend to all the colored fellows."

The appearance of Big Blonde turned Babel aside from his purpose. Big Blonde had been one of his best friends before he stowed away from Marseille and Babel was so happy to see him. He slapped his shoulder and they embraced.

"They say he's a double-crosser," Babel said looking at St. Dominique.

"Traitor hell! Does he look like a traitor to you? All this crazy talk about Lafala is just so much crap. The police will soon find out where he is—if the rats of Quayside didn't drag him into some hole."

The proprietor of the bar looked meanly at Big Blonde out of his lizard's eyes. He had wanted so badly that Babel should beat up St. Dominique. He never got into a fight himself. But he would stand quietly by and watch a quarrel, even quietly abetting it until the antagonists got to blows. Then he would step in and call the police to arrest the one he didn't like. The police would always take his word and arrest the one he indicated. He was sorry to miss getting St. Dominique and thus putting a stop, maybe, to his activities among the seamen in Quayside.

He did not like Big Blonde either. Twice he had had the police put him out of the Tout-va-Bien. For Big Blonde had nothing in common with the real Quaysiders who had a kind of sacred regard for the proprietors of Quayside and their establishments.

Big Blonde was like a hero straight out of Joseph Conrad, an outstanding enigma of Quayside.[1] A big, firm-footed, broad-shouldered man, splendidly built but with the haunting eyes of a lost child. He worked on the docks, a happy worker, active like a madman reckless with his strength, making it hard for his fellow workers to keep up the pace. But he had no interest in the workers' unions and in spite of his natural roughness there was a singular and foreign air of refinement about him.

It was gossiped that he had once held a respectable position in the merchant service, but he never talked about his past life. Because of his quixotic habit of getting into difficulties, he was often in trouble with the police. Sometimes he was jailed for a short term; sometimes he went into hiding.[2] He knew the Seamen's Club and frequented it sometimes ostensibly to read, but really to hide from the police in that district after he had got into trouble at Quayside. And so Big Blonde had come to know St. Dominique and understand his work in which he was not interested.

Once Big Blonde broke up the furniture in the saloon of the loving house of La Créole, because a boy companion of his was insulted there. But afterwards he became a good friend of Madam, the proprietress, and of the boy of the house, Petit Frère.[3] Madam tried to induce Big Blonde to work with her as a bouncer, but naturally without success.

Big Blonde invited Babel and St. Dominique to a wine cellar where wine was kept in barrels and demi-johns[4] only. There they discussed Lafala while drinking. Babel related how they had stowed away together and that he had seen Lafala being taken off the ship to the hospital. He omitted to tell, however, that he had escaped as a stowaway prisoner on his return to Marseille. St. Dominique said he was sorry he did allow Lafala to get out of the taxicab alone when he said he was being followed. But he and his West African friend had not taken the matter seriously, as they felt convinced that the men of whom Lafala was afraid were political secret police.[5] Big Blonde felt certain it would turn out all right.

From the wine cellar they went to La Créole. La Créole was one of the most popular of the loving houses of Quayside. It was Big Blonde's favorite as his little friend worked there. It was much frequented and touted by the colored Quaysiders and they always recommended it to colored newcomers. Madam, the proprietress, a European, had a partiality to colored folk. Aslima was once engaged there and was a good attraction. But she was too savage and Madam couldn't hold her in check and regretfully had to let her go.

There were seven girls in the place, among them a tall mulattress who claimed to be an Egyptian. St. Dominique was surprised to recognize in the assistant mistress a gay girl he used to know at a *bal-musette*[6] near the Seaman's Club and who was very popular among the seamen, some of them even taking her to dances at the club. She whispered to St. Dominique not to gossip to Madam about her former doings because she had a serious position.

There were not many visitors. A middle-aged man was sitting with a girl and two sailors were drinking beer with the girls waiting on them. The player piano was started. The Egyptian was always teasing Big Blonde. And now she pulled him up to dance with her. The two sailors did not get up to dance. One of the girls pulled at the fairest sailor to dance. The dark one put his arm upon his companion's arm and said, "Wait." But the girl playfully gave him a vicious slap in the face and went dancing with the fair sailor.

When the dance was finished the Egyptian said to Big Blonde, "Always the same. You don't dance good with me. I'm going to dance with my tribesman now." (She meant St. Dominique.) "You go and dance with Petit Frère. Maybe it's more exciting." Petit Frère giggled. He was wearing a new blue cache-col[7] knotted around his neck and pushed into the waist of his pants. It was a gift from Big Blonde and it matched well his pale color and expressionless eyes.

St. Dominique refused to dance with the Egyptian girl. He was a little uneasy in the loving house. He preferred to make friends with girls at a popular dance or among his comrades. He continued to talk with the assistant mistress while the Egyptian began a belly-wobble with Babel and Big Blonde danced with Petit Frère.

Two girls in pajamas were dancing together and continually getting in the way of Big Blonde and Petit Frère. "We're dancing the loving omelettes,"[8] one of them said. Petit Frère shrieked and slapped her on the flank.

"I'll cook your omelettes," said the dark sailor and he rushed in and parted the girls to dance with one of them.

Madam the proprietress had heard about Lafala's case and expressed her sympathy, listening to St. Dominique as he told the assistant mistress about it. She asked St. Dominique if he knew whether Lafala had got back to his hotel after he left the taxicab in the Big Square. St. Dominique did not know and thought finding out might furnish a clue. He said he would go to the hotel right then, thus finding an excuse to leave Big Blonde and Babel to their enjoyment.

The loving house was depressing to St. Dominique. He liked Quayside, forever smelling of raw fish, and the contacts with the seamen. But he had radical ideas about the loving houses and often told the seamen that they and all forms of prostitution would be abolished under Communism. And the seamen wondered what their beloved Quayside would be without them. St. Dominique felt sorry for the assistant mistress feeling so important because she had a place of authority in one of the houses. She had been much more interesting to him as a free *bal-musette* girl.

Late that night, or rather towards dawn, Madam, the proprietress of La Créole, was standing in the portal of her palace watching the human shadows hurrying through the dim narrow alley and saw Babel passing in the company of two white men who seemed strange to her as not the type of white men who could be friends of Babel. She called to Babel. He replied, "I'm under arrest. Tell Big Blonde if you see him."

She sent Petit Frère to find Big Blonde. Petit Frère found him in the wine cellar taking a final drink before retiring. Big Blonde went to the police station of Quayside, presenting himself as Babel's friend and asking the nature of the charge against him. He was told that no exact information could be given until the next morning.

In the morning Big Blonde took a holiday from the docks and went to the police station. There he was informed that Babel had already been transferred to the local jail. Big Blonde was baffled. He knew that it was very difficult to see a prisoner in jail unless one was a relative and as his own record was not so pretty he did not like to nose in too much among the police. He thought the best thing he could do was to see St. Dominique and so he waited until noon when the Seamen's Club was open. St. Dominique was not there. Big Blonde waited until he arrived at two o'clock.

CHAPTER EIGHTEEN

There were many little obstacles to overcome before St. Dominique could get to Babel in jail. At the prison he was referred to the police. The police sent him to the judge's office. The judge wanted to know whether he was a near relative of Babel. St. Dominique said he was just a dear friend. He was told to make a written request to see Babel but there was no certainty that it would be granted.

Against all these formalities St. Dominique remembered his white friend who held an important position in a municipal department. This friend had occasionally visited the Seamen's Club. Not as a sympathizer. But only to see St. Dominique. They had attended the same college. The municipal clerk was sorry that St. Dominique had not completed his college course and had swung way over to revolutionary social propaganda.

However, the aesthetic movement towards modern art excited him and even made him curious about the Negroid colony in Marseille and St. Dominique's work. And through St. Dominique he had obtained a few pieces of African wood sculpture and carved masks and sticks from some West African seamen.[1]

St. Dominique went to see his friend about Babel. The friend talked over the telephone to a functionary of another department. This functionary in turn talked to a friend of his who was an official at the prison in which Babel was confined. . . . And so the way was opened for St. Dominique to see Babel.

St. Dominique taxied to the prison and was passed through the gates into a kind of reception building and out into a large court, then into another building and down a corridor ending in a somber place before a wire netting. There Babel was brought to talk to him from the other side of the netting. Babel's black face was invisible because of the obscurity of the place and St. Dominique recognized him by his voice only.

"Lafala is here" was the first thing Babel said. St. Dominique learned that Lafala and Babel had been arrested for the same offense—stowing away. But Babel's detention was apparently incidental to his having been accessory to Lafala's stowing away and his foolhardy return after his escape by diving from the boat. Babel said that when he was taken to the police station on the night of the arrest, there was an officer there from the boat on which he had stowed away and the officer tried to have him admit that Lafala had sick feet before he boarded.

"I couldn't admit no such thing," said Babel, "for all I knowed them Lafala's feet was sound feet and he was one dancing fool at Quayside. So here I is and here I stays tell they let me out."

So St. Dominique saw now that the Quaysiders were righter than he in their conjecture. He wanted to see Lafala then and there, but the order had been given for him to see Babel and the minor official would not make it include Lafala. St. Dominique left the prison and went to a café to telephone his friend, but was informed that the person who had favored him with the first permission could not be reached until the next day.

It occurred to St. Dominique that the afternoon might be well spent if he could get in contact with the shipping company. But he hesitated because he thought that it would probably hinder the thing immediately desired (the liberation of Lafala and Babel) if the nature of his work among the seamen and his connection with the Seamen's Club were known.

There was no doubt that both Lafala and Babel were liable to arrest for the misdemeanor of stowing away. He learned that they could be imprisoned for about six months; besides, they might be held for an indefinite length of time before being brought to trial.

How should he approach these people who had the black boys in their power? It was his functionary friend who suggested the way. . . . After the unhappy ending of his college days, St. Dominique had among other things flirted with the literary muse. And once he had written for a magazine called the *Aframerican*² a colorfully descriptive account of Quayside. As Negroid talent usually has an effect in the close colored world entirely out of proportion to its general significance, St. Dominique had been hailed as the dark star rising in the European literary horizon and achieved a full-sized photograph of himself in the *Aframerican* magazine.

St. Dominique's friend, aware of the respect of local public opinion for the literary mind, which was generally upon a higher level than in any other country, had counselled St. Dominique to present himself with his credentials as a man of letters in the respectable tradition. He added jokingly that St. Dominique's color might help in providing an element of surprise and conviction.

St. Dominique had some express visiting cards printed. And the next morning he got Falope to go with him to the office of the company. The guardians of the outer offices were reluctant about admitting St. Dominique—even in taking his card. But they did finally.

The manager was very courteous. He was acquainted with the different phases of Lafala's case and wanted to know what was the relationship between the young men and Lafala and Babel. At first it seemed he was under the impression that their interest was as practical as that of the New York lawyer who had created the case. He asked St. Dominique if he knew about the circumstances of Lafala's stowing away and the consequences.

St. Dominique said he knew as much as Lafala had informed him and that Lafala's arrest was legal. But he hoped that he would be set free. He didn't want to think that the company was directly responsible for Lafala's imprisonment but even if it were so he believed that a word from the manager might effect his release.

Thereupon the manager explained that his company had no bad intentions towards Lafala. They carried on a big trade with West Africa and were always just in their dealings with Negro traders and benevolent to their Negro employees. Lafala's case had been a very unfortunate one for the company. He had boarded the boat clandestinely. Some officer of the ship might have been careless of attention towards him. But he was sure no one meant to be deliberately cruel to Lafala and lock

him up in a cold latrine to freeze to death. They had acciden-
tally forgotten him. The officer was recognized in the wrong,
of course, but it was possible that something had been wrong
with Lafala's feet before he stowed away. Nothing had happened to his pal, Babel, who had stowed away with him. . . .
Nevertheless the company would have granted Lafala adequate
compensation by installment payments for his lifetime. But
instead he had preferred to institute proceedings against them
in the courts which had cost them an enormous amount of
money and trouble.

St. Dominique said that Lafala was an ignorant uneducated
savage and that in the despairing condition in which he was
after the amputation of his legs it should not be held against
him that he permitted a lawyer to act for him! He had suffered
so much from his illness and confinement in the hospital and
irreparable loss of his legs, he might go insane if he were to be
imprisoned now again.

The manager asked St. Dominique if he happened to have
any writings of his there. In anticipation St. Dominique had
brought that description of Quayside accompanied by his photograph, which he exhibited. The manager looked at the all-
Negro magazine and the article with drawings of Quayside
done by a colored artist and remarked that it was of special
interest to him to see the Negro race developing along intellectual lines and that he wished St. Dominique success in his
work. Finally, he promised to use his influence to have Lafala
and Babel released.

He cordially bowed the young men out, saying to St. Dominique with a smile, "Now don't go away and write anything
bad about the company."

"I couldn't now," replied St. Dominique, smiling back.

Outside, Falope said, "You Bolshy pig. You've missed your
vocation. What you really need is a black kingdom with a vast
court, shaded with palms and ferns and a black king sitting on
his ivory throne with his people around him, and you a media-
tor between the people and the king."

"I'd prefer this or any other Mediterranean port to any kind
of black kingdom," said St. Dominique. "Barcelona, Genoa,
Naples, even Constantinople."

"You're not Negro anyway. You're half here and half there and never will be a whole anywhere," said Falope facetiously.

"Although you're pure-blooded, I'm more Negro in feeling than you."

"And acting not?"

"Well, I have no plumes in my head and rings in my nose."

"But you have chains on your hands and feet. 'Workers of the World, break—.'"

St. Dominique laughed heartily. He was going to the office of his white friend and they were walking along the same avenue where he had first met Lafala.

"Tell me, Dominique," said Falope, "let us be serious now and tell me something. The other day we had an argument in the office about black and mulatto and the white fellows maintained that the mulatto is naturally discontented and divided against himself, that he is half-white and half-black and that the best part of him wants to be white. Do you ever feel that way?"

"I don't believe the best part of the mulatto wants to be white, but we're all divided, all have a dual personality, black, brown, yellow, white."

"But do you feel half of you European and half African?"

"Not as much as you. You're pure-blooded and much more European-minded in a way than I."

"Oh, I'm serious, Dominique, tell me what you think about it."

"Well, seriously, it's all a fallacy. It's a matter of economic determinism—."[3]

"Oh, can that proletarian tripe! This is not an economic problem. It's psychological."

"I'm trying to be serious and you won't let me," said St. Dominique. "To us the psychological outlook is determined by the economic environment. . . . When the white man says the mulatto wants to be white he is right in a way. You yourself told me that in West Africa you have special schools for the children of white and black that neither pure black nor pure white children attend."

"Yes, that's true," said Falope.

"It was the same in the West Indies. The mulatto child is raised in a divided way between white and black. Father belonging to one race, mother to another, both of them of different social standing. But you have the identical thing between Jew and Christian and whites of different nations and classes."

"But color makes the biggest difference with us, you see."

"Yes, but it's because white things are the mightiest things, the richest and biggest material things in the world. The whites don't want to share these things with colored people and so they throw it up to us in a nasty way that we want to be white, as if we want to change our natural skins. When your flattering white friends talk to you that way about mulattoes, you tell them that blacks want to be white too by getting some of the better white things of life."

"But you don't believe that divided allegiance might be psychic? You never had that experience?"

"Mess! I was mixed up in all sorts of feelings before I found myself in this work. Now it's all simple."

"Too simple for me," said Falope. "Why do the whites have all this economic power that you and your comrades worship? Don't you think it was special superiority? Or was it just chance?"

"Economic chance, maybe. But I can't answer your question. You must go and read the histories of the peoples of the world and then think it out for yourself. . . . You've got lessons all around you to learn by if you want to learn. Take this Lafala case, for example. There is little race to it besides his color. It's a stinking proletarian case, from Marseille across the ocean to New York and back."[4]

They were now at the building where St. Dominique's functionary friend worked, and they said goodbye, making a rendezvous for the evening if there were any news of Lafala.

CHAPTER NINETEEN

The next day St. Dominique returned to the prison and saw Lafala. His detention had developed in him a mistrust of everybody. Uncertain of the real cause of it, which had not been revealed to him, he had become suspicious of St. Dominique, of the shipping company, the officers of the boat and even his lawyer in New York. Then Babel joined him in jail and he had no doubt of the cause.

His arrest and short confinement had broken his spirit and he was very fretful. "Why do they keep me here? What do they want of me now?"

"Just to make you suffer a little more," said St. Dominique.

"Suffer some more? Haven't I suffered enough with my legs sawed off and all those months helpless in hospital?"

"But my lad, you caused the company a lot of trouble and expense getting your legs chopped off. They think you're a troublemaker and so they're 'getting even' as you say in English or American. But I think they'll soon let you out."

"Oh, Lord, I wish they would. After all those months in hospital, I just can't bear it anymore. I'll go crazy."

"Oh no," said St. Dominique, "you won't."

"Yes, I will too among all these bloody lot of hard-hided men. I'm tired of being confined with men and I'm sick with dirt. Three of us in one cubbyhole and the stinking slops. Oh, it's an awful odor! Don't you smell it?"

St. Dominique admitted the unpleasant odor. It had affected him the day before and he would have been pleased to avoid a second visit. The aspect of the prison was quite clean. There were flower beds and the paths were shaded with trees. But rising above the sweet flowers was a savage, stomach-turning smell as if many wild animals were brought in from the woods and locked indiscriminately together in one cage out of which escaped their rank mingled odor.

"You didn't expect the authorities to confine you with women? Did you?" asked St. Dominique. "When you are in prison you must do as prisoners do. Find a way out or make one."

"Finding a way is one thing and making it another," said Lafala. "We're all here like a set of old nuts lost off the screws."

"Because the prison bolts are rusty," said St. Dominique. "Prison is no good, lad. Always try and keep out of it."

"It is hell. The food makes me vomit for I can't enjoy it because of the awful smell. Why is a jail so abominable?"

"Because it's a place of punishment. You didn't expect it to be like the Tout-va-Bien?"

"Have you been there? Did you see Aslima?"

"That's what is eating you, eh? I sure did see her and she wanted to tear me to pieces with the gang down there all because of you."

"Babel told me about it," said Lafala. "I got a little note here I want you to give to her. Give it to her herself and don't let anybody know."

St. Dominique took the note rolled up into a little tube through the wire netting. "You never should have come back to Marseille. You should have gone straight back to Africa."

"I had no choice. I was sent back here."

"You should have asked your lawyer to get you sent straight back home. But then, they messed him up. Somehow it's your fault."

"To tell the truth I was crazy to see Marseille again."

"I think it was more Aslima."

That very afternoon Lafala and Babel were released. Lafala went to see his representative and learned that the suit had been won against his lawyer who had been suspended. The balance of his money had arrived. All his affairs were satisfactorily settled. He could now make his arrangements to leave for Africa as soon as he desired. . . . From the office he went to the Seamen's Club. St. Dominique was not there and Lafala left a note asking if he and Falope could keep a rendezvous with him at the Tout-va-Bien after dinner. . . . Then he went to his hotel and bathed and dressed hoping to have an interval with Aslima that night.

That night there was a big reception for Lafala at the Tout-va-Bien. The Quaysiders turned out in a body to welcome him and the café was crowded and exciting. All the old habitués were there, the low-down gangs of old-and-hard youth, girls and men, white and brown and black, mingled colors and odors come together, drinking, gossiping, dancing and perspiring to the sound of international jazz.

Besides the player piano the proprietor had installed a radio set and instead of having to wait a few weeks as formerly Quayside could now enjoy the masterpieces of Broadway, Piccadilly and Montmartre at the same time as the pleasure-lovers of those places.[1]

Titin went up to Lafala and gave him his hand, congratulated him on getting released and said he was sorry for his silly act and that he hoped there was no rancor between them. Lafala assured him that there was none on his part and asked for Aslima.

Aslima was not there. St. Dominique had not had time to give her Lafala's note and tell her that he was expecting his early release.

Titin was jubilant over his approach to Lafala and the results. He slipped out of the café, ran all the way back to his room to tell Aslima that everything was well. . . . He wanted her to go right off to the café. But Aslima did not join in his enthusiasm. She was captious and indifferent. She said that although Lafala might appear genial on the surface, she felt certain that he was on his guard now and that she would not be able to do much with him again.

Titin begged Aslima to try again and use all her art for a success. Finally he promised to marry her if she succeeded. If she really wanted marriage he had no objection so long as she was successful over Lafala. Aslima smiled and appeared pleased at this new capitulation. Titin felt very generous and warm and he took hold of Aslima and kissed her a long kiss full of desire, taking her mouth in his. But Aslima spewed her spittle in his mouth. Titin drew away and spat it out and reproached her. She said it was nothing; it was an African symbol of love. He turned happy for he was very superstitious and believed in all sorts of lucky signs. . . . Afterwards they left together for the café.

St. Dominique and Falope had arrived and were with Babel, Diup and Rock having a reunion drink with Lafala. St. Dominique said the party lacked something with Big Blonde absent. The others agreed and Babel went in search of Big Blonde.

Aslima came in looking rather severe. Lafala beckoned to her to join the party. The evening's business was so good the proprietor had two other assistants beside himself and his lady.

A Martiniquan soldier strolled in with his accordion and began playing beguine tunes. The craze of the Charleston and Black Bottom was about dead and buried. But the beguine was there, always living this heady Martinique dance, blood cousin to the other West Indian folk dances, the Aframerican shuffle and the African swaying.[2]

Everybody was close together in a thick juice melted by wine and music. There was little room for foot play. Just all together, two in one swaying to swaying, shuffling around, bumping and bumping up and down belly to belly and breast to breast.

Aslima sat all the time close to Lafala and showed no desire to dance. Some of the fellows shuffling by tried to pull her up but she resisted. La Fleur was dancing with Titin. He had also made up with her with a friendly word and she had replied, "Let's dance and be happy. Everybody is happy." La Fleur danced with Titin showing Aslima her brown shoulder. But when she noticed that Aslima was really unconcerned (and she had jazzed viciously with Titin just to get Aslima's reaction) she felt convinced that there was some profound relation between her and Lafala.

Babel returned without Big Blonde. He had not been able to locate him. A Senegalese lad, one from one of the boats, entered at the same time with a tambourine and accompanied the accordion player. The beguine mounted louder and wilder. . . .

The music took St. Dominique by the skin and penetrated into his marrow and bone, tickling his joints. But he stiffened resistance, resolved not to dance in the mulatto's café. To have a welcome drink with the rest for Lafala's sake was as far as he

cared to go. And since Big Blonde would not be there he suggested to Falope that they should go.

Aslima also felt the beguine for Lafala[3] and was swaying
and swaying her arm around his shoulder, both of them swaying warmly together. Lafala wanted to dance. He had never
felt the desire so strongly since his accident. The beguine
rhythm caught him by the middle, drop to drop. The music
swelled up and down with a sweep and rushed him off his feet.

"I feel like dancing," he said to Aslima.

"We can try," she said.

And Lafala stood up leaning on Aslima and did the beguine.
He started in timidly, then found it was not so difficult after
all with Aslima carrying him along.

"It wasn't so hard to dance again," he said.

"No, you're doing fine," she said. And she stiffened her
breast to bear him up.

Some of the crowd dropped out of the circle so that Aslima
and Lafala should have more space and standing upon chairs
and tables stacked with bottles and glasses applauded as they
shuffled around.

When the music stopped Lafala called for rounds of drinks
for the tables with whose occupants he was acquainted. With
an exciting flourish the accordionist drew a few long bars of
beguine and Aslima cried out that she would do a native
dance. She mounted a table and started doing a short-stepping,
flat-footed pattering with her right hand held in a straight-up
thrust of triumph. Her primitive flamenco went naturally well
with the music, showing kinship and revealing the African
influence of both.[4] The habitués clapped hands and acclaimed
Aslima, drinking and waving glasses to her, and she finished
with a wild whirling and snapping of fingers amid cries of
"The Queen! The Queen!"[5] and jumped down from the table.

La Fleur felt shrunken to nothing in herself with chagrin
and envy. And Babel was glum and hard-looking like a bull. In
prison Lafala had told him of his intention toward Aslima and
he was stout against it. Lafala had imposed silence on him saying that if the news got around, he would be frustrated in his
plans and Titin would certainly take Aslima's life. It was a
heavy load for Babel to carry. He wanted to share it with St.

Dominique or Big Blonde, anybody who could help persuade Lafala against his folly.

When Babel first heard that Lafala had returned to Marseille a man of means he had not been aware that Lafala had suffered an accident and that his fortune was derived from that. Babel had thought that Lafala had had merely a temporary windfall and he desired to reach Marseille to have a good time with his pal until they were obliged to take to sea again.

But when he arrived at Marseille and learned the big facts, there was a revolution in his mind and all he wanted was to see Lafala cut and away from Quayside. Babel was awed by so much money and felt that Lafala should have a new standard of life according to his means. The vagabond life was all right for a man without property or position, but responsibility and vagabondage could not go together.

It seemed to Babel that if a terrible accident had blown Lafala higher up he ought to start in taking his responsibility in a serious manner. It seemed a crazy thing for Lafala to think of taking a whore out of Quayside to set her up as a lady back home. There were plenty of nice colored girls who would jump at Lafala now. . . . He remembered an ignorant black man in his native city who came into a great deal of money. He could not express himself in a refined way. But the people elected him to the dignified position of city councilor, and he married into a brilliant mulatto family and had two daughters whose velvety beauty was the talk of the town.

Lafala was in a better position than that man. He had a good-enough education. There was a new feeling in the world about and among Negroes. The circumstances were auspicious for Lafala to make a respectable showing. The thought of Lafala returning to his African home after many years' absence with a woman like Aslima was as a bitter orange to Babel's taste.

Although he was a hearty drinker, Babel drank little because of the brooding mood he had fallen into. He was unresponsive to Aslima's performance and the antics of the crowd. It was all at Lafala's expense and Babel believed that Lafala would have a back-breaking bill to pay before Aslima was finished with him. Lafala had offered him some money but he had refused it, saying that however much Lafala had, he would not accept any, because Lafala's legs were amputated and all his funds were necessary to him.

La Fleur noticed that Babel was not in a jovial mood. She guessed it was because of Lafala and was curious to know what was wrong. Because she did not fancy big and aggressive men of Babel's type, she had never taken to him and always repulsed his rough attentions. But now she maneuvered herself to his side and began teasing him to dance. He refused at first but yielded under persuasion. . . . Later he went off with her and La Fleur got what she wanted out of him, learning the exact relations existing between Lafala and Aslima.

Late that night when she was all alone La Fleur wrote three notes, disguising her large, round, heavy and awkward handwriting as much as she could.

The first was to Lafala and ran, "Look out, they're trying to get you with your own plan. Take warning from *INSIDER*."

The second was addressed to the office where Lafala was officially represented and read, "Lafala is menaced by a dangerous gang."

The third was to Titin and sent by hand to a special café: "Attention! Aslima is deceiving you."

CHAPTER TWENTY

From the thought of having an irresponsible gay time in Quayside with Lafala, Babel turned to work. The loss of both legs to which Lafala was now quite reconciled was a fresh and terrible shock to Babel. On Babel's mind was painted a picture of the day when he and Lafala stowed away on the same boat, both of them poor and ragged but robust and happy, sound of legs. He imagined himself painfully in Lafala's place, his huge body without legs. He couldn't imagine how comfortable Lafala felt with his thousand-dollar bonds. . . .

Early the next morning Babel went down to the docks and secured a job with a gang of Senegalese unloading copra. . . . In the evening he looked up Big Blonde. Big Blonde lived near the cathedral midway between Quayside and the breakwater. He was sprucing himself up in his best suit when Babel entered.

Big Blonde was mighty glad to see Babel out of prison and to hear that Lafala was also free. He was sorry he had missed last night's party, but he had gone to bed early to be fit for a hard day's work, for tonight he was going on a special private party himself. Babel said he was hoping Big Blonde could join them that night. Lafala wanted to treat him and St. Dominique and Falope to a little get-together between them only to celebrate their coming out of prison.

But Big Blonde replied that he was engaged for the night with Petit Frère and he became quite lyrical about it. Nothing could make him break that engagement. Not for the love of a drinking party which always delighted him, nor the bouquets of the rarest wines, nor the music of hymen though sweet with the honey of the queen bee and glorious like the songs of

Solomon's loves,[1] no not for the virgin stars of the sky nor a brighter shining moon.

And in the midst of his lyricism Petit Frère arrived, fascinating with his pale prettiness and challenging, deep, dark-ringed eyes and insolent mouth. He had departed from La Créole because of some disagreement with Madam and was now engaged as a bar boy at the Domino café and this was his night off.

Babel's being present was opportune, for Petit Frère had a story to tell. At the Domino he had overheard a little of a conversation between Titin and the Grand Maquereau,[2] who was also entitled the Duke of Quayside. The conversation was about Lafala and the scheme of Aslima to despoil him.

Petit Frère hated Titin. For it was Titin who had been instrumental in getting him the place at La Créole and he had had to pay Titin at regular intervals for it.

Big Blonde was inclined to take the thing lightly, saying that Lafala had experience enough to look out for himself, but Babel insisted it was a serious matter, for Lafala was losing his head over Aslima. He wanted Big Blonde and Petit Frère to go with him to see Lafala. Big Blonde said it was common knowledge that the protectors were well organized and he couldn't believe that Lafala would easily allow himself to fall into a trap. Babel replied that it wouldn't be so hard to believe if Big Blonde was less interested in petit frères and more in petites filles.[3] Big Blonde guffawed and excused himself from joining Lafala and the others that night for just that reason. He and Petit Frère were going to dine together and afterward resort to a certain little café. . . .

Babel felt that he was no longer bound to silence after what Petit Frère had said. Aslima's intentions would soon be common underground knowledge in Quayside. Babel decided to go right then to St. Dominique and ask him to try to talk Lafala out of the crazy idea.

He found St. Dominique with Falope in a little restaurant near the Seamen's Club. St. Dominique was not surprised at Babel's revelation. He had seen enough into Lafala's amorous feelings to understand that he might do something just like that. He said that he didn't think Lafala was wise. Falope thought he was a fool.

Meanwhile Lafala had quite made up his mind about it. He had known a girl or two in his life and Aslima was the only one he had ever felt he could live with. Under her coarse and hard exterior there was always that rare green and fruity quality which had so intoxicated him when they first met. Something was always burning, never consuming itself and going out, but always holding him.

The night before they had talked over a perfect plan of stealing away from Marseille. It would be the easiest thing to accomplish without anybody being aware.

Thus Lafala was full of sweet thoughts and dressing to go to visit Aslima when his room was invaded by Babel, St. Dominique and Falope. . . . Petit Frère's tale did not make much impression upon him. He was aware of the differences and mistrust existing between Titin and Aslima and it seemed natural to him that Titin should seek the counsel of other members of his fraternity. He did not say this to his friends but he was displeased with Babel for revealing his plans to St. Dominique and Falope. Lafala was more apprehensive of Titin getting information from other sources which might stir up new suspicions and endanger his plans.

Babel defended himself: "I didn't say a thing to you' friends heah until the kid done told me and Big Blonde. What was the use keeping me mouth shut when other folkses talking about it?"

"But you're joking, Lafala," said Falope. "You can't really mean to do such a thing."

Lafala said he did.

"Impossible!" said Falope. "Pardon me butting into your private affair, but you don't seem to have any idea of your proper position. You don't seem to realize you're a different man than before your accident—a better man, a bigger man. How could you think of taking a girl like Aslima back to Africa now? You ought to have a colored woman that can stand up against the best European women over there—a woman that can be an example to the native women."

"I think Aslima is all right," said Lafala.

"She gypped you for a white tout once and she'll do it again," said Babel.

"I can't understand you, Lafala," said Falope. "You must be spoiled by civilization. What you're planning to do isn't right at all. It isn't African. It's a loving white way."

"Oh, no, I've passed all through that already," said Lafala.

"But you weren't cured," said Falope.

"Yes, I went crazy once, black fool that I was, but I got over it."

"Better you'd stayed on the crazy side," said Falope, "than doing what you're planning to do now."

"Shut up, you," said St. Dominique. "You've got no feeling for anything. I understand what Lafala is talking about. I've been through the same experience myself."

"Oh, yes!" exclaimed Falope. "Now I know why you're a red."

"Oh, go on!" said St. Dominique. . . . "Look here, Lafala, I thought you were doing a crazy thing at first, but now I feel that if you love Aslima it's all right. I can't see anything so awful happening. Just go right ahead if you love her."

"Love! What is this thing called love?" said Falope.[4]

"Jest a funny little word with four letters," said Babel, "the same as rope with which you hang yourself."

"It's four in your language and Petit Frère's, but it's five in mine," said St. Dominique.[5]

"Five French letters and four English to make love," said Falope. "Enough, my friends, enough for tonight."

"Youse all getting too high-classish literally for me," said Babel. "Guess tha's some moh you' civilization."

"Yes," agreed St. Dominique. "I prefer to think of love without letters."

"Like the time when it was naked and we were too, before we went to school to learn our letters," said Falope. "No, Dominique. You can't be primitive and proletarian at the same time. We can't go back again. We have studied our figures and learned our letters. Now we are civilized."

At that moment a boy knocked at the door and entered with a letter for Lafala. He opened it and read: "Look out, they're trying to get you with your own plan. Take warning from *Insider*."

Lafala's face went blank. He passed the note to St. Dominique who read it aloud.

"That tells its own tale," said Falope.

"Better let's go and find Big Blonde so Lafala can hear the story from the kid himself," said Babel.

CHAPTER TWENTY-ONE

Big Blonde and Petit Frère went to dinner in a Chinese restaurant. Petit Frère was a hearty eater and they ate plenty of several dishes: chopped pork and celery, chopped chicken, fish with thick sauce, rice and tea. Finished feeding they went to the Petit Pain,[1] a little café bar that was Big Blonde's favorite place when he was in a sentimental mood and wanted to spend a quiet evening with his little friend.

The bar was in another quarter of Marseille far removed from Quayside and its hectic atmosphere. It was located in the vicinity of the principal railroad station in a narrow and somber alley. Like the street there was something a little sinister and something very alluring in this café, but difficult to define. It was a quality strangely balancing between the emotions of laughter and tears, ribaldry and bitter-sweetness.

The bar was run by a rather young man and his middle-aged paramour. The man was tall and very thin and his bloodless skin was like parchment upon his flesh and looked as if it were drawn away from his mouth. The woman was a spreading type in happy relief against the sharp harshness of the man.

A few clients were there when Big Blonde and Petit Frère entered. Two men of middle-class respectability were throwing dice for a game called "Pigs" with three lads evidently of the slum proletariat.[2] Two fine and handsome sailors were sipping cognac and sugar with a young man slickly dressed in black like a professional dancer. They soaked the cubes of sugar in the cognac and ate them and the right cheek of the young man twitched at regular intervals like a poor fish out of water and gasping for breath. A soldier was sitting alone over a small beer. And also alone at a table in a corner there was a decrepit woman with half a glass of coffee perfumed with cognac between her sad elbows stuck at a weary slant into the table, her fingers crossed over her eyes.

A phonograph at one end of the bar was wheezing out a popular *bal-musette* song, but the music sounded plaintive as if it were asking why more attention was not being paid to it there.

Big Blonde ordered two coffees and two glasses of cognac and asked for the checkerboard. He and Petit Frère began playing checkers. Petit Frère was a poor player and Big Blonde made bad moves to give him a chance and make the game interesting. Petit Frère won the game and was elegantly preening himself over it when a taxicab slowly negotiating the narrow alley stopped before the Petit Pain. Babel alighted and helped out Lafala who was followed by St. Dominique and Falope. They entered the café adding to the uniformly pale atmosphere a touch of that exotic color for which Marseille is famous.

Petit Frère could add nothing more to what Babel had already said. Lafala asked him about the Grand Maquereau and his relationship with Titin. But Petit Frère did not know anything specific. He was a simple kid and knew nothing of the extent and ramifications of the *métier* by which he ate his daily bread.

And now Falope tried every way to scare Lafala away from his infatuation, magnifying the ingenuity and resourcefulness of the protectors, telling how they outwitted and bribed the police, victimized women, terrorizing timid men and always evading the law which was powerless against them. It sounded frightful, especially as Falope, spending his time between his office and a cheap respectable pension in Marseille, knew nothing about the romantic gentlemen. Lafala knew more because he had lived all of his civilized life in their milieu without ever minding them and how they lived behind their well-dressed facade. There were quite a number of Negro protectors down at Quayside since the Great War, who were seriously competing with the white natives. Only the Negroes were not as closely knit in relationships with the bars and the loving houses as the old natives. Lafala himself had had his chance of being a protector or some approximate thing in well-kept ease. But he had not taken advantage of it, not feeling equal to the job of remaining forever a black god consecrated to the worship of phallicism.

"Let's forget the damned thing," he said, and proposed standing a treat and paying his respects to Big Blonde for his part in helping to get him and Babel out of jail.

They gathered in a circle round two tables and Lafala ordered spumante wine. They drank many bottles. Big Blonde was a heavy, good-natured drinker. Now that the lads had invaded his retreat, he gave himself willingly to the enjoyment of the party. He didn't want to impose Petit Frère upon them when he was invited. But it was all right to have him in the crowd since they had come themselves to find him. And Petit Frère was pleased.

The other clients had left excepting the soldier and the old woman in the corner with her still-unfinished glass of coffee perfumed with cognac. Two little brunettes resembling twins and dressed alike in soiled black frocks and red belts and brown canvas shoes looked in at the door of the café. They were just out on a cruising from a little *bal-musette* in a neighboring alley.

"There is Petit Frère!" said one.

Petit Frère lifted his hand in greeting and the girls entered. They kissed him ostentatiously and one of them drained his glass of wine. Lafala poured the other a drink.

"Play the phonograph and let's dance," she said. The proprietor said they couldn't dance for he had no dancing license.[3]

The girls glanced around and patted their hair and cheeks looking in a mirror.

"Come on down to the dancing when you are finished," said one of them to Petit Frère and they ran out again.

"I never understand why the girls are so affectionate with their little brothers," said St. Dominique to Babel in English. "I should think they would be jealous."

"Lawd no!" said Babel. "They are all young and jolly and working together at the same trade."

"But the little brothers steal business away from them," said St. Dominique.

"And their men too sometimes," Babel laughed. "That's why the little sisters keep on the good side of the little brothers."

"Quayside, it's business above everything else," said Lafala. "Our little brothers are liked and tolerated, because they're good business."

"You're right," said Babel, putting his hand round Petit Frère's shoulder.

Big Blonde removed it playfully, saying, "Keep your hand off that, old man."

Laughing, Babel said, "Lemme sing you all a little song. My song is entitled 'Moonstruck':

> I was stricken by the moon,
> I was smitten by the moon,
> Crazy for the fairy moon,
> It lighted my heart and it caused me to roam
> Far away from my loving wife waiting at home."

The tune was slow and pretty and sounded like a sentimental tango.

The others began humming to Babel's singing.

"Come on, Big Blonde," said Babel. "Let us dance to this thing."

Big Blonde got up and he and Babel began an ungainly shuffle. "Boss," said Babel, "the police can't interfere for this ain't no dancing. We just swaying to the music of the moon."

"Look out the moon madness don't get you too," said Lafala to Babel.

"I'm crazy all ways bar none," replied Babel.

And while they were joking and drinking an old woman entered with a basket of dolls and such baubles that are hawked around all-night cafés and cabarets. She was prematurely grey and her skin was wrinkled and her mouth twisted and she looked like an old cocotte[4] to whom time and people had been cruel.

She offered her wares to the men, dangling a doll by the leg. Big Blonde, happy in his environment and a little maudlin, was going to buy something to be rid of the poor hag but Petit Frère stopped him with a nudge that she did not miss. Babel roughly told her that they didn't want anything, she was in the wrong place.

"Indeed I am, there's no doubt I am when you have that thing there between you," she said fixing Petit Frère with a malevolent finger.

"Whether I was here or not, old cow," said Petit Frère, "it wouldn't make any difference, for you're too God-forsaken old and ugly."

"And you're so pretty, like a doll," said the woman. "You all ought to buy him a doll. He'd be more darling with one in his arms."

"Yes, I'd look better than you selling them," said Petit Frère. "Old useless and jealous has-been."

"Petit *cul-cassé*⁵ and dirty mouth!" the woman cried at Petit Frère. "Little sucking pig!"

"Better to be a sucking pig than an old good-for-nothing sow," said Petit Frère.

Discomfited, the woman left the café and the men laughed hilariously. Big Blonde complimented Petit Frère: "Fine! You were a match for her."

"Come on, let's do the moon-song, again," said Babel.

And he began singing:

"I was stricken by the moon. . . ."

But after an interval the woman returned, looking along the floor as if she had forgotten something. Passing by the group she quickly took a paper full of filth from her basket and slapped it in Petit Frère's face. "There! That is your life," she cried.

Big Blonde jumped up and knocked her sprawling to the floor and flung the basket through the door of the café, scattering the contents. The paramour of the proprietor came from round the bar and picked the woman up and pushed her out of the door. The woman stood in the street, swearing and picking up her wares and demanding payment for them. But the proprietor threatened to telephone for the police and she quickly disappeared. . . . Meanwhile Petit Frère had slipped away to the lavatory to clean himself up.

"Well, that's a pretty ending to your moon song, fellows," said St. Dominique. "I am going home now."

"Oh, don't break the party up yet," said Babel. "Let's finish it up at Quayside. I feel like going up the rags."

Petit Frère returned, well-washed and looking none the worse for his ordeal. "If I ever run across that old sow again I'll cut her twat out and give it to the dogs," he said.

Everybody laughed.

"Here, have a drink on that," said Babel to Petit Frère, "and let's sing the moon-song."

Babel began singing and shaking Big Blonde who had his head down on the table as if he were drunk: "Come on, let's sing together." But he discovered that Big Blonde was crying softly.

"He's drunk!" said Babel.

"Let's go," said St. Dominique.

Lafala called the proprietor and paid the bill. Petit Frère shook Big Blonde.

"He's drunk! Leave him alone till he's sober," said Babel. And the four of them went out, leaving Big Blonde and Petit Frère alone.

CHAPTER TWENTY-TWO

The following day Lafala went to the office of the official and found him with La Fleur's anonymous letter upon his desk. Lafala showed him the warning note that he had also received and wondered if the letters were not a hoax. But Lafala did not get any assurance from him. Whether it was a hoax or not the best thing, the man thought, was that Lafala should leave Marseille at once to avoid further complications. He had thought Aslima was a different kind of girl, a domestic or something, and had never imagined she was just a colored creature of the dives of Quayside.

A few cases of foreign sailors wanting to marry pretty prostitutes out of the cabarets had come under his official notice. But thanks to the local laws that made marriage a difficult transaction, nearly all such persons had been saved from themselves.

But it was the first case of a Negro and a colored prostitute.

Lafala, trying to get right with his conscience, suggested that the anonymous notes might have been written by an enemy of Aslima. But the official said he could have nothing to do personally with the whole matter. He was going to arrange Lafala's passage but he would have nothing to do with his more intimate affairs. He telephoned a shipping company and learned that there was a boat leaving for West Africa the next day and stopping at Lafala's home port. He told Lafala he was going to book his passage or he would wash his hands of his business. Reluctantly, Lafala consented. . . .

But that night Aslima went to see Lafala at his hotel, lovelier and livelier than ever. She was charmingly dressed in native costume and when she took off the coat under which it was hidden, she received the exclamation of admiration she had expected. She had on a long yellow robe reaching to her ankles and a yellow jacket bordered with black braid and blue bloomers.[1] It was one of two dresses she had brought to Marseille and which she had never worn.

"You're fine like that," said Lafala.

"Thanks, my pig," said Aslima reclining beside him. The touch of her burned into him like a sweet fever consuming his body.

"They tried to separate us, but they couldn't for long, eh, my darling pig?" she said.

"No, they couldn't, honey pig. We're true pigs for life."

"Pigs for life," she repeated. "Two loving pigs going away together to hide in the jungle."

Lafala stirred. "You've been sleeping, honey pig," said Aslima.

"Sleeping and dreaming. I didn't sleep last night. Couldn't get any peace in my mind."

"Well, if I brought you peace it's all right, only I don't like you to go to sleep on me. What were you dreaming about?"

"I was dreaming we couldn't go away together. Suppose we couldn't really?" asked Lafala.

"If it's the will of God that we shouldn't—but what's there to prevent us?"

"Suppose Titin should?"

"How could he unless he killed me?"

"Or me," said Lafala. And he told her Petit Frère's story and about the anonymous letters and the opinion of the official.

"Well, if it's as bad as all that, I don't know what to say," said Aslima. "It's up to you."

"Suppose if we couldn't go together, I paid you your passage back home. Would that be alright?"

"What home? I have no home to go back to. No parents, no relatives. I would be a stranger going back alone as much as I am here. I would go with you if you wanted me to, but I wouldn't want to leave here to go anyplace alone."

"Telephone some drinks and let's not talk about this," said Lafala.

"That's better," she said. "It you want to go and leave me I can't stop you, but don't talk about it."

A man entered with the drinks on a tray and set it down on the night table. . . .

"Going to be swilling pigs, tonight," said Aslima. "Forget everything swilling."

"Even Titin!" said Lafala.

"Forget Titin. He's not the same with me since you came out of prison. He's starting to get rough again. But I don't care. I couldn't stand him any longer whether I went with you or not."

"But what would happen if you quit him and stayed here in Marseille?"

"I don't care." Aslima began dancing round the room singing a pig-song in her language which is something like this translated:

> Want to know what's loving sweet,
> Want to know what's loving big?
> When two naughty lovers meet
> And unite in loving pigs.

"Going to be naughty pigs, tonight," she sing-songed. She danced over to the bed and rubbed her burning brown face against Lafala. Lafala hugged her keeping her hot cheek against his and their generated warmth mingled harmoniously, kindling a delicious feeling of ebony in brown, and stirring up in him a riotous sensation of crimson and green, yellow and honey and all the kindred colors of love and passion.

"Oh, you're the darlingest pig in the world," said Aslima, "and you won't find another pig like me in all of Africa."

"I know I won't," said Lafala.

"Then we'll go back together and you won't tease me again about going back alone."

"No," he said.

"For we need one another."

"Yes, we need one another."

"To make pig-honey together, for pig-honey is the sweetest honey. Sweeter than the honey of flowers and bees."

"Yes, sweeter than the damned flowers and the bloody bees," said Lafala.

"Will we be going soon?"

"Yes, soon, very soon," he said. And Lafala meant it then for he was overwhelmed in love. Never was he so happy in sweet loving. It was as if Aslima had all the time reserved a secret cell in her being and had unlocked it now for him alone to enter. And how like a rare tropical garden it was where every fruit was delicious to taste.

Oh, nothing could tear him away from her now. No fear of protectors, nor white respectability, nor native dignity. He would stick to her and be a contented pig in a pen, wallowing with joy in the mud.

CHAPTER TWENTY-THREE

In the early morning Aslima left Lafala as happy as a bird. She went to her room and changed her clothes. Titin was not there; he had not slept in. She tidied the room afresh and went out up on the terrace and sat down gazing over the sea into the horizon, her spirit in a fever and full of the anticipation of a big joy.

The harbor was crowded and busy with yachts moored on the far side and fishing boats clustered together on the near side and through the sunlit blue space between the excursion boats dashed with visitors to the warships and to promenade in the bay.

The fishermen came clogging up the terrace to spread their nets in the sun, and ample women walked with baskets of fish, blue-white sardines gleaming in the sunlight. Little kids screamed and clapped hands around Aslima, yet unmindful of her, digging and rolling in the sand, lifting their short smocks, toddling and pissing. But she remained indifferent to the everyday reality around her, wrapped up in her complete happiness.

She stayed up there on the terrace until lunchtime. In the afternoon she went to the Tout-va-Bien.

The bar of the Tout-va-Bien was a shining affair. Glasses of all sizes were nicely arranged on the little glass shelves over the bar. And behind was the exciting array of bottles stood up or set horizontally according to their contents: white and red wine, whiskies, cognacs, gins, rums, champagnes and a variety of *apéritifs* and cordials. A case of appetizers (olives, anchovies, clams, crackers and other tidbits) at one end of the bar. The piano was dusted and oiled. The marble-topped tables were washed clean and those out on the terrace placed in a neat row.

Everything was in trim for the Saturday afternoon trade.

The mulatto looked well his part of proprietor-waiter in a newly-ironed brown holland coat. His paramour, a broad-bosomed brunette, sat at the desk constantly patting her frizzly crown of cropped hair.

The hour was yet early for business and the customers few. A group of chronic idlers, nearly all blacks, were gaming at cards in a corner. Babel was leaning against the piano and watching the game which he wanted to learn. He had worked only half a day. La Fleur and her friend were sitting on the terrace and an instantaneous photographer[1] was taking a group of sailors and soldiers.

Aslima entered the café and stood at the desk exchanging compliments with the woman. Babel glanced scowlingly at her.

While the women were gossiping, Rock and Diup breezed into the café, each waving a ten-franc note and calling for drinks.

"Come on, Babel and you fellahs," said Rock, "and drink to a safe voyage for Lafala. This is his last treat."

"Last treat!" exclaimed Babel. "Is he gone then?"

"You bet he is. Done sailed away. Diup and me we seen the broad shove off with Lafala and we waved the last goodbye to him and he waved back too without any tears shed."

La Fleur came into the café to hear all about it. Diup and Rock had slept down on the breakwater the night before and in the morning while they were foraging for food along the docks, they espied Lafala on the deck of his ship. Lafala had given them the notes for a farewell drink and asked them to say goodbye to the Quaysiders.

For when he arose from his drunken night of loving in the clear and sobering daylight and began thinking again, the practical side of his nature had reasserted itself over the sensual and decided him to do as his agent wished. . . .

Babel was transported with joy because Lafala had secretly sailed away from Aslima and Quayside. And he began to dance and sing:

> "Oh, the life was sweet but the time is short,
> And I've got to go with the broad alone,[2]
> Oh, the jolly gals in this good ole port,
> Who'll remember me after I am gone."

La Fleur threw up her head at Aslima with a look of smiling satisfaction and delicious triumph. . . . But her manner underwent a sudden change as she observed the terrible expression upon Aslima's face.

Aslima said nothing. She had turned away from the woman at the bar and now she left the café repeating to herself "Mektoub! Mektoub!" (Destiny! Destiny!)[3]

She had gone a few steps only when a uniformed messenger boy came to the café with a letter for her. It was from Lafala and he had sent it expressly in care of the proprietor to prevent it from falling into Titin's hands. . . .

But when Titin came to the café a little later in a chorean state[4] because of the news of Lafala's sailing, the proprietor, like a good ally, gave him Aslima's letter. . . . La Fleur cried out that the letter was Aslima's and Titin had no right to it.

"Shut up, you slut," said Titin, "and mind your own affair."

Titin opened the letter and read it with the help of the proprietor. Lafala had left a hundred dollars with his agent for Aslima which she could claim by showing her papers of identification. She could use the money to return home.

But something else in the letter made Titin's voice trembling wet with tears. It concerned an extra thousand-franc note belonging to Aslima and which she had entrusted to Lafala for safe-keeping, and which he had also left for her with the agent.

"That hard-hearted slut!" cried Titin. "She had all that money saved up from me and there were days when I actually starved. How could any man trust the slut that is a woman!"

"Don't you know better than talking about trusting any woman?" said the proprietor.

His paramour's face grew sharp with anger but she said nothing.

"I'm the last man she'll double-cross," said Titin.

La Fleur slipped from the café and flew to Aslima's room to warn her about the letter and implore her to escape. But Aslima was apathetic. She did not care about anything. She said she would not mind what Titin did now. La Fleur tried to pull Aslima up from the couch where she was lying indifferently but Aslima quietly told her to leave her alone. La Fleur broke down and cried and said she was sorry she had ever been mean to Aslima. Aslima replied that that was all right for she had also been mean and she told La Fleur that perhaps it would be better for her if Titin did not find her there. And so La Fleur left, encountering Titin in the passage who brushed past her like a wild rat with the letter in his hand, hardly noticing her.

He found Aslima in the same listless position in which La Fleur had left her. He brandished the letter and raged until he foamed. But Aslima maintained the same silence. Her manner was even mocking.

"You won't double-cross another man," said Titin. "Your life will pay for this."

"Take it then and stop shouting," Aslima spoke at last. Titin was nonplussed. She had spoken so coolly and confidently, as if life was no longer desirable living for her. It was evident that she had lost her mind and herself to that Lafala. He was not a killer. He wondered hesitatingly if she wouldn't be getting off too easily with death.

Then he began to rage again, but this time more against Lafala. . . . Oh, to be outwitted by a creature of the jungle! . . . A half-helpless savage. . . . A mere black stump of humanity. . . . Escaped. . . . Gone with all the money and the great deep sea between them.

"Better I had killed him that night so his money would have been no use to him either," cried Titin. "Better I had killed him like a dog!"

"Kill him! Kill Lafala?" Aslima started up aroused at last. As if she saw Lafala standing there between them and in danger from Titin. "You'd have to kill me first and kill him over my dead body," she screamed frantically, and drawing the knife she always carried she advanced upon Titin like a madwoman.

He could stop her with the gun only. He didn't want to do it then. There was that money in the hands of Lafala's representative that he would like her to get first. . . . He cried out at her fearfully like a hunter attacked by a precious wild beast that he would rather capture than slay. . . . But he was forced to let go at her or she would bleed his heart. . . .

She threw up her hands like a bird of prey about to swoop down upon a victim and pitched headlong to the door. He shot the remaining bullets into her body, cursing and calling upon hell to swallow her soul.

Suggestions for Further Reading

BY CLAUDE MCKAY

Amiable with Big Teeth: A Novel of the Love Affair Between the Communists and the Poor Black Sheep of Harlem. Edited and introduced by Jean-Christophe Cloutier and Brent Hayes Edwards. New York: Penguin, 2017.

Banana Bottom. 1933. New York: Harcourt Brace, 1974.

Banjo: A Story Without a Plot. 1929. New York: Harcourt Brace, 1970.

Complete Poems. Edited and introduced by William J. Maxwell. Urbana: University of Illinois Press, 2004.

Gingertown. New York: Harper & Brothers, 1932.

Harlem: Negro Metropolis. New York: Dutton, 1940.

Harlem Glory: A Fragment of Aframerican Life. Preface by Carl Cowl. Chicago: Charles H. Kerr, 1990.

Harlem Shadows. Introduction by Max Eastman. New York: Harcourt Brace, 1922.

Home to Harlem. 1928. Foreword by Wayne F. Cooper. Boston: Northeastern University Press, 1987.

A Long Way from Home. 1937. Edited and introduced by Gene Andrew Jarrett. New Brunswick, NJ: Rutgers University Press, 2007.

My Green Hills of Jamaica and Five Jamaican Short Stories. Edited by Mervyn Morris. Kingston: Heinemann, 1979.

The Negroes in America. 1923. Edited by Alan McLeod. Translated from the Russian by Robert J. Winter. Port Washington, NY: Kennikat Press, 1979.

The Passion of Claude McKay. Edited by Wayne F. Cooper. New York: Knopf, 1976.

Trial by Lynching: Stories of Negro Life in North America (Sudom Lincha). 1925. Edited and introduced by A. L. McLeod. Translated from the Russian by Robert J. Winter. Mysore, India:

University of Mysore, Centre for Commonwealth Literature and Research, 1977.

CRITICISM

Bell, Christopher M., ed. *Blackness and Disability: Critical Examinations and Cultural Interventions.* East Lansing, MI: Michigan State University Press, 2011.

Bishop, Jacqueline. "Claude McKay's Songs of Morocco." *Black Renaissance/Renaissance Noire* 14.1 (spring–summer 2014): 68–75.

Braddock, Jeremy. "Media Studies 1932: Nancy Cunard in the Archive of Claude McKay." *Modernism/modernity* 3.2. Web. May 30, 2018. https://modernismmodernity.org/articles/media-studies-1932.

Cloutier, Jean-Christophe. *Shadow Archives: The Lifecycles of African American Literature.* New York: Columbia University Press, 2019.

Cooper, Wayne F. *Claude McKay: Rebel Sojourner in the Harlem Renaissance.* Baton Rouge: Louisiana State University Press, 1987.

Davis, Lennard J. *Bending over Backwards: Disability, Dismodernism, and Other Difficult Positions.* New York: New York University Press, 2002.

Edwards, Brent Hayes. "Vagabond Internationalism: Claude McKay's *Banjo*." *The Practice of Diaspora: Literature, Translation, and the Rise of Black Internationalism.* Cambridge, MA: Harvard University Press, 2003: 187–240.

Etherington, Ben. "Claude McKay's Primitivist Narration." *Literary Primitivism.* Stanford, CA: Stanford University Press, 2018: 135–159.

Fabre, Michel. "Claude McKay and the Two Faces of France." *From Harlem to Paris: Black American Writers in France, 1840–1980.* Urbana: University of Illinois Press, 1991: 92–113.

Hathaway, Heather. *Caribbean Waves: Relocating Claude McKay and Paule Marshall.* Bloomington: Indiana University Press, 1999.

Holcomb, Gary Edward. "'Swaying to the Music of the Moon': Black-White Queer Solidarity in *Romance in Marseille*." *Claude McKay, Code Name Sasha: Queer Black Marxism and the Harlem Renaissance.* Gainesville: University Press of Florida, 2007: 171–224.

Hutchinson, George. *The Harlem Renaissance in Black and White.* Cambridge, MA: Belknap-Harvard University Press, 1996.

James, Jennifer C., and Cynthia Wu. "Editors' Introduction: Race, Ethnicity, Disability, and Literature: Intersections and Interventions." *MELUS* 31.3 (fall 2006): 3–13.

James, Winston. *A Fierce Hatred of Injustice: Claude McKay's Jamaica and His Poetry of Rebellion.* London: Verso, 2000.

Lee, Steven S. *The Ethnic Avant-Garde: Minority Cultures and World Revolution.* New York: Columbia University Press, 2015.

Lowney, John. "'Harlem Jazzing': Claude McKay, *Home to Harlem,* and Jazz Internationalism." *Jazz Internationalism: Literary Afro-Modernism and the Cultural Politics of Black Music.* Urbana: University of Illinois Press, 2017: 27–58.

Maxwell, William J. *New Negro, Old Left: African-American Writing and Communism Between the Wars.* New York: Columbia University Press, 1999.

——. *F.B. Eyes: How J. Edgar Hoover's Ghostreaders Framed African American Literature.* Princeton, NJ: Princeton University Press, 2015.

Newman, Eric H. "Ephemeral Utopias: Queer Cruising, Literary Form, and Diasporic Imagination in Claude McKay's *Home to Harlem* and *Banjo.*" *Callaloo* 38.1 (winter 2015): 167–185.

Posmentier, Sonya. "The Provision Ground in New York: Claude McKay and the Form of Memory." *American Literature* 84.2 (June 2012): 273–300.

Schmidt, Michael David. "A Queer Romance of Materialism: McKay's *Romance in Marseilles.*" *The Materialism of the Encounter: Queer Sociality and Capital in Modern Literature.* Wayne State University Dissertations, 2013, Paper 697: 172–221.

Schwarz, A. B. Crista. *Gay Voices of the Harlem Renaissance.* Bloomington: Indiana University Press, 2003.

Stone, Andrea. "The Black Atlantic Revisited, the Body Reconsidered: On Lingering, Liminality, Lies, and Disability." *American Literary History* 24.4 (winter 2012): 814–826.

Thomson, Rosemarie Garland. *Extraordinary Bodies: Figuring Physical Disability in American Culture and Literature.* New York: Columbia University Press, 1997.

Explanatory Notes

Written between 1929 and 1933, first named "The Jungle and the Bottoms" and then "Savage Loving," Claude McKay's novel was ultimately titled *Romance in Marseille*. With a few minor corrections, our text reflects the 172-page, evidently final typescript of *Romance* kept in the Claude McKay papers at the New York Public Library's Schomburg Center for Research in Black Culture in Harlem. An earlier eighty-seven-page version of the novel, filed as "Romance in Marseille," is archived in the James Weldon Johnson Collection at the Beinecke Rare Book and Manuscript Library at Yale University in New Haven. For more information on the novel's provenance, see "A Note on the Text."

INTRODUCTION

1. Claude McKay, *Banjo: A Story Without a Plot* (1929), New York: Harcourt Brace, 1970, 11.
2. Claude McKay, *A Long Way from Home* (1937), New Brunswick: Rutgers University Press, 2007, 231.
3. Claude McKay, *Romance in Marseille*, New York: Penguin Classics, 2020, 4.
4. Alexandre Dumas, *Impressions de Voyage: Le Midi de la France* (1842), Paris: Michel Lévy Frères, 1887, 171.
5. *Romance in Marseille*, 5.
6. Ibid., 24.
7. Ibid., 28.
8. Ibid.
9. Ibid.
10. Ibid.
11. Ibid., 94.

12. Ibid., 73.

13. Ibid., 74.

14. Ibid., 112.

15. *Banjo*, 316.

16. While in most of the complete typescript of *Romance in Marseille* McKay uses "Lafala," the typed name "Taloufa" appears, redacted and replaced by the printed "Lafala," eight times, on pages 10, 16, 24 (three times), 26 (twice), and 28, to be precise.

17. Claude McKay, letter to William Aspenwall Bradley, Feb. 10, 1928, William A. Bradley Literary Agency Records, 1909–1982, Harry Ransom Center, University of Texas, Austin.

18. *Romance in Marseille*, 28.

19. Ibid., 4.

20. "Champion Escapes from Ireland in Spite of Refusal of English and American Ships to Sell Him Ticket," *Afro-American* (April 13, 1923): 14.

21. "Bring Balto. Boys from West," *Afro-American* (Aug. 18, 1928): 20.

22. "Stowaway Freed When Ship Docked," *New York Amsterdam News* (May 16, 1928): 3.

23. "Jailed on Arrival in England as Stowaway," *New York Amsterdam News* (April 18, 1928): 3.

24. "Three Stowaways Found on Byrd Ship," *The New York Times* (Aug. 27, 1928): 1.

25. "Drop Stowaway on Byrd Ship," *The Pittsburgh Courier* (Sept. 22, 1928): 15.

26. "Stowaway to Carry Appeal to Australia," *Chicago Defender* (Oct. 20, 1928): 4.

27. W. E. B. Du Bois, "The Negro Mind Reaches Out," in *The New Negro* (1925), ed. Alain Locke, New York: Atheneum, 1992, 412.

28. W. E. B. Du Bois, "Review of Claude McKay's *Banjo* and Nella Larsen's *Passing*," *The Crisis* 36 (July 1929): 234.

29. "Kept Manacled on Ship, Says Stowaway," *The New York Times* (May 24, 1927): 27.

30. Ibid.

31. For more on this remarkable public hospital, opened in 1902, see Lorrie Conway, *Forgotten Ellis Island: The Extraordinary Story of America's Immigrant Hospital*, New York: Harper-Collins, 2007.

32. "Ship's Officers Deny Cruelty to Stowaway," *The New York Times* (May 25, 1927): 38.

33. "Kept Manacled on Ship, Says Stowaway," *The New York Times* (May 24, 1927): 27.

34. "Stowaway Fails in Suit," *The New York Times* (May 27, 1927): 41.

35. *Romance in Marseille*, 3.

36. Claude McKay, letter to William Aspenwall Bradley, Feb. 10, 1928, William A. Bradley Literary Agency Records, 1909-1982, Harry Ransom Center, University of Texas, Austin.

37. Ibid.

38. Ibid.

39. *Romance in Marseille*, 19.

40. Ibid.

41. Claude McKay, letter to William Aspenwall Bradley, Feb. 10, 1928, William A. Bradley Literary Agency Records, 1909-1982, Harry Ransom Center, University of Texas, Austin.

42. McKay, *A Long Way from Home*, 185.

43. Claude McKay, letter to "Le Directeur en Chef, La Compagnie Fabre," Jan. 13, 1928, Claude McKay Papers, James Weldon Johnson Collection, Beinecke Rare Book and Manuscript Library, Yale University, New Haven.

44. Ibid.

45. Ibid.

46. Ibid.

47. Ibid.

48. Ibid.

49. Ibid.

50. Claude McKay, letter to William Aspenwall Bradley, Feb. 10, 1928, William A. Bradley Literary Agency Records, 1909-1982, Harry Ransom Center, University of Texas, Austin.

51. *Romance in Marseille*, 100.

52. Ibid., 101.

53. David Levering Lewis, *When Harlem Was in Vogue*, New York: Penguin, 1997, xxiii.

54. *Romance in Marseille*, 130.

55. *Banjo*, 326.

56. The typescripts catalogued as "Romance in Marseille" and "Marseilles," respectively, can be found in two rich U.S. rare book and manuscript archives. The shorter typescript, titled by McKay as "The Jungle and the Bottoms" and likely revised between December 1929 and June 1930, is housed in the James Weldon Johnson Collection, Beinecke Rare Book and Manuscript Library, at Yale University in New Haven. The longer typescript—almost certainly containing what was originally

called "Savage Loving" and produced between 1932 and 1933—is kept in the Claude McKay Letters and Manuscripts at the New York Public Library's Schomburg Center for Research in Black Culture, located in Harlem.

57. Langston Hughes, letter to Claude McKay, July 25, 1925, Claude McKay Papers, James Weldon Johnson Collection, Beinecke Rare Book and Manuscript Library, Yale University, New Haven.

58. The most frequently cited if not quite standard editions of McKay's first two published novels are these: *Home to Harlem*, foreword by Wayne F. Cooper, Boston: Northeastern University Press, 1987, originally published by New York's Harper & Brothers in 1928; and *Banjo: A Story Without a Plot*, New York: Harcourt Brace, 1970, originally published by Harper & Brothers in 1929.

59. *Romance in Marseille*, 4.

60. For basic information on this working history, see Claude McKay's letter to William Aspenwall Bradley, March 18, 1930, William A. Bradley Literary Agency Records 1909-1982, Harry Ransom Center, University of Texas, Austin; and his letter to Max Eastman, June 27, 1930, Claude McKay Papers, Lilly Library Manuscripts Collection, Indiana University, Bloomington.

61. Gertrude Stein, *The Autobiography of Alice B. Toklas* (1933), in *Gertrude Stein: Writings, 1903–1932*, ed. Catherine Stimpson and Harriet Chessman, New York: Library of America, 1998, 900.

62. Claude McKay, letter to William Aspenwall Bradley, Dec. 21, 1929, William A. Bradley Literary Agency Records 1909–1982, Harry Ransom Center, University of Texas, Austin.

63. Ibid.

64. Ibid.

65. *A Long Way from Home*, 214.

66. Ibid.

67. Though St. Dominique was inspired by "this" Senghor, the character is also semi-autobiographical, possibly taking the place that an alter ego named Malty occupied in the now-lost original draft. The fictional St. Dominique fills the office that McKay himself had filled when Nelson Simeon Dede was jailed, acting on Dede/Lafala's behalf when the shipping company plots with the French authorities to imprison the protagonist. This feature of the narrative, however, differs significantly from the Ray-as-verbal-proxy McKay of the previous novels.

68. Claude McKay, letter to William Aspenwall Bradley, Dec. 21, 1929, William A. Bradley Literary Agency Records 1909–1982, Harry Ransom Center, University of Texas, Austin.

69. See W. E. B. Du Bois, "Review of Nella Larsen's *Quicksand*, Claude McKay's *Home to Harlem*, and Melville Herskovits' *The American Negro*," *The Crisis* 35 (June 1928): 202.

70. In his least temperate Harlem Renaissance-era statement on aesthetics, W. E. B. Du Bois proclaimed that "all Art is propaganda and ever must be, despite the wailing of the purists. . . . I do not care a damn for any art that is not used for propaganda." See W. E. B. Du Bois, "The Criterion of Negro Art," *The Crisis* 32 (Oct. 1926): 290–297. For more on McKay's anti-Du Boisian attitude, see his letter to William Aspenwall Bradley, Dec. 21, 1929, William A. Bradley Literary Agency Records 1909–1982, Harry Ransom Center, University of Texas, Austin.

71. Claude McKay, letter to William Aspenwall Bradley, Dec. 21, 1929, William A. Bradley Literary Agency Records 1909–1982, Harry Ransom Center, University of Texas, Austin.

72. Ibid.

73. Ibid.

74. Ibid.

75. Claude McKay, letter to Max Eastman, June 27, 1930, Claude McKay Papers, Lilly Library Manuscripts Collection, Indiana University, Bloomington.

76. Claude McKay, letter to William Aspenwall Bradley, Aug. 28, 1930, William A. Bradley Literary Agency Records 1909–1982, Harry Ransom Center, University of Texas, Austin.

77. Ibid.

78. Ibid.

79. The term "Dreamport" appears in the Beinecke version of the *Romance in Marseille* manuscript, though redacted, with "Marseille" written above it.

80. Claude McKay, letter to Max Eastman, June 27, 1930, Claude McKay Papers, Lilly Library Manuscripts Collection, Indiana University, Bloomington.

81. *Romance in Marseille*, 29.

82. Ibid.

83. Ibid.

84. Claude McKay, letter to Willian Aspenwall Bradley, Dec. 21, 1929, William A. Bradley Literary Agency Records 1909-1982, Harry Ransom Center, University of Texas, Austin.

85. *Romance in Marseille*, 17.

86. Ibid., 41.

87. Ibid.

88. *Home to Harlem*, 128–129.

89. *Romance in Marseille*, 129.

90. Ibid., 55.

91. Ibid., 19.

92. Wayne F. Cooper, *Claude McKay: Rebel Sojourner in the Harlem Renaissance*, Baton Rouge: Louisiana State University Press, 1987, 268.

93. Ibid.

94. George Hutchinson, *The Harlem Renaissance in Black and White*, Cambridge, MA: Belknap-Harvard University Press, 1995, 379.

95. Ibid.

96. See Claude McKay, *Harlem Shadows: The Poems of Claude McKay*, New York: Harcourt Brace, 1922; and Claude McKay, *Complete Poems*, edited by William J. Maxwell, Urbana: University of Illinois Press, 2004.

97. The Garland Fund was officially known as the American Fund for Personal Service.

98. Claude McKay, quoted in Wayne F. Cooper, 212.

99. Claude McKay, quoted in Wayne F. Cooper, 221.

100. Claude McKay, letter to Arthur A. Schomburg, July 17, 1925, Arthur A. Schomburg Papers, Schomburg Center for Research in Black Culture, New York Public Library, New York.

101. Langston Hughes, quoted in A. B. Christa Schwarz, *Gay Voices of the Harlem Renaissance*, Bloomington: Indiana University Press, 2003, 44.

102. Rean Graves, quoted in Langston Hughes, *The Big Sea: An Autobiography* (1940), New York: Hill and Wang, 1993, 237.

103. See Richard Bruce [Nugent], "Smoke, Lilies and Jade," *Fire!!: A Quarterly Devoted to the Younger Negro Artists* 1.1 (1926): 33–40.

104. Wayne F. Cooper, 221.

105. *Home to Harlem*, 92.

106. *Romance in Marseille*, 119.

107. Ibid., 41.

108. Ibid.

109. See Claude McKay, letter to William Aspenwall Bradley, June 25, 1930, William A. Bradley Literary Agency Records 1909–1982, Harry Ransom Center, University of Texas, Austin; and his letter to Max Eastman, June 27, 1930, Claude McKay Papers, Lilly Library Manuscripts Collection, Indiana University, Bloomington.

110. See Claude McKay, letter to William Aspenwall Bradley, July 4, 1930, William A. Bradley Literary Agency Records 1909–1982, Harry Ransom Center, University of Texas, Austin; and his letter to Max Eastman, Dec. 1, 1930, Claude McKay Papers, Lilly Library Manuscripts Collection, Indiana University, Bloomington.

111. See Shireen K. Lewis, *Race, Culture, and Identity: Francophone West African and Caribbean Literature and Theory from Négritude to Créolité*, Oxford: Lexington Books, 2006, 28.

112. Lennard J. Davis, *Bending Over Backwards: Disability, Dismodernism, and Other Difficult Positions*, New York: New York University Press, 2002, 30.

113. Claude McKay, quoted in Wayne F. Cooper, 274.

114. Claude McKay, letter to Max Eastman, Dec. 1, 1930, Claude McKay Papers, Lilly Library Manuscripts Collection, Indiana University, Bloomington.

115. Claude McKay, letter to William Aspenwall Bradley, Sept. 18, 1930, William A. Bradley Literary Agency Records 1909–1982, Harry Ransom Center, University of Texas, Austin.

116. See Wayne F. Cooper, 269, 412 note 16.

117. See Wayne F. Cooper, 275.

118. Rudolph Fisher, "White, High Yellow, Black" [review of Claude McKay's *Gingertown*], *New York Herald Tribune Books* (March 27, 1932): 3.

119. Claude McKay, quoted in Wayne F. Cooper, 274.

120. Ibid.

121. Wayne F. Cooper, 279.

122. Both McKay and Bowles wrote about their Tangier encounter, McKay accusing Bowles of precipitating his troubles with the French colonial administration: see Paul Bowles, *Without Stopping*, New York: Putnam, 1972, 147–149; and McKay's letter to Max Eastman, likely May 1933, Claude McKay Papers, Lilly Library Manuscripts Collection, Indiana University, Bloomington. See also Gary Edward Holcomb, *Claude McKay, Code Name Sasha: Queer Black Marxism and the Harlem Renaissance*, Gainesville: University Press of Florida, 2007, 66.

123. See Claude McKay, letter to Max Eastman, April 21, 1933, Claude McKay Papers, Lilly Library Manuscripts Collection, Indiana University, Bloomington.

124. Ibid.

125. *Romance in Marseille*, 94.

126. Ibid.

127. Ibid., 76.
128. See Dorothy Parker, "Review of *Home to Harlem*" (1928), *The Portable Dorothy Parker*, New York: Penguin Classics, 2006, 503. In his memoir, *A Long Way from Home* (1937), McKay chafed at the allegation that the publication of *Nigger Heaven* had anything to do with his writing *Home to Harlem*, pointing out he had produced a short story of the same title a year before the appearance of Van Vechten's novel, adding "I never saw [his] book until the late spring of 1927. . . . And by that time I had nearly completed *Home to Harlem*." See *A Long Way from Home*, 217.
129. Dorothy Parker, "Big Blonde" (1929), in *The Portable Dorothy Parker*, 187.
130. Claude McKay, letter to Max Eastman, likely May 1933, Claude McKay Papers, Lilly Library Manuscripts Collection, Indiana University, Bloomington.
131. Wayne F. Cooper, 288.
132. Clifton Fadiman, letter to Max Eastman, Sept. 12 1933, Claude McKay Papers, James Weldon Johnson Collection, Beinecke Rare Book and Manuscript Library, Yale University, New Haven.
133. Ibid.
134. *A Long Way from Home*, 193.
135. Ibid., 192.
136. Ibid., 193.
137. Ibid.
138. *Romance in Marseille*, 19.
139. DuBose Heyward, *Porgy*, New York: George H. Doran, 1925, 12.
140. See Ernest Hemingway, *A Moveable Feast* (1964), New York: Scribner, 2010, 15.
141. See Harold Jackman, letter to McKay, June 3, 1927, Claude McKay Papers, James Weldon Johnson Collection, Beinecke Rare Book and Manuscript Library, Yale University, New Haven.
142. See Thomas C. Mackey, *Pornography on Trial: A Handbook with Cases, Laws, and Documents*, Denver: ABC-Clio, 2002, 154.
143. Claude McKay, letter to Max Eastman, 28 June 1933, Claude McKay Papers, Lilly Library Manuscripts Collection, Indiana University, Bloomington.
144. Ibid.
145. Claude McKay, quoted in Wayne F. Cooper, 288.
146. Ibid.
147. Ibid.
148. James Weldon Johnson, quoted in Wayne F. Cooper, 289.

149. *A Long Way from Home*, 261. Thanks to Jack Bruno for noting the reference. See also Nancy Cunard, ed., *Negro: An Anthology*, London: Wishart & Co., 1934.

CHAPTER ONE

1. Lafala: A would-be West African name, as the introduction discusses, derived from the name of the character Taloufa in McKay's earlier Marseille novel *Banjo* (1929). "Lafala" is also possibly tailored from either or both of the Arabic words "fallah"/"fellah" (فلاح), meaning peasant, and "falah," roughly meaning success and well-being. The latter is employed in the daily Islamic call to prayer, which McKay heard often while living in Morocco. Perhaps not coincidentally, over the course of the novel, Lafala rises from something of a peasant to something of a great success—neither, however, as measured in Islamic terms. In any event, his African/Arabic moniker predicts his union with Aslima, a black Moroccan prostitute with a more definitely Arabic name.

2. fine bodies supported by strong gleaming legs: Lafala's tribal memory ironically echoes protagonist Jake Brown's praise of the women of modern black New York in McKay's earlier novel *Home to Harlem* (1928): "'Oh, them legs!' Jake thought. 'Them tantalizing brown legs!'" (8). The reverence of Lafala and his people for physical vitality—a vitality he fears he has lost forever—reflects a dominant theme of the Harlem Renaissance expressed in the work of Langston Hughes, Sterling Brown, Zora Neale Hurston, and others as well as McKay. New Negro authors created portraits of black beauty and robustness, both modern and "primitive," to combat racist myths of black ugliness and physical incapacity.

3. "The Moonshine Kid": The title of this tune, and its association with the erotic pleasures of community, foreshadows Babel's "Moonstruck" song, performed at Marseille's Café Tout-va-Bien in chapter 21.

4. from Africa to Europe, from Europe to America: This passage, among many others in *Romance in Marseille*, may be read through the lens of historian Paul Gilroy's influential theory of a Black Atlantic "counterculture of modernity" in which transnational black identities emerged with the assistance of new technologies of culture and transportation, first among them

rapid transatlantic shipping. Gilroy notes that McKay's own involvement with ships and sailors—he worked as a stoker on at least one ocean journey from New York to Liverpool—offers "support to [Peter] Linebaugh's prescient suggestion that 'the ship remained perhaps the most important conduit of Pan-African communication before the appearance of the long-playing record.'" See Paul Gilroy, *The Black Atlantic: Modernity and Double Consciousness*, Cambridge, MA: Harvard University Press, 1995, 13.

5. It was a time of universal excitement after the war and . . . a dark cry of "Back to Africa" came over the air: McKay here describes the enthusiasm for African origins and Pan-African politics that surged among blacks in the United States, the Caribbean, and elsewhere in the New World after the Great War. It took shape in the populist "Back to Africa" movement of the Universal Negro Improvement Association (UNIA), a group led by McKay's fellow Jamaican Marcus Garvey (1887–1940), and in the international Pan-African Congress of black diplomats and intellectuals first organized by W. E. B. Du Bois (1868–1963) and Ida Gibbs (1862–1957), the initial meeting of which was held in Paris in 1919. See Hakim Adi, *Pan-Africanism: A History*, London: Bloomsbury, 2018.

6. "WC": A water closet or room containing a flush toilet.

7. "Race ain't nothing in this heah hoggish scramble": The "ain't" in this sentence, missing in McKay's original but clearly intended given the context, was inserted by the editors.

CHAPTER TWO

1. girdles: Lafala's girdles are belts or sashes worn across the waist that pay tribute to his West African birthplace. In an effort at cross-cultural sympathy, his Jewish lawyer compares Lafala's handiwork to the girdles once worn by members of the Twelve Tribes of ancient Israel.

CHAPTER THREE

1. Morris chair: A type of solid, wood-and-leather reclining chair first sold by the Arts and Crafts designer William Morris (1834–1896) around 1866.

CHAPTER FOUR

1. *Bellows of the Belt*: Likely a parodic version of *The Inter-State Tattler*, a black-owned Harlem gossip sheet and society newspaper published in "off-color" blue ink between 1925 and 1932, the height of the Harlem Renaissance.

2. *United Negro*: As noted in the introduction, probably a lampoon of the Garvey movement's weekly newspaper, *The Negro World*, which ran from 1919 to 1933. Based in New York and "Devoted Solely to the Interests of the Negro Race," as its masthead declared, the *Negro World* reached up to 200,000 subscribers at its peak, complementing its worldly name with international distribution and regular sections printed in French and Spanish.

3. C.U.N.T. (Christian Unity of Negro Tribes): As the introduction observes, in part an undisciplined swipe at the NAACP, the National Association for the Advancement of Colored People, the leading U.S. civil rights organization launched in 1909. The NAACP's widely circulated monthly magazine, *The Crisis*, was from 1910 to 1934 edited by W. E. B. Du Bois, a vocal critic of McKay's deliberately bourgeois-shocking fiction. McKay hailed *The Souls of Black Folk* (1903), but took Du Bois to task in print for "sneering" at the Russian Revolution, which the younger black writer once went on record to defend as "the greatest event in the history of humanity." See Wayne F. Cooper, *Claude McKay: Rebel Sojourner in the Harlem Renaissance*, Baton Rouge: Louisiana State University Press, 1987, 140–141. In "Back in Harlem," a chapter of his 1937 memoir *A Long Way from Home*, McKay notes that he admired the NAACP stalwarts James Weldon Johnson and Mary White Ovington. But he mocks Walter White, the organization's well-connected assistant executive secretary, for his surname and light complexion, and Jessie Fauset, the literary editor of *The Crisis*, for her "fastidious and precious" novels. In the end, McKay seconds Hubert Harrison's often-quoted radical view of the NAACP as the "National Association for the Advancement of Certain People." See *A Long Way from Home*, 90–92. As the misogynous thrust of "C.U.N.T." indicates, McKay's pseudo-organization also takes unsubtle aim at the historical prominence of women in the African American church and at middle-class black women's groups such as the National Association of Colored Women's Clubs (NACWC), its motto "lifting as we climb," founded by the educator and activist Mary Church Terrell (1863–1954) in 1896.

4. Nubian Orphanage: Nubia, a domain along the Nile River, was home to one of the oldest civilizations of Africa, born as early as 2500 BCE and extending from Khartoum to Aswan. The racial identity of its people, who ruled Egypt in the eighth and seventh centuries BCE, has been debated by ancient and modern scholars. In African American slang, however, the term "Nubian" came to refer to a dark-skinned person of (definitely) sub-Saharan African ancestry. Hence the butt of McKay's satire: this is a "Black Belt" orphanage operating under the blackest of names that refuses to embrace black children. McKay may be targeting one actual orphanage in particular, the Colored Orphan Asylum (COA), founded in 1836 by three white Quaker women. The COA, located in Harlem at the turn of the twentieth century, in fact took in black orphans unable to find shelter in other institutions but long refused to promote black staff beyond menial positions. See Catharine Reef, *Alone in the World: Orphans and Orphanages in America*, New York: Clarion, 2005, 13.

5. He did not belong to any of the two free states . . . and was therefore either a colonial subject or a protected person: By 1914, the close of the European imperial "scramble for Africa," only two never-colonized "free states" remained on the African continent: Liberia and Ethiopia, the latter a central concern of the posthumously discovered McKay novel *Amiable with Big Teeth* (2017). Lafala, his place of birth reminiscent of the "British sphere" of Nigeria but never specified, is not a native of either of these two holdout states, and is thus "a colonial subject or a protected person" of one of the fifteen European powers which divided up or parceled out Africa at the Congress of Berlin in 1884.

CHAPTER SIX

1. a Pyrrhic victory . . . to Aslima: A Pyrrhic victory is one so costly for the winner that it is tantamount to a defeat. Named after King Pyrrhus of the Hellenistic state of Epirus, who defeated the Romans in two great battles during the 280–275 BCE Pyrrhic War yet saw his army destroyed in the process.

CHAPTER SEVEN

1. Marseille lay bare to the glory of the meridian sun: Marseille, the second-largest city in France in McKay's era and ours, is a

major Mediterranean port that recorded a population of 800,801 in 1931, around the time of McKay's writing; Paris, by contrast, was then home to 2,891,020 people, more than two million more. Established as the Greek colonial outpost of Massalia, Marseille remains a port of empire in McKay's imagination, the seaside hub where Metropolitan France, and by extension Europe, communicates with its black and Islamic colonies. It also beckons as an international black crossroads, a not-just-Francophone refuge where one could live among "Negroids from the United States, the West Indies, North Africa and West Africa, all herded together in a warm group" (McKay, *A Long Way from Home*, 213). Both traditionally and in McKay's *Romance*, Marseille is associated with revolutionary history (the rallying march of the French Revolution that became the French national anthem is of course "La Marseillaise"); with the hot, dry climate of Provence (dictated by "the glory of the meridian sun"); and with an outsider culture of regional independence and self-organized crime centered on the bars and brothels of the city's *Vieux Port* or "Old Port" (often called "Quayside," home to the "peddler and prostitute, pimp and panhandler" [29], in McKay's novel).

2. Aslima: A transliteration of the female Arabic name تسليما—"Taslima" is the more common version—that can mean "greeting" or "salutation." In a now lost, initial draft of the novel, Aslima is "Zhima."

3. La Fleur Noire: As the introduction notes, French for "the Black Flower," and perhaps a tip of the hat to the decadent proto-modernism of Charles Baudelaire's *Les Fleurs du Mal* (1857), or *The Flowers of Evil*, which McKay read in the original French.

4. prinked herself up: Adorned or dressed herself with the intention to preen.

5. the rubicund's face: In other words, the face of the rubicund—or blooming and full-blooded—gentleman. McKay goes on to employ this nominalization of the adjective "rubicund" several other times.

6. pianola: A type of mechanical player piano, introduced in the 1880s, that lost ground to the gramophone beginning in the 1920s.

7. Café Tout-va-Bien: French for the "Café Where Everything's Fine," a description not always true of this main "rendezvous of the colored colony" (31) in McKay's novel.

8. Diup: "Diop," close to McKay's variant, is a common surname in Senegal and Gambia. To take just one example, Cheikh Anta Diop (1923–1986) was a Senegalese historian whose studies of

trans-African cultural continuities helped to inspire Afrocentric thought in the United States.

9. spumante: A sparkling white Italian wine produced through the "*méthode champenoise*," or method of secondary fermentation, sometimes favored as a less expensive alternative to certified French Champagne.

10. "La Reine Fleur!": French for "the Flower Queen," here said mockingly of La Fleur Noire by her rival Aslima.

11. when he handed her money, she obstinately refused it: Aslima's refusal to accept Lafala's money for sex recalls an early incident in McKay's first published novel, *Home to Harlem* (1928), when the prostitute Felice returns to the protagonist Jake Brown the fifty dollars she had demanded for a night of love the evening before. "'Just a little gift from a baby girl to a honey boy!'" Felice writes on a note pinned to the cash (16). Realizing that he is as especially fond of Felice as she is of him, Jake spends the rest of the novel searching for her "leaf-like face" tinted "to a ravishing chestnut" in city crowds (11). When he finds her at last, back home in Harlem, the two quickly cohere as a couple and, after a contrived misunderstanding, prepare to shove off for Chicago in the final scene. In *Romance in Marseille*, by contrast, Aslima's gesture of refusing payment from Lafala may be calculated to produce a bigger payoff, at least initially, and is not fully reciprocated. Near the end of this later novel, a cash-rich, love-poor Lafala shoves off for Africa on his own.

12. Titin: A name possibly derived from the gigantic Titans of Greek mythology, somewhat appropriate given Titin's birth on Corsica, a Mediterranean, if not Greek, island, and his reputation as one of Quayside's toughest pimps.

CHAPTER EIGHT

1. stoker: Someone who does the hot, dirty, and difficult job of tending a furnace on a steamship or elsewhere. When perhaps the most famous black poet in the English-speaking world, McKay worked as a ship's stoker to pay part of his way from New York to Moscow in 1922. Jake Brown, McKay's protagonist in *Home to Harlem*, enters the novel as a replacement stoker on a freighter from Cardiff to New York. But Richard Wright's Bigger Thomas, the protagonist of the blunt-force *Native Son* (1940), is the best remembered and most politically pointed stoker-type in African American literature.

2. "all your Lynchburgs in the States": Not just a reference to Lynchburg, Virginia, and Lynchburg, Tennessee, and other towns named Lynchburg in the United States, but a punning generic term for the many locations in the American South where African Americans were lynched, or subjected to extra-judicial killing.

3. bistro: A type of small, modest restaurant, selling alcohol and home-style food, born in Paris in the nineteenth century. As the context of this use indicates, the Café Tout-va-Bien has some characteristics of a bistro as well as a café.

4. "split": Rock and Diup attempt, to the tune of comic asides on the differences between male and female anatomies, to do the split, or "splits," a difficult, gymnastic dance move in which one lowers quickly to the floor with legs held at right angles.

5. the *apéritif* hour: The hour for *apéritifs*, or pre-dinner alcoholic drinks. Common choices for such drinks, meant to rouse the appetite, would in Marseille include vermouth, champagne, and other sparkling wines, and *pastis*, the anise-flavored spirit especially identified with the city. *Digestifs*, in opposition to aperitifs, are taken after the meal is through.

6. habitués: A French term, assimilated into English, for regular, habituated patrons.

7. "'Toujours'": "Always," in French, and here a song title. Perhaps a reference to the hit ballad "L'Amour, Toujours L'Amour," or "Love Everlasting," written by Rudolph Friml, introduced in a 1922 musical, and frequently recorded in the 1920s and 1930s.

8. "the jolly pig": Aslima's dance in imitation of a jolly pig embellishes a long line of flirtatious baby talk in the novel in which she and Lafala compare their erotic satisfaction to the happiness of "sweet" and "darling" pigs. Both they and McKay, then, flout the Islamic prohibition on the consumption of pork, and the letter of Islamic law in general. See this verse, among others, from the Quran: "Allah has forbidden you only carrion, and blood, and the flesh of swine . . ." (16: 115).

9. "Halouf!": A French word, extracted from an Arabic source (حَلُّوف), meaning "pork," and emphasizing the uncleanliness of this meat.

10. Cardiff: The capital city of Wales since 1955, and, beginning in the nineteenth century, a major Atlantic seaport built to facilitate the transportation of coal.

11. cerise: In English, a shade of bright, deep red. In French, the equivalent of "cherry."

12. "pea-eye": As in "P-I," short for "pimp," used in Harlem slang of the 1920s.

13. "*métier*": French for a job, trade, or specialized skill. Aslima's employment of the word suggests that she sees pimping as a line of work much like any other.

14. "Lalla": "Lady," in Berber; a title of respect meaning "Lord" as well as "Lady" used to refer to women in the Moroccan nobility who are descended from the Prophet Muhammad and one of the ten Moroccan noble families; and/or one of "the most widespread terms for a female saint in Morocco." See Issachar Ben-Ami, *Saint Veneration among the Jews in Morocco*, Detroit: Wayne State University Press, 1988, 21. Whichever resonance Aslima intends, she employs the term ironically.

CHAPTER NINE

1. Marrakesh: A Moroccan city founded in 1062 that is set between the Atlas Mountains and the Sahara Desert. McKay, perhaps thinking of its shimmering *khettera*, or ancient irrigation channels, compares the city to "jewels of wild tropical extravagance" (44). Marrakesh impressed McKay as Morocco's most "Negroid" city, a depot of the African slave trade transformed into something "like a big West Indian picnic, with flags waving and a multitude of barefoot black children dancing to the flourish of the drum, fiddle, and fife" (*A Long Way from Home*, 234). If McKay's Morocco can be said to contain a version of McKay's Marseille, then Marrakesh is it. Interestingly, McKay's memoir *A Long Way from Home* observes that it was "the Senegalese in Marseilles [who] often mentioned Marrakesh as the former great *caravansérai* [sic] for the traders traveling between West Africa and North Africa" (234). The affair between Lafala and Aslima symbolically travels between these African regions as well. The third-person narrator's impressionistic guide to Marrakesh and other touchstones in Aslima's past shows McKay's Afro-Orientalism in full bloom. For more of this charmed, fascinated, and exoticizing mode, see McKay's "Cities" poems "Tanger," "Fez," "Marrakesh," "Tetuan," and "Xauen," written around 1934 and collected in his *Complete Poems*, 225–228. And see part six, "The Idylls of Africa," in McKay's memoir *A Long Way from Home*, 227–260.

2. Djemaa el-Fna: A large square and bazaar in the medina quarter, or old city, of Marrakesh, also transliterated from Arabic as

"Jemaa el-Fnaa." Known as "the largest market in Africa," the Djemaa el-Fna's traditional animal trainers, storytellers, and musicians inspired the United Nations to establish the UNESCO Masterpieces of the Oral and Intangible Heritage of Humanity program in 2001.

3. muezzin: One appointed to call Muslims to prayer, often from the minaret of a mosque.

4. marabouts: Muslim religious teachers or wandering holy men, as in Sufi Murshids or guides. Often expert in the Quran, marabouts have been prominent in West Africa, especially Senegambia, and in Morocco and other areas of the Maghreb.

5. hetairai: The hetairai, from the ancient Greek for "female companions," were a class of prostitutes permitted to educate themselves and live apart from male supervision. Though often slaves and foreigners, like Aslima, they were in certain respects, like La Fleur, less housebound and more self-determining than married Attic women. Pablo Picasso, whose Blue Period precedes McKay's novel in its fascination with evocative prostitutes, painted a portrait of a bold, gem-wearing courtesan titled *L'Hétaïre* in 1901. McKay's typescript of the completed *Romance in Marseille* employs the somewhat mistaken term "hetairiti."

6. Fez: An older city than Marrakesh, founded in 808. Thanks to its prestigious Al Quaraouiyine mosque and university, the latter one of the world's oldest continually operating institutions of higher education, Fez became Morocco's earliest spiritual and cultural capital. In his series of "Cities" poems, written in the early 1930s, McKay praised Fez as "Baghdad / In Africa" (1–2), a place of "labyrinthine lanes and crooked souks, / And costumes hooding beauty from men's sight" (3–4). See the poem "Fez" in McKay's *Complete Poems*, 226.

7. Moulay Abdallah: Once a government center under the Marinid dynasty, this quarter of Fez was dotted with brothels and dancehalls and largely closed to foreigners during McKay's time in Morocco.

8. Moorish rugs: Prized rugs in the style of the nomadic North African Muslims who invaded Spain in 711, a people conventionally thought black by Europeans, as in William Shakespeare's *The Tragedy of Othello, the Moor of Venice* (1603). McKay may hope that these rugs underline the complexity of Aslima's mixed black-Arab identity: her mother, *Romance* tells us, was a Sudanese sold as a slave to the Moors.

9. Casablanca: The largest city in Morocco, a port located on the Atlantic coast, Casablanca has long been an economic capital

of the Maghreb. Casablanca was attacked and occupied by French forces in 1907; at the time of McKay's writing, the city was formally colonized, and almost half of the city's population was European.

10. a young Corsican: A young person from Corsica, a mountainous island in the Mediterranean Sea, variously occupied by the Italians, the British, and the French, the last of whom were granted formal control at the Congress of Vienna in 1815. Marseille, from its establishment, contained a significant number of Corsican immigrants, but McKay may have chosen a Corsican origin for Titin because the island's most significant product was Napoléon Bonaparte, born there to a family of minor Italian nobility in 1769. In his fondest, wildest dreams, Titin is a similarly brave conqueror of the wealth and women of France and its possessions.

11. a romantic sheik picture: McKay refers to the Rudolph Valentino silent film sensation The Sheik, directed by George Melford and released by Paramount Pictures in 1921, or possibly its sequel, The Son of the Sheik, also starring Valentino, directed by George Fitzmaurice for United Artists in 1926. In the shorter, earlier Beinecke Library-held version of Romance in Marseille, the sheik picture indeed features Valentino. The finished version of Romance joins both films in relying on an Orientalist palette to paint a racially mixed, erotically charged North African scene.

12. "Pied-Coupé": Sing-song French—the second and fourth syllables are both pronounced "AY" [eɪ], and thus rhyme—for "Chopped-Off Foot," or, less literally, "Stumpy." This is Titin's consistent, abusive nickname for the amputated Lafala. Thanks to the Francophone scholars Jean-Christophe Cloutier, Brent Hayes Edwards, Andrea Goulet, Musa Gurnis, Jane Kuntz, Gayle Levy, and Allan Pero for their help with this and other French terms.

13. "And who're you kidding with that open knife, yourself or me?": The resemblance between George Bizet's opera Carmen (1875) and this scene of a spirited "gypsy" seductress, a jealous three-way entanglement, and a promise of tragic lovers' violence is not strictly accidental. In his 1937 memoir, McKay mentions attending a Parisian Opéra Comique production of Carmen in Toulon in the mid-1920s. See A Long Way from Home, 196. Aslima deepens her resemblance to the character Carmen by dancing flamenco in chapter 19.

14. mulcting: Swindling or defrauding.

CHAPTER TEN

1. yearly festivities: Probably a reference to the annual celebration of Bastille Day, called *"la Fête nationale"* in France, that commemorates a turning point of the French Revolution, the storming of the Bastille prison in Paris on July 14, 1789. Bastille Day festivities in Marseille's Vieux Port are traditionally among the most spectacular in the country, with the holiday in the city spanning several days and including parades, music, and folk-dancing, all represented in McKay's rendition.

2. "beguine": A "beguine," in this sense, is a crush or attraction, as in the French expression *J'ai le béguin pour toi* ("I've got a crush on you"). While the use of the word in this way may date from the Middle Ages, "beguine" also refers to a form of dance and music originated by African-descended people in the French colonies of Martinique and Guadeloupe, its rhythm compared to the rhumba and bolero. In *Romance*, a novel featuring several Martiniquais characters and repeated references to the musical beguine, McKay plays a running, punning game with the two meanings of the term. A few years later, so did the American composer Cole Porter, who legendarily wrote the song "Begin the Beguine" (1935) as a paying customer on a Cunard ocean liner.

3. "when them redskins wouldn't stand being good an' native them ofays had to import us to implace them": Lafala's African American friend Rock laughs to keep from crying about the historical replacement of Native American slaves with imported African captives—the former common in Virginia, for example, between the founding of Jamestown and the end of the eighteenth century. Rock calls white European settlers "ofays," using the African American slang term taken from the Pig Latin translation of "foes."

4. Vin Mousseux: A sparkling French white wine not necessarily produced in the Champagne region in the northeast of France. Like Italian spumante, it is served in the Tout-va-Bien as a cheaper stand-in for true champagne.

5. castaneting her fingers: Moving her fingers as if playing the castanets, small percussion instruments resembling concave shells used by singers and dancers in Spanish folk music, among other styles. Castanets evoke a Spanish atmosphere in the music of Georges Bizet's opera *Carmen* (1875), a significant influence on the plot of *Romance in Marseille*.

6. "'I'm not a Senegambian,' said Lafala": The proprietor of the Tout-va-Bien derisively links Lafala with the royalty of Dakar, the

largest city in Senegal, but Lafala quickly specifies that he is not a Senegambian, a resident of the area of West Africa comprising not just Senegal but also Guinea-Bissau and the Gambia.

CHAPTER ELEVEN

1. serviettes: Napkins—in this case, especially unsanitary ones.
2. a loving feast: Like other aspects of Aslima's dream or vision of "The Sword of Life!," a grandiose prophecy of her love and martyrdom for Lafala, the "loving feast" embroiders and secularizes Islamic tropes and traditions. In this case, the tradition is Iftar, a fast-breaking meal eaten after sunset during the Muslim holy month of Ramadan.

CHAPTER TWELVE

1. the Domino: With some dose of irony, McKay seems to have named this Marseille café patronized by pimps in mind of a haunt of revolutionary artists in the Soviet Union. In his 1923 essay "Soviet Russia and the Negro," McKay recalls visiting the Domino, a Moscow café where young Mensheviks and amateur anarchists shared their poetry and other writings. See *The Crisis* 27 (December 1923): 61–65.
2. a Levantine sort of person: A sort of person hailing from the Levant, in the largest sense a loose cultural region of the eastern Mediterranean stretching from Greece to Libya. McKay may also or instead be thinking of the "Levant States," a term used to refer to Syria and Lebanon in the wake of the French mandate granted after World War I.

CHAPTER THIRTEEN

1. "guillotine": The machine for efficient beheading—thought more humane than the ax—introduced during the French Revolution. It remained France's means of legal execution until the country abolished capital punishment in 1981.
2. the golden age of her people conquering all that . . . earth between the Pillars of Hercules and Marseille: Aslima here identifies with the Moors, the enslavers of her mother, and recalls their emergence from Africa and conquest of Portugal

and Spain that began in 711 in sight of the Pillars of Hercules, promontories in the Strait of Gibraltar. The Moors were turned back from west-central France at the Battle of Tours in 732.

3. a legend that the cathedral was built on the site of a mosque . . . [and] a silent prayer that the lost dominions of her people might be restored: Aslima quietly recalls the legend that Marseille's iconic Notre-Dame de la Garde (Our Lady of the Guard), a Catholic basilica sitting on the highest point of the city overlooking the Vieux Port, replaced a Moorish mosque built over the body of a Muslim holy man. European historians believe that the first version of the Notre-Dame was constructed on the limestone foundations of an ancient fort in 1214; the heavily touristed, Neo-Byzantine structure prized by Aslima, topped with a 135-foot-tall bell tower, was finished in 1864. Her "silent prayer," along with other elements in this scene, indicates that Aslima has come to cast her struggle with Titin as one between Islamic and Christian civilizations.

4. The official's sentiment towards Negroes was based upon *Uncle Tom's Cabin* and David Livingstone: The official's sentiment is therefore built on the antiquated, patronizing forms of nineteenth-century Christian abolitionism expressed in *Uncle Tom's Cabin*, the consequential 1852 antislavery novel by the American Harriet Beecher Stowe (1811–1896), and in the restless African explorations of the Scotsman David Livingstone (1813–1873). Before he shook hands with the journalist Henry Morton Stanley on the shore of Lake Tanganyika in 1871, Livingstone had crisscrossed the continent as a representative of the London Missionary Society, hoping to end the slave trade while converting African souls to Christianity and European-style commerce.

CHAPTER FOURTEEN

1. Seaman's and Workers' Club: This club is modeled on Marseille's Communist-sponsored "International Seamen's Building," a favorite of Lamine Senghor, McKay's Senegalese Communist friend, as the introduction explains. The shorter, Beinecke Library version of *Romance in Marseille* refers to the club as the "Proletarian Hall," a name that, in contrast, highlights its Marxist mission.

2. following the era of the Russian Revolution: McKay ties the formation of Marseille's Seaman's Club, and others elsewhere like it, to the overthrow of Russia's czarist government and the Bolshevik seizure of power in October 1917. Such local radical

institutions were sometimes supported or controlled by the Communist International, or Comintern, a worldwide association of national Communist parties directed from Moscow and founded by Vladimir I. Lenin in 1919.

3. mistral wind: The cold wind that blows with great force—at an average rate of forty-five miles per hour—from the Rhône Valley to the Mediterranean Sea, particularly in the winter, and with special power in Marseille.

4. Etienne St. Dominique: The significance of St. Dominique's name—shared in part by François-Dominique Toussaint Louverture (1743–1803), the military hero of the Haitian Revolution—is discussed at some length in the introduction.

5. brasserie: A type of French eating place more formal than a café or bistro, and thus fancier than the Tout-va-Bien, but still more relaxed than a full-fledged restaurant. Revealingly, "brasserie" also means "brewery" in French.

6. Falope Sbaye: "Falope" is a given name, roughly meaning "thanksgiving," among the Yoruba people of southwestern Nigeria and Benin. It is an appropriate choice for this character, a clerk in a coastal trading business from West Africa.

7. an impressive magnified photograph of Lenin on the right of which there was a smaller one of Karl Marx: Vladimir I. Lenin (1870–1924), the Volga-born Russian revolutionary, initiator of Bolshevism, and founding father of both the Soviet Union and the Communist International, here takes visual and ideological precedence over Karl Marx (1818–1883), the exiled philosopher, historian, economist, and German revolutionary who was the single greatest intellectual influence on modern socialism and communism. McKay, then a Communist who admired what he perceived as Lenin's "simple voice and presence," pulled all the strings in his possession to meet the great Bolshevik when traveling through the Soviet Union in the early 1920s, but was unable to speak with him. Leon Trotsky (1879–1940), the People's Commissar of War, was more obliging, asking McKay "straight and sharp questions about American Negroes. . . ." See McKay's *A Long Way from Home*, 124, 160.

8. "Workers of the World, Unite to Break Your Chains!": An often-quoted digest of the final three lines of Karl Marx and Friedrich Engels' *The Communist Manifesto* (1848), whose most influential English translation closes with this peroration: "The proletarians have nothing to lose but their chains. They have a world to win. Working Men of All Countries, Unite!"

9. "Is it the same as the Back-to-Africa organization?" . . . That was the only movement that had penetrated his ears in the portholes: Lafala wonders if Communism is the same as "Back-to-Africa" Garveyism, the latter depicted by McKay as the radical movement with the better ability to communicate with black sailors. St. Dominique, *Romance*'s specimen Communist, genuinely respects, enjoys, and assists Marseille's black workers, but is a soft-handed, soft-spoken intellectual who makes few converts. So is the president of the Seaman's Club, "a very polite person from the middle class" who "had been a professor" (76).

CHAPTER FIFTEEN

1. Babel: Babel's name evokes the biblical story of the Babylonian city, in which Noah's descendants began building a tower that would reach into heaven. For the sin of their presumption, their single, common language was splintered into many, and they were scattered across the earth. See *Genesis* (11.1–9). Though the opinions of McKay's Babel sometimes speak for the Quayside community as a whole, his name reminds us of the linguistic divisions among Marseille's blacks, and of the forced diaspora that dispersed Africans around the Atlantic world.

2. Genoa: Sitting on the Ligurian Sea, Genoa is the chief port of Italy and one of the busiest of the Mediterranean. Nicknamed "La Superba," or the Proud One, the city is the (assumed) birthplace of Christopher Columbus (1451–1506), the Italian explorer who led the first European excursions to the Caribbean and Central and South America. Babel's canny, frustrating, and partially stowaway ocean journey reverses the path of Columbus with a twist.

3. East-of-Suez rate: The East-of-Suez rate would be one less fair than that offered to a largely European crew—the phrase "East of Suez," chiefly British, referred to the non-European theater of empire east of the Suez Canal in Egypt. Rudyard Kipling, whose collection *Barrack-Room Ballads* (1892) was a somewhat guilty sourcebook for McKay's Jamaican dialect poetry, popularized the phrase in his poem "Mandalay" (1890): "Ship me somewheres east of Suez, where the best is like the worst, / Where there ain't no Ten Commandments an' a man can raise a thirst" (43–44). See Peter Washington, ed., *Kipling: Poems*,

New York: Everyman's Library-Alfred A. Knopf, 2007, 49–51. In the opening pages of *Home to Harlem*, Jake Brown, steaming back to New York from the Great War as a stoker, is said to "despise the Arabs" with whom he works because of their "way of eating" (2). Yet when a white sailor attempts to establish a comradeship based on mutual distaste for "dirty jabbering coolies," Jake demurs: "He knew that if he was just like the white sailors, he might have signed on as a deckhand and not as a stoker" (3).

4. "coolie crew": A crew of sailors from Asia, described using a derogatory term—"coolie"—that emerged in South Asia in the seventeenth century. Such a crew, Babel suspects, would be paid at the "East-of-Suez rate" whatever the initial guarantee.

5. "a darter of a dawg": A daughter of a dog, in distinction to a son of a bitch.

6. one of those miniature republics . . . in the Spanish Main: One of those small states, created from former possessions of Spain's New World empire, in Central America or the north coast of South America.

CHAPTER SIXTEEN

1. Latin peoples: Those peoples with native modern languages derived from Latin, including the French, Spanish, Italian, and Portuguese—and, as McKay conceives it, the Corsicans.

2. a woman whose card of identity was the yellow one of prostitution: Prostitutes in Marseille and elsewhere in France were licensed by the national government and asked to carry identity cards—*cartes d'identité*—noting their profession. Such official recognition, ordered by Napoléon in 1804, came at a price. As Titin's comment suggests, "once a woman was registered, it was difficult for her to resume legitimate work" or to alter her social identity. See Rachel G. Fuchs, *Gender and Poverty in Nineteenth-Century Europe*, New York: Cambridge University Press, 2005, 193.

3. whoreson: A bastard son of a whore or prostitute. Nearly as unflatteringly, "whoreson" can also refer to a wretch or scoundrel.

4. "*une jeune fille de famille*": French for "a young family girl," or, more precisely, a young girl from a decent and respectable family.

CHAPTER SEVENTEEN

1. like a hero straight out of Joseph Conrad, an outstanding enigma of Quayside: Like a hero from the pages of Joseph Conrad (1857–1924), the great realist-to-modernist author of *Heart of Darkness* (1899) and *The Secret Agent* (1907). Conrad's Polish origins, like McKay's birth in Jamaica, helped to make him a perceptive participant-observer of English society and English prose. In tune with McKay's Marseille fictions, several of Conrad's best-known novels employ nautical settings and characters to explore the social and psychological effects of European imperialism. McKay may well be thinking of one famously enigmatic Conrad character in particular, the eponymous hero of the novel *Lord Jim* (1900), in describing the enigmatic Big Blonde. Akin to Lord Jim, McKay's oddly refined dockworker is strong, light-haired, and quick with his fists, in flight from crimes that may have cost him his "respectable position in the merchant service" (95). Much as Conrad's hero retreats from shameful tragedy aboard the *Patna* to a Malay island in the South China Sea, Big Blonde flees from an American ship or port to bury his mysterious guilt amid the variously "colonized" people of Marseille's black Quayside.

2. Sometimes he was jailed for a short term; sometimes he went into hiding: One of several stretches of tough-guy, telegraphic narration in *Romance in Marseille* that demonstrate the influence of Ernest Hemingway's direct, pared-down style. The prose of McKay's previous novels *Home to Harlem* (1928) and *Banjo* (1929) is on average more lyrical and less staccato, its rhythms stamped by the quite different muse of D. H. Lawrence. For more on the shape of McKay's admiration for Hemingway, see the introduction.

3. Petit Frère: This French nickname for Big Blonde's friend and lover means "Little Brother." For the remainder of *Romance in Marseille*, young, effeminate gay men may be called *petit frères*, or "little brothers," in McKay's Quayside idiom.

4. demi-johns: Glass bottles with narrow necks and wide bodies sometimes covered with wicker, from the French *dame-jeanne*, or "Lady Jane." In Britain, a standard demi-john contains 4.5 liters—an imperial gallon—of beer or another liquid.

5. political secret police: As noted in the introduction, the political secret police plot of *Romance in Marseille*, ultimately revealed as a red herring, makes hay from McKay's frightening run-ins with

French and British agents in Morocco. For more on these run-ins, see Wayne F. Cooper's biography *Claude McKay: Rebel Sojourner in the Harlem Renaissance*, Baton Rouge: Louisiana State University Press, 1987, 278–279. McKay's American FBI file, international in scope and the first compiled on a major black author, is discussed in Gary Edward Holcomb's *Claude McKay, Code Name Sasha*, Gainesville: University Press of Florida, 2007. It can be read in full at William J. Maxwell's online *F.B. Eyes Digital Archive* (http://digital.wustl.edu/fbeyes/).

6. *bal-musette*: A popular type of café or bar, first found in Paris in the 1880s, in which patrons danced tangos and *"bourrées"* to the sound of an accordion or musette, an instrument of the bagpipe family. The (originally) working-class dancers and musicians of *bal-musettes* were painted by Pablo Picasso (1881–1973), Georges Valmier (1885–1937), and other French-based modernist artists. In addition to this visual inspiration, the *bal-musette* may have appealed to McKay as the indigenous French equivalent of the jazz club.

7. cache-col: French for a scarf or muffler, in this instance worn with style.

8. the loving omelettes: Not a tender breakfast, but apparently McKay's humorous coinage for a style of close dancing. Like the eggs in an omelet, beaten together into a single mass, the pajama-clad girls sharing this dance seem to blend into each other indistinguishably.

CHAPTER EIGHTEEN

1. And through St. Dominique he had obtained a few pieces of African wood sculpture . . . from some West African seamen: St. Dominique's white college friend, now a municipal clerk in Marseille, has become interested in his city's black population thanks to his passion for modern art. In this, he resembles the European modernist artists he admires, many of whom were enthralled by the traditional African art they first encountered in the early 1900s. In France, Henri Matisse (1869–1954), Pablo Picasso (1881–1973), and their colleagues in the School of Paris studied West and Central African masks and sculptures that offered lessons in abstraction, vivid stylization, and pictorial flatness. Examples of so-called *"art nègre"* could be seen at the Musée d'Ethnographie on the Trocadero near the Eiffel Tower, but McKay's municipal clerk joins Matisse, André Derain

(1880–1954), and the Belgian painter James Ensor (1860–1949) in purchasing African carvings for his own collection. McKay complained, sharply and precociously, about the unscrupulous and alienating display of African art in Western collections in his 1923 study *The Negroes in America*, written for Soviet use in the Soviet Union. The Benin bronzes in the British Museum, he charged, doubled as tokens "of British piracy, exploitation, and deceit. . . ." In the same book, McKay suggested that Fauvism, Cubism, and other Parisian avant-gardes were hatched by those who "followed the [French] tricolor into the African jungles and returned to Paris with samples of Negro art." See *The Negroes in America*, translated from the Russian by Robert J. Winter, Port Washington, NY: Kennikat, 1979, 56–57.

2. *Aframerican*: With its American emphasis, its fondness for generous author photographs, and its coupling of black art and black advancement, this magazine is reminiscent of the NAACP's *Crisis*, one of the two "chief journals of African American literature and criticism" during Harlem Renaissance. (According to George Hutchinson, the Urban League's *Opportunity* magazine was the other.) See Hutchinson's *The Harlem Renaissance in Black and White*, Cambridge, MA: Belknap-Harvard University Press, 1995, 127. Whatever the *Aframerican*'s inspirations, McKay carefully and self-referentially situates St. Dominique as a foreign survivor of the New Negro movement's American publicity apparatus.

3. "It's a matter of economic determinism—": St. Dominique, a Marxist, believes that the psychology of racially mixed "mulattoes," and of everyone else, is finally determined by economic relationships, the basis of all other social ideas and arrangements.

4. "It's a stinking proletarian case, from Marseille . . . to New York and back": Much as St. Dominique's Marxism leads him to view race consciousness as an economically determined matter, it instructs him to consider the case of Lafala's stowaway, amputation, and jailing as a "stinking proletarian case"—a case, that is, more closely linked to the victim's working-class identity than to his racial one.

CHAPTER NINETEEN

1. a radio set . . . at the same time as the pleasure-lovers of those places: The Tout-va-Bien's new radio instantly familiarizes

patrons with the popular song "masterpieces" introduced in the vaudeville houses of Broadway in New York, the theaters of Piccadilly in London, and the cabarets of Montmartre in Paris. This aside represents one McKay contribution to the deep vein of attacks by literary modernists on supposedly alienating new sound technologies, a vein running from T.S. Eliot's *The Waste Land* (1922) to Richard Wright's "Long Black Song" (1938). Guglielmo Marconi's design for a radio transmitter was first patented in the United States in 1901.

2. The craze of the Charleston and Black Bottom was about dead. . . . But the beguine was there, . . . the Aframerican shuffle and the African swaying: McKay's narrator observes that the fad for the Charleston, an African American–authored dance that peaked in the mid-1920s, had nearly passed at the Tout-va-Bien. (Whatever its legal status, this café sometimes serves as a showcase and blender of various national black dance styles.) The fad for the Black Bottom, a similarly exuberant African American dance, commercialized by the Broadway show *George White's Scandals of 1926,* had faded as well. (McKay's Pan-African Quayside, called "the Bottoms" in the first draft of *Romance,* is a different kind of black Bottom.) But the narrator notes that another black step, related to the most basic moves in African and "Aframerican" dance, survived to take their place. This was the beguine, the slow, rhumba-like dance style identified with the island of Martinique, St. Dominique's birthplace in the French Caribbean.

3. Aslima also felt the beguine for Lafala: For this alternative but still-music-related sense of "beguine," see the note for "beguine" in chapter 10.

4. Her primitive flamenco went naturally well with the music . . . revealing the African influence of both: Aslima may feel the beguine for Lafala, but she flaunts her love through the flamenco, among other things a highly syncopated, formally demanding dance form pioneered by Andalusian "gitanos," the Gypsy, or Roma, people of southern Spain. Aslima's "primitive" interpretation of the dance reveals its African ties and its kinship with the beguine. Modern scholarship has tracked McKay in detecting Moorish influences on flamenco.

5. "The Queen!": Embarrassing La Fleur, the patrons of the Tout-va-Bien elevate Aslima to royalty after her flamenco performance. Earlier, it was La Fleur who was hailed as "La Reine," or the Queen, if in jest.

CHAPTER TWENTY

1. nor the music of hymen . . . glorious like the songs of Solomon's loves: Nothing will keep Big Blonde from his date with Petit Frère—not "the music of hymen," erotic songs and poems celebrating marriage, as glorious as "the songs of Solomon's loves" found in the Hebrew Bible and the Old Testament. Solomon's songs in the *Song of Songs* or *Song of Solomon* celebrate, in intensely sensuous terms, the love between man and woman and of the Lord for his people. Big Blonde's love for his Little Brother is thus stronger than the most captivating literature of straight and sacred Eros.

2. the Grand Maquereau: French slang for "the Big Pimp." Less colloquially, a "maquereau" is, as it sounds, the fish known in English as "mackerel." Karl Marx included the exploitative, human sort of maquereaux in his famous roll call of bottom-dwelling types—the "maquereaux, brothel keepers, porters, literati," etc.—belonging to the so-called "lumpenproletariat," a political anxiety for Marx but for McKay a choice fictional subject. See Marx's *The Eighteenth Brumaire of Louis Bonaparte* (1852), New York: International Publishers, 1987, 75.

3. if Big Blonde was less interested in petit frères and more in petites filles: In other words, if Big Blonde was less attracted by little boys and more by little girls.

4. "What is this thing called love?" said Falope: Falope's question salutes Cole Porter's song "What Is This Thing Called Love?," an eventual jazz standard introduced in the musical *Wake Up and Dream* (1929). "What is this thing called love?" asks the first line of lyrics, "This funny thing called love?" (1–2). With this allusion, McKay rivals the radio-listening habitués of the Tout-va-Bien in rapidly absorbing the latest popular music. Porter claimed the tune was suggested by witnessing a native dance while visiting Marrakesh. See Charles Schwartz, *Cole Porter: A Biography*, New York: Dial Press, 1977, 143.

5. "it's five in mine," said St. Dominique: With "five in mine," St. Dominique points to the five letters in "amour," the word for love in his native French. The English word "rope," like "love," has four letters, a commonality Babel cleverly notes.

CHAPTER TWENTY-ONE

1. the Petit Pain: French for "the Little Bread," or more exactly, "the Bread Roll."

2. throwing dice for a game called "Pigs" with three lads evidently of the slum proletariat: "Pigs" is a craps game of folk origins. See John Scarne and Clayton Rawson, *Scarne on Dice*, Drake, Ohio: Coachwhip, 2017. Aslima and Lafala speak of their love affair as another kind of piggish game.

3. The proprietor said they couldn't dance for he had no dancing license: Though dancing breaks out there, the Petit Pain café is not licensed for it. In interwar France, only businesses such as a *bal-musette*, a club usually featuring an accordion band, were sanctioned for dancing.

4. an old cocotte: An elderly, once-fashionable prostitute.

5. "*cul-cassé*": Likely McKay's reversal and back-translation of the French slang term *casse-cul*, used to refer to a coward, a villain, a "pain in the ass," and a "bugger" (one who engages in anal copulation). The last of these meanings is particularly significant in view of the context, a desperate character's effort to insult a gay man. A *caisse-couilles*, meanwhile, is a "ball-buster."

CHAPTER TWENTY-TWO

1. bloomers: An alternative to the skirt, bloomers are a pant-like, roomy woman's garment covering the lower body. Introduced to Western women in the mid-nineteenth century, they were named after the American feminist Amelia Bloomer (1818–1894). Significantly for Aslima, bloomers were associated with exotic "Turkish dress" as well as with enhanced liberties for women.

CHAPTER TWENTY-THREE

1. instantaneous photographer: A term introduced during the nineteenth century for a photographer who captured life in motion with a quick exposure, in this instance to profit from the tourist trade. The English photographer Eadweard Muybridge (1830–1904), famous for his stop-motion pictures of animal locomotion, was sometimes labeled an instantaneous photographer in his day.

2. "And I've got to go with the broad alone": Babel's song exploits the double meaning of "broad" as both a woman and a ship in early twentieth-century American slang. Lafala, for his part, finally goes with the latter sort of broad alone.

3. "Mektoub! Mektoub!" (Destiny! Destiny!): McKay explicitly self-translates the Arabic term "mektoub" or "maktoob" (مكتوب), meaning fate or predestination, as "destiny." In his memoir *A Long Way from Home*, he interpolates his poem "A Farewell to Morocco," which concludes with another common translation of the term: "It is written." See *A Long Way from Home*, 341. With Aslima's cry of "Mektoub!," McKay's novel too has been written, and has nearly reached its destined end.

4. chorean state: A state characterized by nervous, involuntary movement. The highly unusual word "chorean" is most likely McKay's attempt to adjectivize the noun "chorea," which refers to a neurological disorder that causes irregular bodily contractions.

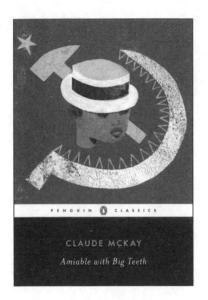